Elixir of Life

I0562601

Lyndsay Tobiyah

Purple flower books

Typeset in Palatino linotype

To offer feedback, please visit the author at

www.lyndsaytobiyah.wikidot.com
www.myspace.com/statsinparis
or via facebook (as Lyndsay Coomber)

ISBN 978-0-9558543-1-6

Elixir of Life

Lyndsay Tobiyah

Purple flower books

Other books by the author

The Dream Catcher

To P.S.H., who it was meant for from the very beginning, even if I didn't realise it.

Acknowledgements

There are people who inspired this tale, people who have fame and fortune in their own rights, but whose brilliance has given me the courage to keep working.

Firstly, the skaters who were at the forefront of their sport when this tale was only retrospective by a year or so. Gwendal and Marina, the French Ice Dancers, who were brilliant beyond belief, and whom I miss watching immensely. Also, the beautiful Russian boy, Evgeni Plushenko, who will always be recalled by my mother and I.

Secondly, I would very much like to thank Angela Lansbury et al, for every single episode of Murder, She Wrote, which I can watch over and over again, even when I know who did it. No other show has ever entertained me so much. Also, thank you for Mrs 'Arris Goes to Paris.

Prologue

Time had disappeared. The century was coming to an end, and this time there was so much more at stake. He could still recall the last time the year had changed with such dramatic effect, and the fear on the faces of those who had seen it. There had been no cause for concern, but who could have told them that?

It was a long time since he had entered the world. Lives had come and gone within his own, and he had watched with the assured knowledge that he would survive them all. If only he could still claim that.

For the world was changing. Worse still, there was no place for him within that new world. He couldn't see where he belonged anymore.

Perhaps, given time, he could have found a new niche, located a safe place. But The Old Man had run out of opportunities, and now it was all he could do to hold on while he still had time.

Lyndsay Tobiyah

Chapter

one

The whole class was watching her, waiting for her to make a mistake, which would never come. Swinging back and forth, she gathered speed, knowing that there was only one way to land after such a performance, and that was perfectly. There was no room for error in the Olympics, as her father had so regularly pointed out since she was first able to walk. The ice was the only thing that mattered, or so she had been led to believe. Even though this was a high school phys. ed. class, there was no reason she shouldn't be the very best that it was in her ability to be. Plus, if her father ever got a hint that she'd had a less than perfect dismount off the uneven bars, there would be hell to pay.

It was amazing that Electra Philips had enough time to rationalise all of those thoughts whilst she was swinging in mid air. As she leapt from the bars, aiming for the mat, she wondered what would happen, what her father would do, if she slipped and broke her leg. It might at least keep her from Nagano, she thought. But as she twisted first once, then twice, and landed perfectly, she knew there was little chance of that particular thought coming to fruition.

An apathetic round of applause broke out, with the coach the most enthusiastic participant. It wasn't that they didn't like Electra, but most of them would not have cared whether she was there or not. The teachers treated her as the star they believed someone with gold medal potential *should* be treated. It had taken her a long time to prove that she had more than athletic ability, though. She did, in fact, have a rather higher than average IQ. When she passed her SAT's in the top three percent, she seemed to finally put the whole question to rest once and for all.

After the class finished, she changed slowly back in to her uniform. She always wondered how her father had managed to locate the only high school in the whole of the bay area that imposed a school uniform, and a particularly vile one, at that. It comprised of a brown wool skirt, with a mustard yellow blouse, and either a blazer or sweater option, depending on the weather. A brown and yellow tie completed the ensemble, along with knee high socks and brown shoes. It would have been almost bearable if the fabric had not been itchy. It could have been worse, Electra had decided early on, because they could've chosen maroon or orange, which would have clashed gloriously with her red hair, which was now long enough to sit on, and curled just a little at the end. And besides, the outfit suited her small frame, even if the blazer was a little too boxy, and the skirt a little too full.

She had a free period after P.E, so she made her way out to the area behind the school where kids could be found in the fine weather. A large fountain occupied most of the space, and the sound of the water was loud in her ears. The water splashed over the top of a dolphin's head, before falling into a pool, where it rippled across the surface to meet whoever might be there to watch it. For now, Electra was the only one there.

She spent the time reading a letter from her brother, Cain, who was at college over the bay at Oakland. He was the luckier one, so far, as he had managed to escape the programme her father had imposed upon her since she was old enough to walk. He had faked a complete lack of athletic ability, and now was free, while Electra continued to train for the forthcoming winter season, when she would take on the world's finest on the skating rink. She was already dreading what it would be like if she didn't get the gold.

Mr. Philips had once been a gold medal gymnast, but had failed to make the Olympics after an injury had ended his career. When first Cain, then Electra, were born, he did his best to push them into a programme of enforced training, which seemed set to succeed for Electra. And if she failed, then she would endure what her father no doubt viewed as the wrath of God. That had been a strong theme in the Philips' household after their parents had found religion, almost ten years before.

Now, though, Electra had to move on to her next period, before she was late. There was no point in rocking the boat, especially when she was trying her hardest to stay in line. Her reason was her new found cousin, Gideon, who had appeared only weeks earlier, on a dark night when even the moon was reluctant to show Her face. He had come from New Orleans, and Mr. Philips did not approve of him. He did not really approve of anyone, though, Electra realised.

Mr. Philips had decided early on that Cain and Electra were to save themselves for marriage, and even, then it would be at his arrangement. Electra had longed for romance when she was in her early teens, but as eighteen fast approached, she was starting to give up on the notion.

It would have been fantastic to have someone to share her dreams with, but it was an unrealistic fantasy on her part.

To be honest, the programme took so much of her time that she doubted that she really even had time for a real romance. Instead, she dreamed of famous actors, musicians, sports stars; any one who might sweep her off her feet for an evening of dinner and dancing at the Top of the Mark, or some other place where there was valet parking, and the waiters wore bow ties, and she wouldn't have to worry about the amount of carbs in her meal. It was only a dream, though. No one was coming to whisk her away, and the Olympics were her only future.

Chapter

two

Vagan Elison woke up with the taste of blood in his mouth, salty and metallic. For the third morning in a row, he had woken up in the small shack just off the campus grounds. It was still only the end of his second week at UC Oakland, and this was the fourth time it had happened since the previous Saturday. Somehow, he had managed to lose several hours, and could hardly even remember what he had been doing the evening before. Now, here he was yet again, curled up on the floor amongst the old machinery that was stored in the shack.

He couldn't help but wonder what was going on. He had always been very healthy, having grown up on his parents' farm just outside Salt Lake City. He had dedicated all his spare time to his studies, which had earned him a good GPA, but also helped with the everyday running of the farm. He was an only child, and he had helped with everything.

Now, he tried to stand up, but found that his legs were sore. His muscles contracted painfully, as if he had spent the night running. He tried hard to remember what his actions had been as he struggled to work his legs into movement. Glancing down at his watch, he realised he was going to be late for his first class if he didn't get a move on. He shook his left leg, then his right, hoping that the action might loosen the muscles sufficiently for him to be able to walk at a slightly quicker pace. He couldn't really afford to miss any of his classes if he wanted to keep his partial scholarship for Photographic Studies.

He made it back to the main campus quickly, walking off the pain, when he came face to face with his roommate, Billy. Where Vagan was the studious type, Billy was pure jock. He had been awarded a sports scholarship, even though his father made enough to put a whole fleet of kids through college if he wanted to. Some kids had all the luck.

"Hey, Elison, where'd you get too? I saw you with that girl, Geena, last night. Good work, man!" Billy greeted Vagan. He felt his mind go blank for a moment. He was trying hard to remember who Geena was, so the fact that he had been with her, was an even bigger mystery to him.

"Are you sure it was me?" He asked, trying to sound mischievous, but a little uncertain that he wanted to know the answer.

"There aren't many around here that look like you, Elison." The jock grinned. Vagan had to admit to himself that it was true. He didn't look like many others on the campus. He had not followed the recent trend to let his hair grow long, but kept it cut short. He may not be a jock, but he was fairly muscular in a way that most others could not guess at how to achieve. It had come from many years on the farm, and a lot of games of ice hockey on the pond out back in the winter. His nose had been broken and fixed when he was fairly young, but his Jewish heritage was still

14

fairly obvious in his appearance. "I figured you got lucky, so I hope you don't mind that Stacey and Olivia shared your bed, last night."

"Something like that." He smiled noncommittally, wishing that Billy didn't pick up quite so many girls each day. He was starting to get aggravated now, knowing that he was already running late, and that Billy was holding him up further. He had to stop by the dorm room to collect his book for the psyche. 101 class that was due to start in about seven and a half minutes. He might have to forget the book, any way, because he wasn't sure that even if he ran he would be able to get there and back to the lecture hall. "I've gotta go, Billy. Catch you later."

As he ran across the campus, he realised that his legs seemed to be working better than they had done for a while. Perhaps he *had* spent the night running. That would certainly explain a few things. It wasn't until he reached the lecture hall, book under his arm, with a minute and ten seconds left to go, that he remembered who Geena was, and a strange sense of dread spread through him.

Later, as he returned to the dorm room, the dread was forgotten. Vagan could hardly even remember what he had been doing all morning. He had spent the afternoon working on his first photo essay in the college dark room. He had spent his first weekend taking photographs of the city, hoping he might get to know the area as quickly as he could, trying to complete the project set before the beginning of the semester ahead of schedule. It had taken him an afternoon to develop the films, then he had looked over the contact sheets, choosing which would become his first submissions of the semester. Now, he was exhausted, and he wasn't really sure why. The faint throb between his shoulder blades could have been to do with moving the enlarger around, he rationalised. But the head ache? Must be to do with the chemicals.

The next day, the throb was still there. A couple of aspirin cut the worst of it, and he tried to go about his day. When he spotted Geena Du Pré heading toward him, though, the sense of dread that had spread through him the day before, returned.

"Seven hours, Vagan. That's how long I lost. All I know is I was talking to you, and now I've lost *seven hours* of my life." She was crying. Her face looked pale under her freckles, her hair unwashed and limp. He wasn't really sure what he was supposed to say to her, so he simply walked away. The feeling of nausiation that filled the pit of his stomach grew with every step he took toward the shack. He didn't collapse when he got there this time. Instead, he fell to the floor, and started to cry.

What if he had done something to Geena? The thought kept running through his head, along with all the different scenarios that he could come up with. *What the Hell is happening to me?* He asked himself. In the end, he wasn't sure where the scenarios ended, and the dream began; the dream of the beautiful girl that he didn't know, and the burning house that was falling down around him.

Chapter three

Gideon stepped into the twilight. All around, streetlights were starting to flicker into life. He hadn't lived in San Francisco for very long, and was weary of the rest of the residents of the city. Now, walking amongst them, he found himself shivering, a slight panic filling his being. He was slightly agoraphobic, and he preferred the safety of his house. If it weren't for his new found relative, Electra, he would not have gone out at all. But he had promised her he would meet her, at 7:45 in the Golden Gate Park. From there, they were going on to a nearby ice skating rink, where she would no doubt display her talents.

As he made his way there, he thought about Electra. He knew they were cousins of a sort, but he couldn't figure out the degrees of separation. Somewhere in the past, the lines of the family had splintered, and it had taken Gideon a long time to find any relatives. After all, he was the last of his own branch. From the moment he had first met her, he had realised that things were going to start happening. There was something special about her. She radiated beauty and warmth, and he found himself attracted to it. She seemed very strong, possibly because of all the athletic ability she had, but it also seemed to be an inner strength. Perhaps she had developed it over time because of her parents.

He hadn't had the pleasure of meeting them, yet. According to Electra, they were very good, and very religious. Despite the fact that Gideon didn't really give much thought to God one way or another, he suspected that this meant they would not really like him much. He also knew that the father was rather over baring when it came to Electra's athletic aspirations. He knew instinctively that she must have a great deal of talent. Just by looking at her, he could tell her grace must be immense.

He arrived in the park as the sky turned indigo. He had a few minutes before he was due to meet her, so he made his way to the Shakespeare monument, where they were meeting, and sat on an iron bench, trying to relax a little, despite the few people who were still around.

"Gideon!" Called a voice from behind him. He had heard her coming, but chose not to react until she made herself known. In the past, he had been too eager when people he knew were near to him, and had scared them from him. He smiled and turned to where she was approaching from.

"Good evening, Electra. How are you?" He asked in his careful manner. He always chose his words carefully, letting them flow in his heavy southern accent. He watched her as she crossed the small area in front of the monument, and sat beside him. Her long red hair was loose around her shoulders, and her green eyes were sparkling.

"All the better for seeing you!" She smiled brightly, and tucked a strand of hair behind her ear. "I booked the rink for eight, so we should get a move on. They like to call home if I don't turn up on time, and then dad goes mad."

"We wouldn't want that." Gideon chuckled gently. They started out of the park, and toward the ice skating rink that was located a few blocks away. "How *are* your parents?"

"Same as they ever are. Dad has a new topic of argument, which is that if I don't take things seriously, I'll never be able to coach when I'm older. The joke's on him, because I don't care. I don't really want to coach, but he thinks it's a good point. Mom has decided that her new project, which is her usual project when it comes to me, is to dress me in so many sequins that the cameras go into solar flare mode. And she wants them to be pink! I mean, does she not realise that I have *red* hair? To be honest, I'm just so glad to be old enough to get here without them transporting me any more. I used to have to get rides from them, and that meant *punctuality* was my middle name, rather than Sarah, which *is* my middle name. Not that they mention that so much any more since they found God, because it makes my initials ESP." She was talking rapidly, excitedly. He liked the way she talked. It reminded him of his wife, God rest her soul.

The ice rink was housed in a large building, brightly lit from all angles. His biggest fear, bigger even than crowds and open spaces, was that of light. Photophobia, he was told it was called. He often wondered whom it was that had decided all these names for things, but never for very long. As they got closer, he could feel his anxieties growing, but tried hard to suppress them. There was a loud whirring noise in the air. He could hear it already, knowing that his hearing was acting in its most sensitive manner. The closer they got to the building, the louder the noise became.

"Did I mention that Cain is coming to join us, this evening?" Electra asked, sounding excited again. He shook his head to indicate that she had not, and she continued to talk. "He's showing some new kid around, so I told him to bring the kid along, too. It should be a fun evening."

"New to whom?" Gideon asked, a gentle mock in his tone.

"To the college; a freshman from out of town, apparently. I think Cain is trying to palm him off on me, but I might be wrong." She laughed. Gideon felt a little stab of fear, realising that he was going to have to meet these people. He had met Cain before, of course, but only briefly. This other person may be nothing, but he had to try and prepare. He was also a little concerned. If it were true that Cain was trying to pass this young man over to Electra, then Gideon may not have as much time with her as he would have liked any more.

"Well, you just make sure you still have enough time for me, Cher. I hate to think that you won't have time to show me the sights of the city." He smiled gently, knowing that very few females had ever been able to resist his charms. They were now making their way into the main rink area, through a dimly lit corridor, and the noise was getting louder. Finally, he had to ask her. "What *is* that noise?"

"What noise? Oh, the Zamboni; it resurfaces the ice so that it's all nice and smooth for me to skate on. If you take a spot in the bleachers, I just need to go change and tell the rink manager that I'm here for my session." She told him, still smiling, and pointing at the rows of wooden benches that circled the rink. Having stepped out of the darkness, he now found himself engulfed in light so bright it rather hurt his eyes, and to add to the enjoyment, he was going to have to sit on one of these rough wood planks.

As Electra disappeared back into the dark corridor, he made his way between the benches, looking for one which did not look quite as rough as the others. Once upon a time, he had been nowhere near as neurotic, but time had changed him. He sat, waiting patiently, hoping that the machine – Electra called it a *'Zamboni'*? – would stop soon, because it was doing something very near impossible. It was giving him a headache.

When it *did* finally stop, Electra was just getting ready to step onto the ice. She had changed from the long green dress she had been wearing. Now she was dressed from head to toe in black. Even her skates were black apart from the blades, which were shiny and sharp. Her outfit was extremely tight, and if he'd had much of an imagination, he would not have required it right then. She was gliding across the surface of the ice, now, forward and backward with the ease of much practice.

"Would you like to see a triple toe loop, Gideon?" She asked, as she slid gracefully to the barrier in front of him.

"I have no idea what that is, but I would love to see it." He replied, hoping that it was something exciting, because he was feeling slightly disinterested by that point. As she began to skate quickly around the centre of the ice, he tried to concentrate on what he was seeing. She leapt into the air, landing perfectly on one foot, swinging the other out behind her, and he was actually rather impressed. He clapped his hands together, and was pleasantly surprised by the warmth he managed to generate with the action. He decided that he could bear to show a little enthusiasm, so he stood, and made a little cheer.

"Won't you join me, Gideon?" She asked, her voice clear in the crisp, chilly air. This was what he had been afraid of. He had never really been near ice before. New Orleans was a warm place to live, and not prone to cold

21

weather. He may have travelled to a few places, but rarely anywhere that was cold at the time. So the thought of stepping onto the ice, which he knew was slippery (after all, he wasn't unintelligent), didn't fill him with fervour. Still, he didn't think that she was about to take no for an answer. "Come on, you can borrow some skates from the office."

A few minutes later, Electra was pulling laces tight across the boots that now encased his feet. He was starting to feel even more self-conscious than he had in a very long time. The piece of metal she used to pull the boots tight was shiny, glinting in the lights. He tried hard not to catch a glimpse of his reflection in it, knowing that it would show a distorted version of him that he did not care to view.

Pulling him by the arm, she led him on to the ice. He had been correct; it was very slippery. She could obviously tell that he was tense, because she attempted to tickle him. It was a brave move, although she didn't realise *how* brave. If she had known him a little longer, perhaps she would have resisted the motion. He made an attempt to giggle, but it sounded false in his own ears.

"Electra, how exactly does one stand in these things? They make me feel rather clumsy." He told her, hoping that his protestation may lead to his release. He gripped her hand tighter than before, and she dragged him a little further on to the ice. "I shall slip, Electra, any moment."

"You complain endlessly, Gideon. It's easy. Just hold your head high, and try not to think about the ice being slippery. Push your feet back and forth across the ice for a moment, just to get used to it. Don't worry, I'll catch you if you fall." She smiled up at him. He wasn't convinced that this was true, but he felt he must trust her if he wished to continue his companionship with her. "Relax."

"You make it seem so effortless. I think perhaps I would be better off sitting back down." He protested further. But he was not going to get out of it, he realised, as she started to move a little faster, still holding his hand tightly, and he had to either follow or fall. "You said your brother was coming?"

"He should be here soon. Now, are you going to relax, or am I going to have to ditch you here?" She grinned, starting to pick up more speed than he thought was reasonable in the situation. Within moments, and before he even really knew it was happening, they were making their way around the rink. The barrier that ran around the circumference of the ice seemed distant, too far for him to grab for if he felt his legs begin to buckle beneath him.

Minutes passed slowly, and he was now regretting leaving the safety of Louisiana, where he didn't have to worry about things like this. As Electra pulled him around the surface for the third time, he became aware that they were no longer alone. The knowledge came to him as it normally did; he could feel their presence, smell their individual scents, hear them breathing in the cold air. The sound of footsteps on the concrete steps confirmed that two other people had arrived.

Electra pulled him over to the barrier on the opposite side of the arena, before turning to look at her brother, and the young boy who seemed to be his companion. The smile on her face spread a little wider than before.

"I'll be back in a moment." She smiled, before turning from him, pushing her lead foot forward, and moving away across the wet, white surface. He watched her as she went, knowing that her strength was what made her shine, that her real beauty was her grace. "Hello, honey!"

"Electra," the older of the two boys called back to her. Gideon was grateful for the sensitivity of his hearing for once. "You look fantastic this evening, as ever, of course."

"Flattery will get you everywhere! I've been trying to teach our cousin how to skate, with a little success. I think I may need your help, though." She was telling Cain. The other boy seemed to be a little withdrawn from the conversation, unsure as to where he fitted in with them.

"Well, I'll get some skates and join you in a moment. In the mean time, Electra, I'd like you to meet Vagan Elison." Cain announced. The younger boy stepped into the light, and Gideon realised instantly that he was going to lose Electra to him.

Chapter four

Vagan wasn't sure what he had really been expecting, but it certainly wasn't Electra Philips, the girl his mother thought had the most potential out of all the prospective Winter Olympians. She was stunning, but he had known that she would be, if only from the descriptions that Cain had supplied him with before hand. He had rather imagined a more feminine version of Cain, and although he had been told she had red hair, he had pictured it being the same sandy colour as his new friend's.

The long red hair, which had caught his eye when his mother made him sit and watch the American championships earlier in the year, was tied up. He knew that when she let it fall, it would reach most of the way down her back. This close up, he could finally confirm that her eyes were green, flecked with blue and gold, as he stepped down to the barrier, taking her outstretched hand gently in his own. She smiled, revealing her perfect white teeth. But it was her lips that he noticed most of all, plump and well formed. Within that instant he decided that they would taste of chocolate and green apples, both sweet and sharp at once. He could feel his own mouth water slightly at the thought.

"Hello, Vagan. Do you skate?" She asked. He felt a small laugh forming in the back of his throat, allowing it to escape in a low chuckle. He was star struck, he decided, unable to talk to this beautiful creature whose form was so familiar to him.

"Sorry, I didn't mean to laugh. Yes, yes I can skate. I'm not much of a dancer anymore, although I can hold my own I guess. I played hockey until I finished high school, but I'm a little out of practice at the moment." He found himself babbling, unsure of how to stop himself from looking foolish in front of her. She was still smiling, so he decided he was all right so far.

"Come on, Vagan," Cain grinned at him. "We'll go get some skates."

Cain led him through a dark corridor to a small room lined with skates. There were all sorts of sizes and colors of boots, and it took them a moment to find ones that would fit them. Vagan was trying very hard to keep his voice even, and his breathing steady, when Cain started to laugh.

"She's only a girl, Vagan." He laughed loudly.

"I'm star struck, aren't I? Did she realise?" He asked, looking at his new friend, who nodded, still laughing. "Tell me I didn't get all red. I should've guessed you would have *her* as a sister. If I told my mother I just met Electra Philips, she would scream down the 'phone at me, and tell me to get an autograph. I'd never hear the end of it."

"She could do with a little fun now and then. You could be just what she needs." Cain told him. "There had to be some reason for them making me your 'older brother'. It may as well be this."

"I wouldn't even know where to start." Vagan sighed, feeling his face start to turn red, hoping that, as he could feel it this time, it hadn't happened before when he was actually talking to her. He knew what Cain was thinking, but in all truth, Vagan wasn't sure it was even a possibility.

"Just get out on the ice and impress her. She will respect you if you can stay upright for more than a couple moments." Cain told him, standing on his blade guards, and making his way toward the door. "Take a deep breath, and smile."

A minute later, Vagan Elison stepped onto the ice for the first time in months. Normally, he would have spent the off season on his inline skates, but he had spent the last days of his high school career dedicated to his studies, making sure that his scholarship money was safe. Now, here he was, in front of this girl, knowing that he had the chance to show her what he could do.

As he pushed off, his left foot leading as always, he knew that speed was his greatest asset. Moving faster and faster across the ice, flowing backwards, feeling his legs find their familiar stance, he hoped he had what it took. He knew she was watching him, as he passed the group, which now included the other guy, the one Cain described as 'the cousin'. Finally, he slid to a stop, his back turned to the group, his body a little breathless.

"You're so fast!" She exclaimed. He turned to look at them, smiling a little. Cain gave him a wink, as he skated back to them. "Sorry, Vagan, this is Gideon, Gideon, Vagan."

"Pleased to meet you." Vagan greeted the other man, and realised that there was a look in the other man's eyes that gave him a slight sense of fear.

Now, standing beside Electra, he decided that she was the perfect height. She stood at about 5"10', including her skates, which added a couple of inches or so. As he was 6" even, he thought it was just about right.

"Cher, please can I sit down, now? I am not meant to be on ice, I think." Gideon requested. She agreed, and led him back to the far barrier. Vagan tried not to watch her as she went.

"I think that might have done the trick." Cain whispered loudly, conspiratorially, to Vagan.

"She's going to Nagano, right?" Vagan asked, trying to remember, because he hadn't really been paying attention to her score card; he'd been too busy trying to see her through all the sequins (they had been pale blue).

"Yeah. She did well at the Americans earlier this year. She placed second overall, even though she doubled out on a triple Salchow, and then she caught her toe pick on a rough bit of ice. That bit of ice got Maggie Treat a fine, too. Almost half the skaters in the final group had a problem, after she gouged a bit of ice out at the end of her routine. She didn't deserve to take first, but her skate was almost perfect other than a wobble on a camel spin." Cain told him, watching his sister, too.

"My mother isn't keen on Maggie Treat. That much I *do* know. You should've heard her when they announced that Salt Lake City was getting the games in 2002. She was more excited than anyone, *ever*. We live about ten miles away, so she has plans to camp out for tickets. Dad will probably tell her to get back on the farm right away, but I don't think it'll happen." Vagan told the other boy.

"Great, maybe El can stay with you guys instead of at Olympic village. She hates having to bunk with fifteen girls she doesn't know."

"Well, mom would love that, but I think your sister would probably run screaming from her within ten minutes." Vagan tried to sound as if the idea was just that, while in his mind, he was already imagining what it might be like to have her staying on the farm. She was done with helping her cousin to the barrier, and was now on her way back to them. For the first time in a few weeks, he felt fairly normal. It was a month since he'd started college, now, and things were starting to fall into place. His only worry was that there were still large gaps in his days, ones that he could not account for. All he knew was that when he woke up in the shack, he had always lost at least an hour or two of his day. Mostly, it was more, though - anywhere up to a day, so far.

It was an entertaining evening. They spent nearly an hour on the ice. Electra showed them a few moves that she had been working on, including a variation on the Biellmann spin, which, she informed, them was completely unique. He made an effort to try and do a couple of the moves he had learned when he was younger, when his mother had taken him on the ice on the pond out back. He was not as practiced as she was, but he could manage a double toe-loop, still, and the odd sit spin if he really pushed himself.

After they were all skated out, the group of four found themselves out in the fall air, heading for Haight-Ashbury, where, they informed Vagan, there was a diner where they could get a great burger, and Electra could get a salad. She protested loudly at the idea, but Cain reminded her what their father was likely to say if he found out that she had eaten carbs on a Tuesday.

After that, Gideon made his excuses, and they watched him walk away in the other direction, while the others started off toward Steiner Street, where, Cain told him, Electra and his parents lived in a Queen Anne, in pale blue.

"So, how *did* you learn to skate that fast?" Electra asked him as they made their way up a rather steep hill. Cain was walking a few steps ahead of them, allowing them to talk freely.

"Practice. Lots, and lots, of practice. My mom taught me a bit when I was a kid, then I played hockey for most of my high school career. I liked the speed rather than the game." He confessed.

"I wish I could get that kind of speed going. It's easier to do some of the jumps when you have a little more speed. I would rather like to go to Japan with a quad toe-loop if I could. I know a lot of the guys are doing quads, now." She spoke rather rapidly, and he found he liked the way it sounded. He watched her out of the corner of his eye as she pulled out the pin that had been holding her hair up. A sheaf of red hair fell around her shoulders, and she ran her fingers through it, letting it sit in soft strands around her face.

"The speed is easy, the jumps are the hard part. I envy that talent. I could always show you mine if you'd show me some of yours." He responded, hoping he didn't sound stupid. She let out a little laugh, but didn't seem put off; that must be a good sign, he thought.

"How did you end up here, anyway?" She asked, twisting a lock of her incredibly long hair around one of her slender fingers.

"I was lucky, I got a partial scholarship, and a small award from the college, after I had a little exhibit run in a local gallery. Photography, pictures of things that people didn't really understand, so they thought I had talent. It gives me enough money to get through four years, but they have to be spent here, or they don't give me anything. My folks thought it was a great chance, so they put up a little cash, too. They put in the couple grand a year it would have cost to send me to the local tech college." He replied, feeling a little self-conscious again, telling this girl about all the monetary problems that had plagued his early years.

"Do you miss home?"

"Not really. I don't miss getting up at five to feed the cows, or making sure that the chicken coop is bolted at night in case the coyotes come round. I do miss the way the sun hits the pond in the evening, though. I miss my mom's apple pie, I guess."

"You don't miss any friends, or anything?" She pressed gently.

"No. To tell the truth, other than the guys on the team, I barely knew anyone. I was a bit of a bore, if you really want to know." Vagan admitted.

"How is that possible? Even your name is interesting. I've never met a Vagan before, and I've met people from all over the world. How did you come by it?"

"Long story, or short?"

"Whichever is the least dull."

"Firstly, I try never to be dull, anymore. I only tell interesting stories these days. As for my name, well, it actually *is* a little interesting, I guess. At the end of the Second World War, my grandmother left Poland after her husband, my grandfather, was killed. She was pregnant with my father. When she arrived in America, in Salt Lake City, of all places, she gave birth to Julius, my father. Julius was my grandfather's name. But after a few years, my grandmother met a man named Vagan. He was Polish, and Jewish, and a very good man. He married my grandmother, and adopted my father as his own. When I was born, rather later than planned, as a mark of respect for the stepfather who had raised him as his own, he named me after him. So, it is a Polish-Jewish thing, and I apologise now, because I realise it really was a rather dull story after all."

"That wasn't dull. You underestimate yourself. Cain, don't look so worried." She called to her brother, who had come to a stop in front of one of the houses. The fact that it was pale blue led Vagan to guess that it must be the Philips' residence. "For some reason, my brother fears my parents."

"This is where I leave you, El." Cain told her, turning to look at her. "Come on, Vagan, I'll spring for a cab back to campus."

"It's pot luck at the church on Friday. You wanna come keep me company?" Electra asked her brother, placing her hands on his shoulders and looking directly at him. "I'll make pop corn, and we can watch movies."

"Sure. Call me and tell me when they go out." Cain agreed.

"Vagan, it was nice to meet you. I'm sure we'll meet again, if my brother has anything to do with it." She smiled again, those lips gently parting as the corners of them turned up. He watched her as she wandered up the walkway to the house, a gentle sway in her step that made her hair dance in the night air. He could tell that things would get interesting if he managed to get that close to her again.

Chapter five

The Old Man sat in the house alone. He had not called on the boy that evening; he had not needed to. He had managed to get what he needed by himself. That didn't happen very often; not at the moment, anyway. Things changed from decade to decade.

He had bought the old house on Prescott long before, and had it renovated to his own requirements, restored to a glory it had not known since its original construction. The workmen had been paid a great deal; more than was sensible, at any rate. That had ensured they worked around his schedules.

Other than the workmen, who had really not counted, he had known few. People had come and gone from his life. It had been a long time since he had experienced love, or even friendship. There had been others in his life, of course, but they had been few and far between.

Sometimes, he liked to think back to a time when he was free and happy, and in love. For he *had* been in love, so many years ago, before the world had forsaken him, before he had given up everything. There was no way out for him, now. He would have given anything to see her face again, but Heaven would not have him, now.

Chapter

six

E lectra, The principal needs to see you in his office."
The woman at the front of the room announced.
Study hall was half over, but Electra didn't have any
complaints about leaving. She stood up, pulling her book
bag on to her shoulder, and made her way out of the room,
ignoring the sound of the rest of the class mumbling about
such things as 'special treatment' and 'false celebrity status'

The principal of Electra's high school was Mr.
Spring. He was a good man, a friend of the Philips', and
Electra's Godfather. He was a strong, distinguished man,
and many of the other students feared him; Electra
respected him, instead.

"I'm here to see Mr. Spring." She told the secretary
as she entered the small office entrance. The young male
secretary, Dylan Adams, had only joined the school that
semester, but he had quickly become one of the most
popular people in the place. For some reason, he seemed to
rather like Electra, though.

"Hi, Electra, he'll be with you in a moment. He's on the phone to the supply teacher place. Ms. Abelwhite is out with a personal complaint, again. But I didn't tell you that, okay?" He smiled, and she understood what he was saying. "Won't you sit and visit with me for a few minutes. I could do with some intelligent conversation for once."

"Well, I'm not sure what you will get from me, today. I have to say, I'm not feeling terribly bright right now." She responded, taking a seat across the desk from him. He was one of those people it was easy to see would be a heart breaker when he was out of his work environment. He had the looks of a silver screen movie star, and he spoke with a voice that seemed much older than his age should allow, a slight accent from who knew where rounding some of his words in unfamiliar ways. He seemed to have a knowledge of the world that came from experience. Electra liked him.

"You have been training too hard, again? I suppose you have to spend many hours training if you want to be the best." He sighed, understanding more about her resentment than she normally admitted to herself.

"You have no idea. I have Skate America in a couple of weeks, so I have to be ready for that. My trainer keeps telling me to keep focused, that if I don't get my quad toe-loop right in the next week, I may as well forget it altogether. I have no idea if it is even possible for me to *manage* a quad toe-loop. If I get the take off wrong once more, I think I might just tell her to shove it where the sun doesn't shine, and be done with it." Now it was she who sighed.

"You don't mean that, I'm sure. All you need is a little luck, and perhaps a little confidence in yourself. I know that you have talent. I've seen you skate, before; I know you can do it. I know the competition is normally intense, but don't let it get in the way of what is within

36

your power. Who really worries you?" He asked. She thought for a moment before answering.

"The Russians, at the moment at any rate. They have more skaters than is sensible. The mere volume of them is a problem. I'm just glad I'm not an ice dancer at the moment. The French pair is brilliant, and I would hate to even try against them. There's a young Russian guy who I think is worth watching for a while; he was a junior champion last year, but I think he'll be going senior this season. I think the next few years could be really interesting. Of course, the home side is tough this year. Nagano would be a nicer prospect if Jo Fox were coming with me, instead of Maggie Treat. I won't complain about Maggie, because she is really talented, and it's nice to be there with someone as good as she is, but I do get on better with Jo. Mind you, when there are a dozen of you, and only the best get through, I suppose something has to give somewhere." She responded truthfully.

"Well, hopefully what Mr. Spring has to say to you will make you a little more at ease. Don't take it personally, though. I shouldn't really say anything, but I should warn you to take a deep breath, and let the words he has for you meet your ears without too much thought to what difference this will make to you. And be warned, the rest rooms on this floor are out of order. You'll be wanting the ones downstairs, preferably." He told her cryptically, as he made a mental note of all she had said. As he finished speaking, the intercom on the desk made a static crackle, then buzzed loudly.

"Dylan, is Electra here yet?" A voice asked through the speaker. Dylan leaned forwards and pressed one of the red buttons on top of the device.

"Yes, sir, she's right here." He replied, wishing he could repeat his warning, as he realised she was going to forget it.

"Please, send her in. And could you put a call through to Roses are Red for me. Actually, forget that; I'll do it myself in a minute." The older man said. The intercom went quiet again, and Electra took that as her cue to go in and see the principal.

Her Godfather was a handsome man, only just 40. His hair was beginning to grey at the temples, but his frosty blue eyes were clear. As she entered the room, he stood and greeted her warmly.

"Electra, please, sit down. I need for you to sign a few papers for me, and I have a little news for you, also." He greeted.

"That sounds ominous." She smiled, taking a seat; inside, her stomach churned. Was this what Dylan had been talking about?

"I'm afraid it's bad news, of a sort. The thing is, it may not be such bad news for you." He seemed unsure how to broach the subject that was on the tip of his tongue. She watched him as he paced for a moment, then sat down heavily in his desk seat. "I'm not really sure where to start, so I shall be blunt and to the point. It's about Maggie Treat."

"What about her?" She asked, feeling her stomach churn again, this time rather more painfully. She was starting to guess why Dylan had warned her about the rest rooms.

"It seems she was staying in LA with a few friends before the start of Skate America. One of the friends found her this morning. She seems to have decided that there was no way out for her; she cut her own wrists." He told her. She felt her body sag in her seat, nausiation rising in her throat.

"Why? Maggie had more talent than most of us put together. She would've won just about everything this season. I don't believe it! Why?" She exclaimed.

"I really don't know why, Electra. There was no note, apparently. What I do know is that after Jackie Slater had her accident, it leaves you as the only medal winner from the American championships still in the running for the Olympics."

"I can't believe she did it. I didn't really know her that well, but we met a few times. She kept herself to herself, even had her own special dorm at the games because she hated to share with anyone. You know, for the rest of us, competition is like a big sleepover, without the pizza because we can't afford the carbs, of course." It was true to a point that Maggie was the better skater, but there were things she couldn't do. She'd still had problems landing a triple Salchow, and her Biellmann spin was far from actually looking like one, but artistically, she had a certain quality, unmistakable in style. One thing did spring to mind, though. "My father will be pleased."

"That's a little harsh, Electra."

"Sorry, but it's also true."

"Yes; yes, I suppose it is. I'm arranging some flowers from the school, as we're partially sponsoring your entry in Nagano."

"Speaking of which, don't you need me to sign some papers for them?"

"Yes, just some release papers for the winter semester. They release you for about two months. I know you won't have any problems with the finals; with your history, you shouldn't have any, though." He told her, opening one of the desk drawers. He dug around for a moment, before pulling out a sheaf of forms for her, handing them across the desk. "Take your time over them. As long as I have them back before Christmas, that's fine. I see no point in you going back to study hall, now. Stop by Dylan for a hall pass."

"Thank you, sir." She tried to smile, but her lips would not behave for her. As she made her way out, Dylan simply handed her the yellow slip of paper that excused her from class, as she started to pick up speed toward the staircase. She couldn't remember which way Dylan had told her to go, so went up. The rest rooms were at the end of the hall, and either side there were classes full of students, all trying to finish whatever it was they were doing before the end of the period. Electra ignored them, and kept walking in as straight a line as she could manage.

She hurried as she got closer, feeling her stomach flip entirely. Finally, the wave of nausiation that had been lingering, threatening to pounce at any moment, overcame her. She ducked into one of the stalls just in time to see the content of her stomach end up down the toilet.

She collapsed on the floor next to the toilet bowl, the acrid smell burning in her nostrils. She closed her eyes, and pressed her head against the cold concrete wall. She felt wretched.

It wasn't fair. People like Maggie weren't supposed to kill themselves. She was beautiful and talented, and expected to win most of the gold in the coming season. It was true that she had done a few things that Electra had disliked, especially her trick with her toe-pick, but she would not have wished her dead. Electra knew, probably better than most, the pressure of having to keep to the programme, but she had never even contemplated ending her life because of it.

Minutes passed, and she started to feel a little better. The nausiation began to retreat slowly, and she managed to flush the toilet. She got to her feet slowly, her legs shaky, and stepped out of the stall. She stood in front of the mirror, and found her reflection too hideous to look at. Her eyes were puffy and blood shot; she hadn't even realised she had been crying.

Her hair was a mess. She had let it down before leaving the house that morning, knowing that when she did so, she managed to keep slightly more of her own personality instead of the one imposed upon her by her father. Now, it was all over the place. She ran her fingers through the roots, hoping as she did so that it would lay flat. She turned on the faucet, and let it run cold. She cupped the water in her hands, and took a long drink, rinsing her mouth before spitting it back out, trying to rid her mouth of the taste of vomit.

In the hallway outside, the bell rang, signalling the end of the period. Electra held a paper towel under the faucet, pressing it to each eye, then across her forehead. The door swung open, and 3 girls, a junior and 2 sophomores, walked in.

"Who died?" The junior asked rather indirectly. Electra thought for a moment before replying.

"Maggie Treat, gold medallist skater, and a friend of mine." She said rather bluntly. The effect was perfect, as the girl stopped smiling, and looked down at her black and green espadrilles.

"Sorry." The girl mumbled. The other girls both looked a little sheepish now, too. Obviously the sight of their leader being wounded in battle was too much for them. Electra merely shrugged, turned back to the mirror to check her appearance, then left. That was when she remembered that Dylan had told her to go down, and now she guessed why. It may have been a lie that she had told the girl, but it had, at least, had the desired effect.

The hall was now crowded, packed with students trying to get to their next classes, trying to remember where they were supposed to be. Electra wasn't sure she could handle biology, but it had to beat sitting on the floor next to a high school toilet bowl. This was going to change things.

In some small part of her brain, she knew that the loss of Maggie would clear the way for her, and the others, too. Maggie would have been the winner, the one to beat. There were few who could've matched her anymore. Still, she was five years older than Electra, and her time in competition would have been coming to its end naturally within a few years anyway. It was true that Electra would now be entering the Olympics as the only remaining Americans' medal winner, but that didn't mean that she was any more likely to win.

Only three of them were able to go to Nagano, and they had to be the best, the reigning champions. Jackie Slater had taken her fall just after the American championships took place, dislocating her knee, tearing two muscles in one leg, and fracturing her arm in three or four places. That had ensured she would not be able to compete again for some time, possibly not until the 1999 season started. Her medical problems had made space for the girl who had taken fourth, a pretty girl who had just turned sixteen, and was competing at senior levels for the first time. Now that Maggie was gone, Electra wasn't quite sure what would happen. That was the decision of the ISU, she guessed, but she had to hope that it might make space for Jo Fox.

Biology was not one of Electra's strongest subjects; she disliked the old male teacher who tended to leer at the girls, and the fact that she almost always had to work on her own because her lab partner managed to spill something, or drop something, or explode something (even in biology, where that should have been fairly difficult). She made up for these things by sitting at the back of the class, keeping her head down, and staying in line.

The period, being the last of the day, dragged on for what seemed an eternity. There was a window in Electra's little corner, and she spent a good deal of the class looking out at the busy road that ran beside the school, at the top of a hill from where it was possible to see most of San Francisco, and all the way out to Oakland, on a clear day. The sun was shining, warming her through the glass. It would have been so easy to just open the window and jump out. She knew she could make the landing with ease; she also knew that it was never going to happen. When the bell finally rang, she was out of the room quicker than any one else, and before long, she was out in the afternoon sun.

It was early October, though, and there was the start of a chill in the air; the approach of fall, already. Within the next week, she would be leaving for Detroit, and Skate America. It signalled the start of the new season, one in which Electra felt she was going to discover many new things about who she was, and who she was meant to be.

Chapter seven

D ylan Horatio Adams had lived in San Francisco for three years before he managed to secure his job at the high school. He liked it there. People didn't question him, didn't ask who he was or where he came from. Everywhere else he had worked, people had wanted to know all about him. Then he would normally have to leave.

He had lived all over the world before coming to San Francisco: Paris, Hong Kong, Zagreb, Geneva. So many places; a year here, a year there. When he first started out, his parents were with him, but now he was alone.

Sometimes, he wondered if it had been worth roaming around the world without aim. But he liked the city. It was a wonderful place, where he could be any one or any thing without raising any eyebrows, or receiving the damnation of people who didn't know him. Even the fog didn't bother him as it did others. In fact, there were times when he would simply go and stand on the Bay Bridge, and let the fog roll in around him.

The job at the high school paid well enough that Dylan had been able to move from the small studio he had been living in, and into a large apartment on Haight Street. It was the first real apartment he had ever owned. He'd even purchased furniture and a TV. It wasn't that he'd not had money. His parents had left him a fair amount, but he had been careful with it, knowing that it would have to last him a long while. But the job seemed to be steady, and the money would be coming in for a while. It was time to settle for a spell.

He had his reasons for coming to the city. He had spent years searching for someone, following someone. He was still chasing after the man who had killed his parents. Now, he had tracked him down, and he wouldn't leave San Francisco until he had done what he had set out to do.

The city was the ideal place to take revenge. He could be anyone he wanted to be. He could change his face, blend into the crowed with ease. For what it was worth, if he chose to, he could walk around the Golden Gate Park dressed as Carmen Miranda, and nobody would care.

No one cared about him anymore, anyway. Sure, all the girls at school seemed to think he was hot property. They all came to him in groups of three or four, asking for their hall passes, and staying for ten minutes, attracted by the strange magnetism that he had been given a long time ago, and which he had been thus far unable to break away from. It was a good thing he had mastered the art of typing without touching the keys, because other wise he would never get his work done on time.

The only person he ever encouraged was Electra Philips, that beautiful creature who reminded him of someone he had known long ago. She was more rebellious, though. She had a mischievous streak running through her, which he found very attractive. She was an important part of his plan. All he had to do was figure out what that was.

Chapter eight

The body of 23 year old Maggie treat was discovered this morning at a residence in Sun Valley, Los Angeles. There is no evidence of foul play, but no suicide note was left. The police are currently not seeking anyone in their investigation into the incident. The friends that Ms. Treat was staying with are said to be shocked at the death of a girl they describe as talented, beautiful, fun loving and brilliant. There has been no comment made currently by her parents." It was the radio in Vagan's room, the one that Billy usually had switched to some sports show. Vagan preferred a bit of music.

He had been with Electra Philips just the evening before, skating and having fun. Now, he recalled what Electra had said about the other girl, and what Cain had mentioned about her little toe-pick trick. Although they didn't seem to be worried about finding anyone else to talk to about her death, he wouldn't be surprised if there weren't a few people who would not take a moment to mourn her loss.

It had been a long day after the evening he had spent with Electra and Cain. His legs were in fairly good shape, for some reason. It was almost as if he had never stopped skating in the first place. He had managed to bruise his knee when he slipped during a particularly fast twizzle, but it would not hold him back. He had rediscovered what it was that he had always loved about skating; freedom, the feeling that he was not held by the bonds of gravity.

Having to come back to the reality of college was the last thing he really wanted after that. He had spent the day in and out of classes: psychology, literature, photographic history; he wouldn't have minded if he had actually been allowed to *take* some photographs, but his professor for that class was still putting them through a basics course. The promise of a challenge he had found in the pre term essay was missing now that the actual course was underway.

It was not as if Vagan was a beginner to the art. He had been given his first camera when he was ten, along with a few pieces of equipment, by a local farmer who couldn't afford to keep up the hobby. Vagan's father had made space in one of the sheds for a darkroom, and within weeks, Vagan knew how to print his pictures, to develop rolls of film; it became his passion.

Now, the day was finally coming to a close. He realised that he had not been called on for a while, not that it bothered him. He was quite relieved, if he was being honest. He had no idea what happened to him when he lost time, where he had been or what he had done, only that the pain had come, a splinter of a burn between his shoulder blades, pulling him toward the small wooden shack where he fell into the oblivion of darkness. The truth was, he could have been out battering old ladies on Haight Street without realising it. He did rationalise that this was unlikely, as there had been no reports of old ladies being battered on Haight Street. But there were countless other possibilities.

Even so, there was a part of him, however small it might have been, that felt lost without it. Somewhere in his subconscious, he wondered if he might have come to depend upon being called, that he might have needed it to make him feel real.

'Real' wasn't the word he felt, though. In fact, he wasn't even sure which word described accurately what he felt when he was waiting for the pain between his shoulder blades to start. The closest he could find was 'anticipation', but even that didn't really do it justice. It was like being both scared and excited at the same time. He likened it to the feeling he got when getting ready for a date, not that he really knew that feeling very well.

That was part of his problem. When he had been in high school, he had been a bit of an outcast, the farm boy that few wanted to know. It had helped that he had been on the hockey team, because if he had not, he would never have been a part of anything at all. He had missed out on the most important rites of passage; homecoming parties, spring dances, even his senior prom. During each of those events, he had stayed home, avoiding the looks of his classmates when he failed to secure a date for them. He had, in the end, managed two dates during his junior year, with a girl that had nothing better to do. When he realised she had only gone out with him because one of her friends put her up to it, he decided it was probably better to avoid putting himself through the situation ever again.

Still, there was something new in his mind, now. It was Electra that had started to invade his thoughts. He had even dreamed about her the night before. One meeting with her was all it had taken, and now she was the face of the girl in the dreams, the one that called out to him from amid the flames, the one that wanted to save him.

The news came to an end, and Vagan flicked off the radio. His room was cold, and he pulled on a sweater, trying to cut out the worst of the chill. He felt sure it must be colder inside than it was out, so he resolved to leave, shutting the door behind him as he went.

It was just about dark, but parts of the campus were lit by huge floodlights, painting the world with an unnatural glow. He wasn't even sure where he thought he was going. He simply wandered aimlessly for a while, before coming to a wooden bench, and flopping down on it. Now, he wasn't even sure why he had felt the need to leave his room. It wasn't as if Billy had been there, and he had loads of work he could have been doing. Things were under control, though, and an hour wouldn't make any difference overall. Of course, he was now starting to realise that it really *was* colder out than it was in.

Once again, he found his mind returning to the dream of the night before. He was not sure that Electra was supposed to be the woman from them, but her presence there had made him feel calmer. The thing that worried him was the man, the figure of darkness that felt so familiar to him, like someone he knew, someone who he had known for all his days. It was almost as if the dark man was a father like figure, trying to guide Vagan in his ways. Dread filled Vagan's mind when he thought of it: the tall backed chair, the candles that spread into flames although there seemed no reason for them to do so. And the man himself, hiding in the shadows, a mask of white obscuring his facial features, a dark cloak covering his head and body. The only thing Vagan could make out was the tip of a tan boot.

He always watched the dream as a spectator, able to see himself sitting beside the man's feet. The man's hand rested on the top of Vagan's head, not in a protective manner, but one of aggressive force.

"Vagan?" The female voice came from behind him, so quiet he wasn't sure it was not imagined. He turned, and looked up at the blond girl that many would have thought attractive, but Vagan saw as rather plain.

"Geena? What's the matter?" He asked, noticing the tears in her eyes. "Sit down."

"I don't know what's wrong with me." She said quietly, sitting beside him on the bench. "I wish I did, because I'm not sure how much more of this I can take."

"What is it?" He asked again.

"Well, you remember when I went missing?" She asked, looking directly at him. He nodded yes. "I don't. I have no idea what happened to me. I don't remember where I went, or what I did when I got there, or anything else. All I *can* remember is talking to you, then waking up in my room with a headache that won't go away. Then I started having the nightmares, and now I can't sleep at all."

"What are the nightmares about?" He asked in a whisper, almost afraid to hear her reply, but knowing that he had to.

"I'm trapped, in the dark, and I can taste blood in my mouth, like I bit my tongue or something. It feels like it lasts for hours, until the door opens, and a guy comes in. Then I wake up." She cried. "Why is this happening to me? What have you done to me?"

"I haven't done anything to you, Geena. If I could tell you what was happening to you, then maybe I could explain what is happening to me. I can't, though. And I know how scared you are, because I feel just the same. It *is* happening to me, too." Vagan lied. He knew what was happening to him had nothing on what was happening to her.

"I'm scared, Vagan." Her dark eyes peered out at him. She looked ill and tired. "I even went to see a doctor, had some tests done. He told me I'm anaemic, but he has no idea why. And he can't explain why I can't sleep, either. Told me that with anaemia like I have, I should be falling asleep all over the place. He gave me iron pills, and a prescription for sleeping tablets, but they don't seem to be working. How the hell is he going to fix me if he can't even find out what's wrong?"

"I don't know, Geena. I wish I did, but I don't; I have no idea." He sighed

"You don't know very much, do you?" Geena practically yelled at him. "I feel like I'm going nuts, and all you can do is sit there and say you don't know. I have to go, Vagan. Thanks for being so helpful, but I think that I might get more answers out of that tree. See you around."

He watched her as she walked away. Possibly, he could have given her some better answers, but that would have meant he had to admit to himself that he had some idea that he was changing, becoming something different. He didn't know what was wrong with her, though. Christ, he wasn't even sure he knew what was going on with *him*. How was he supposed to solve her problems for her?

He sat in silence for a long while, trying to clear his mind, to just drift away, but it was impossible. Thoughts kept coming. He was so tired, he just wanted to sleep. But he knew that sleep would bring the nightmares, and that frightened him too much.

All the same, he resigned himself to the fact that he was going to have to make his way back to his room. He went slowly, though, breathing in the chilly night air. When he finally got back, he found Billy on the couch with his latest conquest, a blond girl with a huge chest. He didn't stop to say hello. He went to the other side of the room, to his bed, lay down, and put his headphones on. He switched on the CD player, and tried to sleep, immersed in music that he hoped might block out the sound of the screaming within his dreams.

Chapter nine

E lectra flopped down on her bed. She could hear her father shouting about getting her speed up. By the sound of things, her coach had been on the 'phone straight after their session, telling him that Electra was a hopeless case. All right, maybe she hadn't used those terms, exactly, but she may as well have. After the day she had had, she really wasn't in the mood to listen to it. If he were in one of his strict moods, then he would probably go on for several weeks.

Her prediction had been right. As soon as she had arrived home from the rink, she had been subjected to the 'you don't know how lucky you are' speech, with a good deal of emphasis on the fact that her path was now a lot clearer than it had been. Then the 'phone rang, and the speech changed. She didn't like to tell her father that she thought she might have found the answer to her speed issues, and that it turned out to be a boy. He would have hit the roof.

He had moved on to yelling about the Russians. The words 'do you think Slutskaya has that problem?' and 'a quad toe-loop would put you ahead of all of them' filled the house. She had heard all of it before, and it had never made a difference to her then. She tried to tune it out, wondering if it wouldn't just be easier to drop out altogether. It would not happen, though. He'd never let her.

She allowed herself to imagine what it would be like to run away from it all. Maybe she'd head somewhere a little cooler, or maybe someplace like New Orleans, with Gideon. Outside, it had started to rain heavily, but she ignored it, pretending she really was someplace else.

Her bed was big and warm, and smelt of a thousand memories. She had slept in it since she was twelve, beneath the comforter that was older than she was. Now, lying across the bed, she allowed herself to continue with her daydreams of being in New Orleans with Gideon, Cain, and Cain's new friend, Vagan. She may have only met him once, but she felt she already knew him.

They had talked about many things the evening before, including their tastes in music, books, films. He had told her a great deal about his life, and where he had grown up, on a farm just outside Salt Lake City. The way he looked didn't hurt, either. He had the nicest nose she had ever seen, a little crooked, but rather pleasant. His brown eyes were nice, too. She felt almost as if she could lose herself within them. She had resolved that she needed to see him again within moments of watching him climb into a cab behind her brother. Even if nothing else, she wanted him to teach her how he managed to make such speed on ice.

"Electra, are you even listening to me?" He called through the door. She hadn't been, of course.

"Yes, dad." That would cover most things, she figured. She sat up, and swung her legs over the side of the bed. She walked over to the window and looked out. She watched the droplets of rain making their ways down the pane of glass, rolling slowly to the sill. Her father was still talking.

She decided that if she was going to have to think about her sport, then she might as well do so in a productive manner, so she moved to her desk, and flicked open her note book. It contained all her ideas for moves. There was a list of spins and jumps, which she could perform, and another of the compulsory moves she had to use in a routine, mostly imposed by her father and her coach. She was on the verge of a breakthrough on a couple of new moves she had been working on. Even if she didn't have the quad for Nagano, she would have a couple of things unique to her.

"You have so much potential, Electra. You need to apply yourself more, and you can go all the way. Give up on all these foolish pursuits, like that cousin of yours. He is bad news, Electra, and he is distracting you. I know all about you skating with him last night. It isn't right, Electra. That boy is evil." Her father continued. At this, she could stand the torrent of words no longer. She got up, and went to the door, pulling it open, and came face to face with him.

"Dad, Gideon isn't evil. He is just a little different from us. We went skating, didn't we? And apart from a few minutes at the beginning, it wasn't as if he was even skating. He just sat and watched." She told him, being careful not to mention that the others had been there. "And you know what, that spin I've been working on, it *will* be ready by next Monday. I'll be at the rink all weekend, but I *will* make that spin, and take it to Skate America next weekend."

"But that boy..." He started again.

"Isn't evil. I know he's Cajun, but he has promised me that he has never performed any voodoo." She lied. She suspected that if Gideon wished to do voodoo, he probably could. After all, there was something in his manner that seemed – *enchanting*.

"I just hope you know what you're getting yourself involved in, because if you think that the Lord will forgive you for getting involved with the Devil, then you are much mistaken, daughter." He told her, seeming to have come to the end of his speech on the matter. He turned and made his way back down the hallway to the stairs. Electra sighed with relief, leaning back against the frame of the door.

She moved back to the desk, and slammed her note book shut. She knew that there was little she could do on paper at this point. What she needed more than anything else was a day off, but there was even less chance of that happening than there was of her managing to get that dinner at The Top of the Mark. Besides, winners, as she was so frequently reminded, didn't take days off. They were meant to live as slaves to the profession, never able to cut loose unless it was at the proper time, in the correct place. That was why the gala performances were so important. There was nothing better than being on the ice when there was no pressure to perform perfectly. That was another thing she had managed to learn from her illicit skating session.

It wasn't fair of her father to make her feel like she didn't deserve a life away from her sport. If it were up to her, she would never have got involved in the first place. But there was no way she could take it back, now. And besides, she wasn't even sure what else she would do if not for the ice. She was bright enough to do most anything, but she had never stopped to actually think what she would choose instead.

Perhaps, she had thought once, she might be a writer, or an actress. She could have been a fair musician, if she'd been allowed to continue piano lessons past the age of ten, but she had been told in no uncertain terms that it was not an option. The only thing she had decided was that she would have to live in student accommodation when she went to college, because there was no way she was staying at home if she didn't have to anymore.

Later, as she slipped into sleep, she began to dream, of Vagan, caught behind a screen of flames, and a dark figure that sat silently, holding its hand toward her, asking her to join them within the fire. And as she slept, she screamed in silence.

Chapter
ten

The halls were packed with pupils, all trying to get out in time to catch the bus to a weekend of freedom. People called to each other over the throbbing crowd, making last minute plans for the following 48 hours. Electra hung behind, taking books from her locker, looking at her watch, and trying to pass the time. She was in no hurry to start the weekend, knowing that this was the last time she would be in the halls for a week. Still, there was the promise of seeing Cain in just a short time. As long as her parents were ready to leave on time, she should get a few hours with him.

She spent an extra minute rummaging in her book bag for her umbrella. It had been raining rather heavily for most of the afternoon, and now she was starting to face the fact that she was in for a very wet walk to the rink. The rain showed no sign of letting up, and the umbrella was not there. She turned back to her locker, and surveyed the contents. There were books, a spare pair of tennis shoes, and a gym skirt that was too big for her. No umbrella, though.

"Hi. Lost something?"

Electra spun around, almost losing her balance, and came face to face with Dylan. She frowned, then smiled.

"My umbrella. I think I must have left it at home. Well, I guess I'm going to get wet." She shrugged, still smiling.

"Me, too. And I really have no excuse for that. The weather is such a fixed thing, I should have known." Dylan laughed.

"Well, you're welcome to get wet with me if you like. I have to walk right past Haight to get to the rink. I hate the week before competition; I spend more time there than anywhere else. Then I should manage to freeze to the ice, so it should be fun all round." She grinned.

"I hope you have a change of clothes rather than that! I assume you use the rink just off Ashbury, then?" He enquired, sounding interested. She nodded, and together they started to walk away from the bank of lockers. It took her a moment to remember that she had left her own locker standing open. She apologised quickly, and turned back to slip the padlock through the hasp, before rejoining Dylan. Together, they walked out into the rain, which was falling in huge droplets, splashing into large pools strategically placed across the ground to make sure they caught as many feet as they possibly could. "Hmmmm, we're going to get very wet."

"I don't mind so very much. It'll save me having to shower when I get home." She laughed, knowing that she was going to have very little time to get back home before her brother turned up.

They walked slowly, in silence, for a long while. Within a few minutes, they were wet through. Even

Electra's heavy wool blazer did not keep her dry for long. The cold wet droplets seeped through, making the fibres even heavier than normal. Her braided hair was saturated, and where it hung down her back, the water ran through, drenching the nape of her neck.

"So, how are you feeling now?" Dylan asked her. She had been wondering how long it would take him to ask how she had been dealing with the news of Maggie's death.

"I've been better, but also, far worse. Next week should really be the big test, because it will be the first competition without her. I have a weekend of practice ahead, though, so I can't relax yet." She sighed heavily, wiping her hand across the top of her head to keep the water from running down her forehead and into her eyes.

"So, it's all practice this weekend, then." It wasn't a question.

"Mostly. My brother is coming over tonight. We're being rebellious, and I'm having popcorn." She answered him quickly, smiling again. Dylan was easy to talk to, she found, and his presence tended to put her at ease.

"Ah, to have family. I could have done with siblings, once. Still, I couldn't really have asked for more than I had." He didn't seem sad, more that he was resigned to the fact that he was alone. This surprised her.

"You don't have anyone?" She quizzed, feeling a little self conscious to be prying.

"Not for sometime, now. The closest I had to siblings were Maria and Amennette. They were good friends, but that's another story, and not one for today." He sounded as if he were recalling something from a distant past. She looked at him, and he gave his head a slight shake before the smile returned. "So, it's just you and a brother? No others?"

"No, although I have a cousin as well, now." She would have stopped right there with thoughts of Gideon if she had been at home, but with *this* company, she felt no guilt at mentioning him.

" 'Now'? You didn't have one before?" He seemed curious.

"We didn't realise he existed. He turned up a couple months back, part of the New Orleans branch of the family, on my mom's side. We thought they had died out in the early seventies, but then he appears out of the blue. Mom says he's the spitting image of his father, who she met a couple of times, before there was some kind of accident or something. She didn't realise he had any family. So, now, I have a cousin. It's cool, but my dad thinks he must be some voodoo priest or something, because of the New Orleans t-hing. I can't convince him otherwise."

"Interesting theory."

She could sense the silent laughter that he did not give, but was oblivious to the dark shadow that flitted across his mind for the briefest of moments. As they continued toward Haight Street, they chatted about nothing in particular, and as she left him, making her way for the short session she was running a little late for, she did so feeling nothing of the storm that was soon to come.

Chapter eleven

I hope it's okay that I brought him with me." Cain was grinning when Electra opened the door for him. The young male he was referring to was standing by the kerbside, his back turned to them, but she recognised him immediately. Cain dropped his voice and continued. "He talked about you most of the way back the other night. I think you've made a new friend."

"Just don't tell dad. He'll hit the roof. Don't worry; they'll be out for the next four hours. Their minister is giving some sort of speech about the perils of meat on Fridays or something. I don't mind not eating meat on a Friday, if it means I can have carbs instead." She responded in a similar volume, before raising her voice, and calling to the boy. "Come on in, Vagan."

She led them into the house, and into the den where the TV stood. For a long time, it had only been used for watching material of either a religious or an educational nature. Luckily, when their parents were out, Electra got to view what ever she liked. Better than anything else, Cain had a large collection of bad horror movies that he loved to share with his sister.

"Okay, so I got my new favourite, Killer Klowns From Outer Space, and I'll take it you haven't seen it yet. Also, I got a pack of Cokes, because I know what dad would do if he saw you drinking the stuff. Just don't tell him, all right? Did you get popcorn?" Cain asked as they went. She nodded, and watched as Cain and Vagan sat on the huge pink couch. She left them there for a moment, and went to the kitchen where she had already microwaved some popcorn. She would have to ask Cain to take the evidence with him when he left. As she made her way back, she could hear them talking. "Because I rarely get to do anything nice for her, so just shut up, and let her sit next to you."

"I have no problem with her sitting next to me, but she might have one. I'm not sure what to say to her. In fact, my palms are sweaty, and I'm absolutely petrified of her. Not that she's scary, but, you know, she's *her*." Vagan was talking in little more than a whisper, but she could make out every word he said. "I'm really not good with girls, Cain. And she's not just any girl, she's Electra Philips."

"Amazing, that, her being my sister and all. Calm down, Vagan. She doesn't bite." Cain laughed quietly. Electra waited a moment, then went back into the den. "Hmmm, popcorn."

"I hope you don't mind salted, Vagan, because I am not allowed salt, or butter, so this has both." She announced, pretending that she had heard nothing that they had said. She squeezed onto the couch between the pair, the bowl on her lap, and waited for either of them to respond. When they both just looked at her, she let out a laugh, and pushed her brother. "Put in the movie, Cain."

The movie was just as bad as Electra had expected it to be; it was about as scary as a three-week-old puppy. When it finished, Vagan excused himself rather quickly, leaving Electra and her brother on the couch.

"Jumpy little guy, isn't he." She commented.

"You have no idea." He responded. "Are you okay? I mean, I heard what happened to that girl, and, well, are you okay?"

"Dad acted as if I won the lottery when he heard. He's unbelievable sometimes. Yeah, I'm okay. I didn't really know her all that well, anyway. To be honest, she was a bit of a pain in the ass, if you know what I mean, but I wouldn't have wished her dead. Maggie had talent, and she'll be missed by many, but to be honest, I can't get too upset." She told him.

"Did dad tell you that 'suicide is a mortal sin'?" Cain questioned.

"No, but it's about all he missed out." She shrugged.

"You remember when Nicky Travers from my homeroom killed himself?" Cain asked. Electra nodded, remembering the short, rather rotund, boy that her brother had referred to. "Well, for about a month after that, dad told me every night that 'suicide is a mortal sin, and you'll end up in hell if you do it'. For a while, I wondered whether he thought I was really going to jump off the bridge like Nicky did. It didn't help any that I was up to my eyeballs in revision for my SATs at the time. Besides, Nicky was never happy, not even when we were in kindergarten."

"And when were you ever happy at school?" She asked, knowing that her brother had been somewhat of an outcast.

"Ah, well, that brings me to my point. I did want to check with Vagan first, but as he seems to have disappeared, I'll just go ahead. Do you remember when we were kids, and we went camping at that place a couple hours north?"

"Yeah, the place with the stream and the pool surrounded by redwoods. What about it?"

"Well, Vagan and I are planning a weekend trip away. I've roped in one of my other friends, too. Thing is, I'd really like it if you could come."

"When are you going?" She asked, feeling a sudden sense of dread that she would have to ask permission.

"The first weekend in November. I figure you could tell dad it will give you a chance to relax after Skate America. I know what you're thinking, but it would be so nice to have you there with us. I know Vagan wouldn't mind, and Devon, well, he doesn't mind anything much."

"You know he'll never fall for that. Dad's not easily convinced of anything anymore."

"Well, to sweeten the deal, I'm willing to come to a family dinner on Sunday." He pushed. Her mother would be very grateful for managing to get Cain in the house for once; she may even be able to invite Gideon. "Thing is, after Skate America, you have a couple weeks before the next competition, so you deserve to have a break after this one. Otherwise, all you have for the next however long is practice."

"Hey, I'm not the one who needs convincing, Cain!" She sighed, then changed the subject. "Do you think he's okay?"

"I'm sure he's fine. He probably got over excited when I made him sit next to you. He seems to be a little star struck. He'll get over it, though." Cain laughed a little. "I'll go find him."

She watched him as he walked out of the room, and made his way to the kitchen, where Vagan had obviously headed. She was starting to think about how nice it would be to go off into the wilderness with her brother and this young male who seemed so alluring all of a sudden. She wasn't sure she would manage to convince her father, but she was sure going to give it a go.

"Well, that's what you get when you eat too much popcorn, man. We should really get going soon anyway." Cain's voice signalled their return.

"Cain, I'll talk to mom, tell her you called while they were out." She called to him as they came back into the den. "Can I invite our new friend here, too?"

"Sure, and he'll even accept." Cain grinned.

"What am I being roped in to?" Vagan asked her brother. Electra answered before Cain could.

"You are agreeing to dinner on Sunday, and to a favour I need from you." She responded, making a snap decision, which she would probably live to regret if her father heard about it. "Come to the rink, tomorrow, at eleven. I want you to show me how you manage that speed, and I don't have long to learn, but I pick things up quickly."

"How will you get Frau Hitler to leave you alone?" Cain asked, referring to her coach with the nickname they had given her before they had found better words to describe her.

"That's where you come in. You place a call for her, and keep her talking for as long as possible. I only need five minutes." She grinned at them both. "Please, tell me you'll be there."

"This is going to get me in trouble, isn't it?" He sighed. She was impressed he had figured out her father, and his wrath, so quickly.

"Maybe, but I really need this." She pleaded. He seemed to process her request for a moment, but the smile that started to turn the corner of his lips up showed that he was coming around. Rather more impulsively, she rose onto her toes, and kissed him lightly on the corner of his mouth. He blushed wildly for a moment. "Thank you."

"We really should get going," Cain interrupted. "Try to act surprised when I raise the subject on Sunday, okay? Now, I have four empty Coke cans, and a microwave popcorn package. Is there anything else I should take with me?"

"If you could take me, I'd be grateful. Otherwise, no." She told him, walking with them to the front door. "Vagan, thank you for coming, and I will see you tomorrow at eleven. Cain, take care, and remember, five minutes."

She watched them walk away, then made her way up to her room, switched on the radio, and tuned it to the Bobby Dee show. It was the most popular show on the airwaves, and everyone listened to his voice every night.

"Hello, bay area. You're listening to KW-SFR, and this is the Bobby Dee show, bringing you all the best rock from the rock. That was the mellow tones of Aerosmith, and up next, a little Alice Cooper. Make sure you stay tuned throughout the night. Rock on, fans."

Chapter twelve

O h dear, I think I've just figured out who killed Eloise, and who *tried* to kill Marlene!" It was the TV. Vagan was watching 'Murder, She Wrote', and had already figured out who did it twenty minutes before the female super sleuth did. Now would ensue a detailed and well thought out entrapment scheme, where by the heroine, Jessica Fletcher, would unmask the criminal. There would then be a happy conclusion for someone, normally with one of her friends, or many relatives, finding themselves very happily in love. It was fairly cheesy, but Vagan adored the whole thing.

If only life could really be that simple, Vagan thought. He wished there was someone to figure out all the answers to the questions that he had about life and love. Unfortunately, there wasn't; Jessica Fletcher was only a TV character.

The show came to an end, and Vagan had correctly predicted whom the perpetrator was. Even the ending was what he had expected. He watched the closing credits, listening to the theme tune, then switched off the set. It was Friday, and it was very close to midnight.

Having spent the evening with Cain and his sister again, he was now back in his room, waiting for the night to pass. It was taking its time, though.

He went to the icebox, and pulled out a carton of juice that he had been hiding from Billy; his roommate had a tendency to consume everything in sight. With Billy out, he decided to switch on the radio, and actually listen to some music. He tuned the dial to his new favourite station, KW-SFR, and found the DJ talking over the last moments of a song.

"Well, that was the Violent Femmes, with 'Blister in the Sun', and up next is Wheezer, with 'Suzanne', as requested by our very most favourite listener, Electra P. Keep listening, and calling our beautiful little lady, Frankie. She just loves to talk to you guys. This is, as always, the Bobby Dee show, and I'll be here with you till one am. Stay tuned and rock on." The DJ spoke in the kind of chilled, laid back voices that Vagan associated with movie characters of the same persuasion.

Now, he took a deep drink, and realised that Electra was starting to enter his life from every angle. He was not only seeing her in his dreams now, but in just about everything he saw and did. Her face seemed to be everywhere, her name spoken so very frequently. He knew that within the next week, she would be on TV again, as her next competition began. For the first time ever, he would actually take the time to watch the sport without the pressure his mother put on him to view it.

The song was good; he recognised it from somewhere. He took another drink from the carton, before stashing it back out of sight, and grabbing a cookie from the little box behind the sink.

Outside, it was still raining fairly heavily. Billy had been out for hours, and Vagan didn't expect him back much before dawn this time. He could look after himself, Vagan had decided fairly early on.

There was always the option of heading to bed, but he couldn't bring himself to do it. He knew that there were dreams waiting for him there. The fact that she was now there with him helped with the prospect, but even so, he knew that as soon as he fell into the darkness, the flames would engulf him. Instead, he resigned to listen to the Bobby Dee show for as long as he possibly could.

"So, this guy, Karl, he took my car and sold it, then he tells me that he did it because Dr Seuss told him that the Devil was coming to earth, to take young virgin maidens for their blood. Obviously, the guy's a complete nut, but luckily, I'm not a virgin, so he doesn't want *my* blood. But what can I say? He looks like a young Lloyd Cole, if you remember him, Bobby. So, what should I do?" It was a young girl talking to the DJ about her psychotic boy friend.

"Get away from him. Even if he does look like a young Lloyd Cole. And yes, I remember who Lloyd Cole is. The question is, how do you? Really, kids, psycho maniacs do not make good mates. Now, I wanna play some tunes, so please, lets go back in time, with this classic track from Guns and Roses with Paradise City. Keep listening, keep calling, and sometimes, keep running."

He couldn't stop himself from laughing. The idea that Dr Seuss could tell someone anything other than how to clear pink cat rings off a bath was ludicrous. Still, the girl obviously believed that there was some truth to the idea; she wouldn't have called if she didn't.

The track was good and heavy, and Vagan found himself getting lost in the noise. It was nice to find himself drifting into a reverie that saw him back on the farm. It was a fantasy that had seen his parents retire to a smaller house, leaving him to run the farm with his beautiful young wife, Electra. He knew it was only a dream, but something felt so right. Something told him that there was a chance if he could just get past the fear that she was out of is league. It was only a dream; it harmed no one.

The song was just coming to an end when the door swung open, and Billy came in, accompanied by three girls. Vagan looked at his roommate in wonder. He couldn't figure out how he managed to do it time and time again. Billy wasn't even attractive. He *was* a jock, though. For some reason, girls seemed to like that.

"Vagan, I'd like you to meet these very fine friends of mine. This is Sarah, Gigi, and Luisa. Girls, this is my Vagan roommate. Sorry, I mean my roommate, Vagan." Billy hiccupped. He was highly inebriated, to the point that Vagan would not have wished to light a match for fear he may be inflammable.

"Billy, can we go to bed, now?" One of the girls – Vagan thought it was Gigi – asked.

"Of course, honey, we're all going to take a nice, long, relaxing trip to paradise." Billy responded, laughing. They all went over to Billy's side of the room, leaving Vagan to come to the conclusion that it was probably best he wasn't tired, because he wouldn't be getting any sleep.

Chapter thirteen

The sound of the 'phone ringing woke him. Gideon reached out, trying to find the receiver without having to open his eyes, but in the end, he had to relent. He found that the room was far too bright for his liking, but he didn't have time to dwell on the fact, as he lifted the receiver to his ear. "Hello?"

"Gideon, It's me." Came a familiar voice. He smiled despite himself.

"Cher, what are you doing calling me at this ungodly hour?" He asked his cousin, shading his eyes, despite the fact that the drapes were drawn across the large window.

"It's nearly eleven. Besides, I have to call you now, because I only have ten minutes break before I have to get back on the ice." She told him. He felt himself groan before he had the chance to stop the sound leaking out. If she asked him to do *that* again, then he was going to pack up and head back to the French quarter right there and then.

"Don't worry, I have far too much practicing to do on my quad toe-loop. I can't afford to help anyone else on the ice today."

"So, how can I help you, then?" He asked, starting to feel a little frustrated with her now.

"I have to ask you to dinner tomorrow. Cain is coming, and he's bringing that nice young friend of his, too. I've spoken to mom, and she says you have to come. Besides, if dad doesn't get to know you soon, he will start telling everyone that you are in league with the Devil, and you won't ever be allowed to see me again. Mom is making roast beef, as rare as possible, so get to mine by eight, and don't be late, alright?"

"I think I got most of that. Be there at eight, tomorrow. Not a problem. Can I go back to sleep now, Cher?" He yawned.

"Of course, but I hope you don't make a habit of sleeping all day." She responded.

"Bye, Electra." He called down the line, and replaced the receiver before she had a chance to say anything else. He wasn't in the mood to start explaining why he tended to sleep during the day rather than at night; he really didn't feel like explaining any of his habits to her. She may have questions about how he managed to live in such luxury when he had no visible way to support himself. He hated to have to admit that his wealth came from outliving many people when it was really they who should have witnessed his demise.

Chapter fourteen

The smell of man-made ice was different to the natural version. It was a fragrance he had known well for a long time, but one that had begun to fade from his memory, until now.

He watched her, red hair flying around her shoulders, as she flowed effortlessly around the rink, seeming to pay very little attention to the barked commands of the coach. She moved with such grace that he was sure she was made of liquid, rather than being a solid entity.

He had managed to conceal a pair of skates he'd borrowed from one of the guys on the college team, and entered the arena as quietly as he could, then climbed into the stands to watch her and wait for the call to come through. At twenty to eleven, he watched as she was dismissed for ten minutes, keeping as close to the shadows as he could in order to avoid being observed. When she came back onto the ice, he took the opportunity to take a couple of shots with his ever-present camera, knowing that he would shortly be on the ice beside her. He hoped he would have enough time to show her what she wanted. At eleven o'clock precisely, there was a crackle of static over the PA system.

"Coach Alderton, telephone call in the office. Coach Alderton, telephone call." A female voice recited, her tone distorted by the old speaker system.

The older woman looked frustrated, but called to Electra to stop for a moment. This was what he had been waiting for. The phone was in an office, and the office was far enough from the ice that the round trip would take about four minutes. Cain would keep her talking as long as he possibly could.

"Vagan?" Electra called, as the coach disappeared through a heavy, white door. He was on the ice within seconds, trying hard to conceal the fact that his pulse quickened when he stood next to her.

"I've been trying all morning to figure out how it works, but I can't put it into words. I'm going to have to show you, instead." He grinned, and carefully took her hand in his own. He pulled her gently, moving his feet backwards and forwards with such precision that within two steps, they were moving with more speed than he guessed she was normally capable of alone. He was reluctant to take the next step, knowing that it would mean her moving away from him. Still, he knew it had to be done. "Now, let go of my hand, but keep moving."

"Okay." Her voice was caught in the breeze their movement was creating. He felt her warm fingers slide from his own, and made his way back to the barrier as quickly as he could. The whole thing had taken only two minutes. If she could keep the momentum going, she would be fine.

He slipped back into the shadows, watching her move again, now with the added speed. The coach came back through the door after only four and a half minutes. As she did so, he watched Electra take off, rotating four times in the air before landing with perfection, as if she had made the jump many times with just as much ease.

He fought the urge to jump to his feet and applaud her, knowing that it would cause difficulty for her. Instead, he watched quietly as she landed the quad toe-loop a further three times before she started to spin, pulling her right foot high above her head, where it remained as she rotated for almost a minute.

He had never been quite so impressed or excited in all his days. She was the one.

Chapter fifteen

L ast night, some one asked me if I remembered who Lloyd Cole was, and I told her yes. I realise that most of you are under the age of twenty, and therefore have absolutely no idea who Lloyd Cole is. That's why this morning, when I finally got out of here, I went and saw my sister. She has a fantastic collection of rather old records – on vinyl, I kid you not – which just so happens to include a rather wonderful album by the man himself. From the 1984 album 'Rattlesnakes', by Lloyd Cole and the Commotions, which I gave her on her fourteenth birthday." Bobby Dee paused for breath. "This is the title track, 'Rattlesnakes'."

Billy was out, again, so once more Vagan was alone. It was close to midnight again, but still he refused to sleep. He had been awake for almost 36 hours, now, doing all he could to avoid the dreams.

He realised that he hadn't been called on in over a week now. He was starting to miss it, the gentle pressure between his shoulder blades that signalled he was being drawn from normal life to the little shack where he had spent so much of his first week at the college. Now, he wondered why it had worried him so much, and why it had been so long since it last happened.

It was one more day before he would see her again. He had been telling himself that all afternoon, since her hand had left his on the ice. He would endure anything to see her again. He had spent the journey back to campus the night before trying to get over his affliction. Cain had told him the real secret was to remember to breathe when she was close by, and to forget that she was anyone important. He wasn't sure how that was going to work out, but he intended to give it a try. It had almost worked earlier that day, but he wasn't sure he'd ever pull it off entirely. He wasn't even sure why he had been invited for dinner, but he supposed it might have something to do with the fact that both Cain and Electra felt more at ease with their family life when there were others around them. Besides, he was hopeful that he may get another one of those gentle kisses if he played his cards right. Cain had watched with great amusement as he found the tips of his fingers returning to the spot her lips had touched. He had a feeling it may mean more to him than it would to any other guy.

Vagan stifled a yawn, telling his brain it wasn't tired, but that it merely wanted a little extra oxygen. He had learnt the reason behind yawning when he was in high school, and now tried to convince himself that he was yawning because his brain needed stimulation.

Boredom led him to pick up the black cell 'phone that Billy had left lying around – the one his father paid for – and quickly dial the number so familiar to all the kids in the bay. 555-27-27. It was the only number he knew locally. It was the number for KW-SFR.

"Hello, KW-SFR, Frankie speaking, how can I help you?" The young female voice asked from the other end of the line.

"I have a request for the Bobby Dee show." Vagan replied.

"Could I take your name, please?" The girl asked.

"Vagan Elison." He responded, starting to worry about what he was going to request.

"Okay, Vagan, I'll take your request and pass it to Bobby as soon as he's finished the messages."

"Thanks, Frankie. I'd like to request 'Free', by The Martinis. And can I dedicate it to Electra P, please." He smiled, hoping the gesture was brave rather than foolish. It was a song he knew from happy memories, and he hoped she would also like it.

"Our favourite girl. No worries. I'll pass this through to Bobby in a moment. Thank you for calling KW-SFR, and keep listening." The woman hung up the other end, and Vagan pressed the end button, placing the cell phone back in about the same place as it had been.

He looked at the radio for a moment, then turned his attention to his camera. He had been cleaning the main lens, having dismantled the body to get to a loose screw that was doing nasty things to his aperture settings. Now as he tightened the screw to just the right degree, he took a moment to make sure that there was no dust caught in the thread. The old manual SLR had seen him through a lot of important events. He had been photographer for his high school yearbook, and had taken hundreds of thousands of shots for the student newspaper, *'The Bernard High Gazette'*, mostly all of the football team. When he had taken his award winning photo essay, he had used that old camera, developing the film and the prints with assorted chemicals that left his hands fragranced with a very individual scent.

"Hey all you young things, I've just had a request come in for a tune. The request came from Vagan, and he's dedicated it to our girl, Electra P. I have no idea where you get these names from, but I'm glad to have you listening. So just for Electra, this is The Martinis, with 'Free'. It's soft, it's sweet, it's just for you, girl."

"It really is." Vagan breathed, as he turned out the light, lay down on his bed, and drifted into a brand new daydream.

Chapter sixteen

The sound of rain falling in the night air outside reminded him of the day she had been laid in her tomb, cold and empty as death itself. It had changed everything for him. As long ago as that was, he could still remember the scent of her fragrance, the way her breath felt when they slept at night. He may be old now, but he could still remember everything with the clarity of the last moment.

He sat in his chair, waiting for the decay of passing time to take him. There would come a time when he would want back his old glory, he knew, but for now, he was content to let it all slip away as easily as it had come in the first place. It wouldn't be long now.

Except that there had been some change within him recently. He had actually managed to get what he required for himself, for the first time in many years. In fact, the thrill had been so great that he had not even bothered to call on the boy for a week. It had been so simple; he wondered why he had avoided the game, the hunt, for so long.

He had long ago discovered how to conceal himself within the shadows. He moved as silently as a mouse, hiding within the cracks in the surface of the world. The prey he had chosen had been easily charmed, her life stolen before she had even realised it was in jeopardy. He had fed until he was full, and left her to fade within the loving arms of the people who did not know, or understand, the truth of just how tragic her short life had really been.

For days, the hunger had been sated. For the first time in many years, he did not long for more. Still, now he understood that part of this was to do with the fact that he had got what he wanted for himself, and that he had not had to control his hunger to avoid the possibility of discovery. Now, he came to conclude that he would have to continue with this if he wanted to keep his contentment.

So the boy's days went on undisturbed for a while. The old man went for a prowl whenever the mood took hold of him. So it was hardly surprising that he now found himself more tired than he had been in a very long time.

As he sat in silence, listening to the rain falling, he finally decided that he was ready to fight to regain a little of what he had lost.

Chapter seventeen

A s he bit into the dark red meat, he could feel that he was being watched. He raised his eyes to meet the gaze of Electra Philips, and tried not to smile too inanely. If he got the chance to speak to her alone, he hoped that he might be able to keep his voice steady for once. Cain, sitting next to him, was trying hard not to laugh. He had never felt so out of place as he did right then.

Sitting next to Electra was the cousin, Gideon, who seemed to be rather bothered by something. At either end of the table, the parents were watching every movement made. They seemed polite enough when he had first arrived; Mrs. Philips was pleased with the flowers he had presented her with, just before she had asked Electra to take his coat from him. Mr. Philips had shaken both his and Cain's hands, before leading them into the large room that he referred to as the 'drawing room'. Electra had referred to it as the den the other evening. Looking at Electra and

Cain's parents, he was rather at a loss to see what had brought them together in the first place. Mrs. Philips was a youthful figure, with hair like Cain's – sandy strawberry blond, much paler than Electra's. Her hazel eyes were open and honest, and he supposed that when she was her daughter's age, she would have been almost as beautiful. Mr. Philips, on the other hand, was rather oppressive to be in the same room with. His once athletic figure had aged with maturity fairly well, but his stern face and stark white hair gave him the appearance of someone who had seen far too much to greet the world with a smile, anymore.

"How are you enjoying San Francisco so far, Vagan?" It was Mrs. Philips who thought she should fill the void of silence that had started to become deafening around them.

"It's certainly bigger than where I come from. I live just outside Salt Lake City, in a town called Bernard. My parents have a small dairy farm there. I guess it's great here, but I do get a little *overwhelmed* by the scale of everything. I'm getting used to it, though." He replied, trying to keep his voice calm. He wasn't used to talking so directly to people he was unfamiliar with, especially when in company.

"A dairy farm? How nice. And what about your parents?" This time it was Mr. Philips who addressed him, watching him with intense blue, hawk like eyes, ready to pounce on any information that was slightly less than perfect.

"Well, they're good people, hard working. My mom loves her home; it's all she ever wanted when she was a kid. My dad is very giving, and would do anything for his family. I'm lucky, I guess. My folks have always done what's best for me, and I couldn't ask for any more. I feel bad, at least slightly guilty, for leaving them. I know what this season is going to be like, and I wish I could be there for them, but they wouldn't let me give up college for that, so here I am." He gave his response as quickly as he could, avoiding, as instructed, any information about his religious and social background. Cain had warned him that if he got on to the subject of faith, he might never be able to get away from it. Besides, he wasn't that devoutly Jewish, so he didn't think it would make any impact on their views of him overall.

"What drew you to photography?" It was Electra's voice that gave the question across the table to him. He gave a slight smile, feeling that this was a question she may well have been intending to ask before, but which she now felt more comfortable asking because there were others to hear the response. He raised his eyes, and looked directly at her, resisting the urge to smile too broadly at her, feeling his cheeks flush ever so slightly, and hoped that no one else noticed.

"I would have been a painter, but I had no talent. There is something comforting in raising the viewfinder to my eye, choosing the perfect view, and capturing it forever. There are so many things in the world that need to be seen. I have hope that somehow, I can manage to show them to others. I have managed to find beauty within the grotesque, to view the changes of the seasons, and bring them back to glory. I will always be able to find something to capture my interest. Colours and textures fill my sight, and I would do all I can to let others see things as I do. I apologise if I come across too – impassioned – about this little hobby of mine. Really, one day, there will come a time when I can use this skill to make a living, and what more could anyone ask for?

"I've already had a small amount of success. I sold a few prints off the back of my small exhibition back home, which has helped out a lot over the past few months. Photojournalism is a well-respected profession, now. And if all else fails, I can go back to the farm, eventually." He frowned at the end, before adding "it would be a little more responsible of me, I guess, when I have a family of my own."

"Well, at least one of you youngsters seem to have thought ahead to your futures." Mrs. Philips commended. He thought about pointing out that Electra seemed to have hers all planned out for her, but decided against it.

"Who could really want more than a family?" He asked quietly. He looked down quickly to avoid meeting Electra's glance.

"How very refreshing. You could learn a lot from this young man, Cain." Mr. Philips nodded his approval of the response. Vagan suppressed the laugh he felt gathering in his throat, and smiled.

"Talking about family, dad, I was thinking about taking a trip to that parkland where we used to go when we were kids." Cain started. Vagan had been warned that this might get uncomfortable for the viewers.

"The place by the river?" It was Mrs. Philips who spoke first.

"The very same. Well, I was wondering," he paused, taking a deep breath, "if Electra could come too."

"She flies to Detroit in the morning." Mr. Philips practically barked.

"Not until the weekend after next, dad. I was hoping she might make the numbers up. One of my buddies from college is coming, and Vagan will be there. Don't you think it would be a good chance for her to relax before the next event? I mean, the flight to Paris alone is bad enough, but to do it twice within a week? Plus, it would be really nice to spend some time with her before the holidays." Cain's voice was surprisingly persuasive, but Vagan wasn't convinced it would do the trick. "It will leave her plenty of time for practice in between."

"I'm not sure, Cain. Electra's programme is fairly intense at the moment. She *is* working toward the Olympic dream, here. She needs to remain focused." Mr. Philips didn't sound willing to give an answer either way.

"She's focused to the point of insanity. Two days - 36 hours - that's all. There's a week after Detroit, and then another before Paris either side. She'll be at school longer than that. Dad, she managed the quad today, that puts her ahead of the others already. " Cain argued. Vagan made a mental note not to get on his wrong side any time soon.

"You're partly right, because that's very impressive, but it doesn't mean she doesn't need to concentrate still." Mr. Philips seemed able to argue just as fiercely. The talk about the quad toe-loop had been fairly constant in the early stages of the evening, but it had fallen by the wayside at some point. When Mr. Philips had announced the news that it had been accomplished, Vagan had acted impressed, even though he had seen it first hand. He hoped she could recreate the speed on her own. Two minutes was not really enough time to have shown her well enough that she would recall the technique when she went solo.

"Well, we'll be going anyway. Just, think about it, okay?" It was a final request on the subject, at least for the time being.

Dinner continued with a lot of small talk, about the weather, how the economy was fairing, the state of the education system. Mr. Philips made a lot of comments about how he was glad Electra went to a good school. Eventually, the plates of beef and other various items were cleared, and replaced with warm apple pie and ice cream. The conversations continued, and finally, the parents and Gideon left the table. Gideon excused himself, leaving into the dark night. Electra, Cain and Vagan remained at the table.

"Well, that went well." Cain grinned. Electra rolled her eyes. "Just keep working on dad, okay?"

"Sure. He's never going to give in, you know." She sighed, then turned to Vagan. "Are you guys sure you even want me there?"

"Of course we do." He gave his reply quickly but quietly, looking directly at her for the first time since she'd asked him about his course choice. He could feel his cheeks

colour again.

"I'll be back in a moment." Cain announced rather abruptly, standing up and leaving the dining room. For a minute, neither of them said anything, then Electra laughed.

"Could he have made that anymore obvious?" She murmured. "I think we're sufficiently alone for me to say thank you, now. I just hope it's enough."

"Just remember how to keep the momentum, and you'll be fine." He assured her.

"Sure, you make it seem so easy. Alderton couldn't believe it when I pulled it off. I thought she was going to call the press and get them down there to see for themselves. If I can perform that jump next week, then I'm home free. I'm not going to pin all my hopes on it, though. I've been in the game too long for that." She sighed quietly.

"I'll be watching, though, cheering you on as best I can. I may have to get rid of my roommate for the evening, because otherwise, he's likely to make fun of me." He was already imagining the ribbing Billy would give him for watching girls ice skate in a decorative manner. "He isn't normally around much, anyway, but knowing my luck, he'll decide that he suddenly has an undying need to study for his football midterms."

"I'm sure that's very academically geared." She laughed. "I'll wave to you from the kiss and cry if you like."

"Thanks." He could feel his cheeks start to colour again, just a little.

"I'm pretty sure that should be my line. Thank you for the song, too. It was nice." She was looking down at her hands, now. "Nice doesn't seem good enough, to cover it. It meant a lot to me. Thank you."

"The title made me think of you, and I hoped you would hear it. You deserve to be free, because from what Cain tells me, you have far too much pressure to be. I hope you get to come with us, because I really want the world to treat you right." He was sure this was too much to be saying, but for some reason, he couldn't stop himself. "Plus, I have a feeling you photograph really well."

"I'll do everything in my power to get him to agree. I'm not sure it will be easy, but I will do my best." She smiled, levelling her eyes to his.

"Vagan, it's time we got back. Sorry, El, but we really should get going." Cain's voice interrupted from the doorway. Electra let out a large, low sigh. "We'll visit soon, honey. In the meantime, good luck this week. Come on, see us out. I've all ready said goodbye to the folks, so all that's left is for us to go find a cab."

"Shouldn't I say goodbye to them?" Vagan asked, looking back and forth between the two.

"No." They both chorused at the same time, then laughed. Together, the three walked to the front door, and out into the night air. There was a chill of Autumn in the air, but at least it was dry. Cain stepped in to the street, and waved down a cab that was thankfully just pulling away from a house up the street.

"Good luck." Vagan told Electra, softly, before climbing into the cab behind Cain. He was so over whelmed with his evening, he didn't even notice the first hint of a throb between his shoulder blades.

Chapter Eighteen

D ad, I'm exhausted. Can we please just talk about this in the morning?" Electra sighed, hoping that just this once, he might listen. She wasn't even sure *why* he was so aggravated. It wasn't like she hadn't placed at all. Still, in his eyes, unless you got the gold, you hadn't achieved anything.

"But silver, Electra!" His voice followed her into the house and up the stairs.

That's right, dad, Silver, and I was lucky to get that! She thought as she climbed another step. He had been trying to get her to listen all the way from the airport. The flight from Detroit had, at least, been quiet, but only because there were other people on the plane.

She reached the bedroom door, pushing it open, relieved to have reached a safe haven, at last. The bed was inviting her to climb in and forget everything. But that was not going to be an option, she realised before she even thought it could be. Instead, she flicked the light on, finding that in the glare from the bulb overhead, the bed was far less inviting.

A small stack of envelopes lay on the bedspread, making up the post she had missed during her week away. She shuffled through them, noting an official looking thin white envelope with the five Olympic rings on – that was sure to be an early reminder about Olympic village protocol, no doubt – and a couple of letters inviting her to take out credit with different banks. There was a magazine detailing all the latest in sequin placement, and her monthly subscription to Hair Styles. The final item was neatly addressed in blue ink, on pale blue stationary. It was familiar handwriting, because she had seen it many times before. It was Cain's disguised script, the one he had used whenever he had been talked into doing someone else's homework. It may have fooled her parents, but it would take a lot more to fool her.

She slid her finger under the flap, pulling the top of the envelope off in her haste. There was a small, folded piece of paper inside, and something else. As she pulled out the photograph, she smiled, realising that it had been shot by some one who actually cared that she had taken silver.

The image was of herself gliding across the glassy smooth surface of the ice. The smile across her face had been offered to him, in those moments before he had joined her on the ice, even though he was so very new to her. She closed her eyes for a moment, searching her mind for the right image of him, and settling on one that made her smile increase.

Opening her eyes again, she propped the picture against her bedside lamp, and turned to the small slip of paper. Unfolding it, she found the less neat version of her brother's handwriting, and smiled again as she read the words.

*Don't be mad at me. He wanted me to keep this one, but I
thought you should have it, instead. He'll kill me if he
finds out. You have yourself a proper little fan, here.*
Cain
*Ps I think dad is going to cave on the trip. He called to
make sure it was all above board.*

Electra grabbed the phone's oversized receiver from
its cradle, and dialled the familiar number quickly, waiting
for Cain to answer.

"Hello?" His voice came after the third ring.

"Cain, it's me. I just got home, and I got the note."
She grinned into the receiver.

"Keep that quiet, or Vagan will kill me! Oh, and I'm
sure I'm supposed to say something about congratulations
or something. How is the old man taking it?" Cain asked,
and she felt herself sigh. "That well, huh?"

"Anyone would think that silver meant last place!
He's been ranting since the airport. He doesn't show any
sign of stopping yet. But, and it is a rather *big* but, he did
say he was willing to let me come on the trip with you
guys." She responded, finally unable to keep the news to
herself any longer.

"What are his conditions?" Cain's voice was
suddenly dubious.

"Well, he wants to see the van you're renting, but I
think he just wants to make sure that I won't have to bunk
with a 'boy'. Also, he wants me to do some training whilst
I'm there. Finally, he wants me back by midnight on the
Sunday. That's probably so that he can make sure that if
I've been sullied he can get me re-blessed on the Sabbath."

"Well, as long as Vagan is still doing his
disappearing act whenever you're around, I wouldn't
worry too much about your virtue. You aren't Devon's
type, I promise." She could hear a hint of a laugh in his

voice, but didn't really think much of it. "Hey, is that him yelling?"

"Yeah, he's still at it. I wish he'd just give up for a while. Okay, so I tripled out on the quad, but at least I tried. And three and a half rotations is more than any of *them* could manage. If only I'd had more than a few minutes with Vagan last week, I might have stood a chance at figuring out how he does it. I think dad brought this on himself!" She grinned. But her father's voice was getting louder again, and she knew he was outside her door now.

"Do you hear me Electra?" He yelled.

"Yes, dad!" She yelled back, holding the receiver away from her as she did so. "I should go, Cain. He's not going to give up anytime soon. Thanks again for the picture. If you see Vagan, make sure you tell him I say hello, and watch him turn red for me. I find it rather attractive on him."

"No worries. See you soon, bye." The click at the other end of the line came so quickly that she didn't even have time to respond. She sighed again, placed the receiver back in its cradle, and moved over to the door.

"Dad, I have two weeks till the next competition, and by then, I'll have it down cold, okay?" She asked the glowering man whose stare met her as she opened the door. His face didn't even *try* to soften as he looked at her.

"Fine, but at the moment, we have a new situation, which you would know if you'd been paying any attention to me. It seems that the police have decided that Maggie's death may not have been quite so clear cut as they thought. They are now treating the circumstances as suspicious. I need for you to come down stairs, please. There is a call for you from the authorities dealing with the case." His face was a rather strange shade of red, the one he reserved for when she had displeased him more than normal.

While he had been talking, though, the bottom had fallen out of her stomach, making her glad for once that she had not been permitted to eat the complimentary peanuts on the flight. Even the bottled water wasn't sitting well, right now. She followed him slowly down the stairs, into the living room, where the main house phone was located. Her father took a seat in the green easy chair, while her mother sat silently on the couch. Yet again, she held a phone receiver to her ear.

She listened numbly as an officer from somewhere in Los Angeles told her that they were now treating the death as suspicious, and that they would be contacting everyone who had cause to have been in contact with Maggie Treat during her short life. The whole conversation lasted for only a few minutes, and it was mostly all one sided, but as Electra sat there, she realised that she was suddenly being seen as a suspect.

Chapter nineteen

The Old Man stared at the portrait above the fireplace. It had been painted a long time before, by an unknown artist who'd shown great potential. The face it held was his only company, now. Day in, day out, he existed alone. Visitors were rare, and the few who called, he managed to ignore most of the time.

The image in the picture was his own. He had no other mementoes of his past, but that painting. There were no photographs to speak of, no objects of value. The only thing to remind him of what he looked like was that painting, because he had discarded all mirrors long ago. He did not want to know what he had become, now, didn't want to be confronted with his own face as he was.

The strength he had found had drifted away almost as quickly as it had been discovered, so he had been forced to start using the boy, again. He did not care, though, because something new had come to his attention. He was being hunted, by someone who would not be willing to give up until he no longer inhabited this world. Although he was tired, although he had waited for a century to be released from this existence, he found that he was not yet willing to give up with out a fight. He would hold on to it as long as he possibly could, and would take as many with him as he could when he had no choice but to succumb to the darkness that was waiting for him on the other side of his demise.

Chapter twenty

Vagan was stacking food in the cupboards of the RV when Electra and her father arrived. He had spent the afternoon packing, and then at the stores getting supplies.

"Hello?" Electra called, knocking on the open door of the van. Vagan smiled at the voice, so familiar to him all ready, and turned to greet her. Cain had warned him that Mr. Philips would be coming, so wasn't surprised to find him there. He extended his hand to the older man, who shook it firmly.

"Come on in, I'll show you around." He welcomed, and led them into the main seating area. "As you can see, the van is well equipped, and plenty big enough for all involved. There is a nice little stereo, so we can play some CDs later. There's a fridge with an icebox, and a two-ring stove. Through this way, there are a total of three bedrooms, one twin, one bunks, and the big one at the end is a double. Then, the shower room. It's not huge, but it will be fine for a couple of days."

"Well, it all seems very comfortable. As Cain has assured me that he doesn't mind his sister coming, I think that everything should be fine. Now, I want you back here before midnight, and your assurance that you will be doing some training whilst you're away." He sounded stern. Vagan made his way back to the seating area, trying to give them some privacy.

"I know, dad. You have my promise." He could almost hear her rolling her eyes at her father as she responded to his request.

After a few more minutes, Electra's bags were out of the trunk of Mr. Philips' BMW, and on the pink velour couch. With one last mention of the midnight curfew, Mr. Philips left them, and Vagan went back to stocking the little fridge.

"We had a discussion," he started, not turning to look at her. "We think you should take the double at the front."

"That doesn't seem very fair." She objected quickly.

"Sure it is. I'm happy with a bunk, and Cain and Devon are fine with the twins, so you get the double. It makes sense to me. Besides, no one would give up the double in favour of the other options." He argued back. It was true. He'd tried the bunks, and they were about as comfortable as rocks, and the twin beds weren't much better, but there were few other options. "Come on, we'll get you all settled in, then I just have to pop out for a little while. Cain and Devon shouldn't be too long, though."

He lifted her light bags from the small couch, and carried it down to the end of the van, where the door to the big room was. Pushing it open, he led her into the small space, dominated by a large bed. There were a couple of small cabinets above it, where he had found a stash of sheets that had seen many better days. A small, lacy curtain covered the one window, letting in the pale afternoon light. A pink bedspread and three rather lumpy pillows completed the room, which was wallpapered with a beige textured affair that seemed better off in the seventies than the current time.

"Adorable, isn't it." He chuckled, placing her bags on the bed. "I'll leave you to it."

He was going to have to get a move on now, not sure how long it may take him to go, do whatever it was he had to do, and get back to the van before they decided to go without him. Hopefully, this would be one of those times when he got away with only an hour of missing life; if not, there were sure to be questions.

Whilst he had begun to miss the pain, he had also begun to hope that the nightmare was gone for good. Now, though, it was back with more force than he would have thought possible. For the past week, he had spent more time in the shack than he had in his own bed. Even Billy had noticed that he seemed to be gone more often, and Billy was hardly the most observant person Vagan had ever met. Now, as he headed back to the tiny building, he hoped that he would be free of the pain for the weekend.

He was surprised when he woke up less than an hour later, pain gone, feeling better than he normally did after one of these episodes. By 5:23, he was back at the van, where he found Cain and Devon just arriving, with a large stash of boxes, that Vagan could guess the content of.

"I thought I was going to have to drive this thing myself. That would have been a problem as I still only have a learner's permit." Electra greeted them as they climbed up into the vehicle. She had obviously been busy while she had been waiting, because the table was covered with maps, showing the route they would be taking, and the area they would be staying in. She had also marked a couple of places where they could stop for gas if they needed to. Cain was going to do most of the driving, as the RV was in his name, although Devon had offered to take over if the need arose. "Hi!"

"El, this is Devon; Devon, Electra." Cain introduced. Electra shook hands with the other male, then sat back down to look at the maps again.

"Dad says it takes about two hours to get to the park, and then about another ten minutes to get to the right place for the stream. That means that if we left now, we could be there before eight." Electra told the room. "I did mention I have to be back by midnight Sunday, didn't I?"

"If we didn't get it from you, we sure as hell got it from him!" Cain called back to her, carrying his bag through to the room with twin beds. Vagan had taken one of the boxes from Devon, and was now stacking bottles in the fridge, and the small cabinet under the sink. He wasn't sure there was going to be enough space, or that the quantity of alcohol was really necessary, but he wasn't about to start making a fuss over it.

Less than ten minutes later, they were on the road, Cain at the helm, while the others played a couple hands of cards. They stopped to refuel after an hour, and then pressed on, all eager to get to their destination as quickly as possible.

The parkland was north and a little east of the city. As Cain drove into the area, Vagan realised that this was just the right environment for him. The air was clean, and the land beautiful. Redwoods grew tall all around them, with small clearings appearing naturally hear and there. The stream that ran through the park, toward the lake, was not huge, but it was fairly fast flowing. The sound of the RV's engine was loud, but they could still hear the call of birds.

Finally, Cain pulled over into a larger clearing, right beside the stream. It was a beautiful spot, where the trees were far enough spaced for them to build a fire. The ground was covered in years worth of old pine needles and fallen leaves, carpeting the space with a crisp, brown surface. Although it was dark already, Vagan could tell that the place was stunning.

They climbed out of the van, and stretched various limbs. Vagan had decided to gather some wood in order to build the fire, while the others started to set up the table and chairs that had been supplied with the van. It didn't take long to gather a large selection of wood pieces, and some dried leaves and pine cones. He built a pyre, and lit the lower edges, watching the flames as they spread upwards slowly. He tried not to think about the dream, pushing it as far from his mind as he was able.

As the four of them talked easily into the evening, stopping only to take mouthfuls of hot dogs they had roasted on the fire, the sky above them darkened into a sea of stars that was almost as beautiful as the one he had grown up with.

Chapter twenty-one

It had started in 1907, in London. He could still remember that cold winter, the way his hands felt cold even when they were wrapped in leather and held against the fire. His parents had insisted they return from Paris for the season, trying to out run the fear, the demons that were watching them so closely. If they had only known what they would find there waiting for them, they would have fled further.

By the time that Christmas came, and their escape may have finally been secured, it was already too late for them. The Old Man had consumed them, leaving little but the shadows that had once surrounded them.

For nearly ninety years, the search had proved fruitless. He had always tried to stay as close as possible, following any lead that might be of any value. It had led him back across the globe, back to many of the places he had been.

The closest he had been, until now at least, had been in Memphis, during the late 1940s. The Old Man had stayed put for several years, put down some roots for a while. He had watched from afar, as The Old Man had taken on a new boy, young, and beautiful as always, but with more potential than he had seen in a long time. A bright future lay ahead for this soul, but it would be at a price, now that The Old Man was involved in it. They were the ones he normally sought - the brightly burning souls, who would eventually have the whole world before them. His own future would have been just as brilliant, had he not decided to ignore his vision of it, and gone after The Old Man, instead. And so he had waited during those five years, but the chance to strike never arose.

Eventually, they moved on. For a while, The Old Man went missing, and he had to assume he had gone home. By walking the land where he was first at home, The Old Man became invisible to him. There was no way to follow there, into the lair of a killer, and remain.

When he finally sensed The Old Man moving again, he knew that the time was coming sooner than he had anticipated. He climbed on to a bus, and headed for San Francisco.

224 years to the day since he had first taken breath, Dylan Horatio Adams had come to the conclusion that the days had disappeared far too quickly, but that he was still no closer to the end of them than he had ever been.

Chapter Twenty-two

T he air was cool, clear, and fresh. It was almost as sweet as the air at home, but there was a quality to it unlike any he had felt before; it was almost as if an electric current ran through the atmosphere.

He spent nearly ten minutes making sure he had everything he needed for the day ahead. His hiking boots were a little stiff from lack of recent use, but they would soften quickly. He had decided that they were his best option, realising that the best views would probably take a little effort to reach. He wore them with an old pair of shorts, and a t-shirt, not wanting to over heat in the warm fall sunlight.

His camera was encased in its rigid leather shell, and he now took a moment to check that all the settings were correct for the type of film he was using – black and white, a fast film in case of any action taking place – and adjusted the speed setting. His lightweight titanium tripod was carefully stowed in a long green weatherproof bag. He was all set; so why did he hesitate to start moving?

"Good morning." The soft, feminine voice from behind him was what he had been waiting for, he realised as soon as he heard it.

"Hi." He smiled, and turned to look at her. A tumble of red hair was falling around her shoulders, waving gently after being braided the day before. Her green eyes seemed to have a dreamy focus to them, and her lips were slightly parted in that smile he had grown remarkably fond of in such a short space of time. The pale, muted lime green dress she wore was a little sheer in the early sun, and hinted at the gentle curves of her athletic frame. He tried to conceal his blush by ducking his head, but he knew as he did so, that she had seen enough of it to guess what it was in response to.

"When are you heading out?" Her voice didn't give away her thoughts, although he was fairly sure he could have guessed at them, and been right.

"A few minutes. I was planning to follow the river a little way. After that, I'm not sure." He shrugged, looping the camera strap around his neck, slinging the tripod bag across his shoulder.

"I was going to walk to the lake, if you don't mind some company." She sounded a little hesitant, but possibly – hopeful?

"You're more than welcome." He was trying not to sound too eager, but realised he was failing badly. "Which way do we head?"

"That way." Her voice was confident, now, and he was willing to follow her wherever she may lead – whether that was to the lake, to the closest strip mall, or round and round in circles back to camp for the next three days.

The stream was clear, crystalline in the morning light. They walked in near silence most of the way. A few times, Vagan attempted to start a conversation, but he kept on failing. He wasn't used to being alone in the middle of nowhere with nothing but the wilderness and a beautiful female. It was far more difficult than he could have anticipated.

"The path starts to climb a little, just here." Electra warned him. "It helps with the waterfall. It's a really low gradient, and the water runs fast enough to keep it flowing. There's quite a drop into the lake, anyway, but I guess it helps."

"Cain said it was years since you last came here." Vagan responded, glad that she had spoken first.

"It has been." She confirmed, then seemed to think for a moment before continuing. "I have few memories outside of skating. I guess I retain more detail for the memories I *do* have."

"Has it been hard?" He asked, feeling that he may be prying, but still wanting to know, wanting to understand more about her.

"Not always. I may have missed out on a few things, rites of passage or whatever, when I was a kid. My social calendar was never particularly full, I guess. I never noticed, though. I was always too busy with some thing or other, mostly training. Plus, I was never really overcome with friends extending invitations my way." Her tone was impassive.

"Why do you think that is?" He pressed gently.

"That's easy, although you're the first to ask." She smiled wistfully, her clear green eyes becoming a little glazed. "I was destined to be different. When I started kindergarten, I was already on the first stages of the programme. While the other kids had milk and a cookie before naptime, I had a protein shake and a multi vitamin tablet. At lunch, they had sandwiches; I had steamed rice and cabbage. They all knew I wasn't one of them.

"All through grade school, I kept myself to myself, tried not to draw attention. It was hard, though. When I was in sixth grade, I was junior all state level, seeded higher than anyone else in my age range. When news got round at school, they hated me more than they ever had before. Then, this year, the American championships, and I placed silver, bronze at worlds. That was the hardest semester ever. They all think I'm stuck up, and that I get preferential treatment because of who I am. They have no idea that all I ever wanted was to be one of them; all I wanted was to be normal."

"I'm not sure that would be possible, but you deserve the chance to try." Vagan gave a sad smile, understanding the way she felt more than he would be willing to admit.

"I know. I'm rather resigned to the fact, now. I still have hope, that the future will somehow be better." She sounded far more optimistic for a moment.

"Would you have done it all differently, if you'd been given a choice?" He was eager to keep her voice in the air.

"Some of it, sure. But I also realised a long time ago that some things are vital in leading us to others. For example, if I couldn't skate, Cain would not have dragged you to the rink, and we would not be here now." She spoke softly.

"True, but I'm sure Cain would have found some other way to throw us together." Vagan objected quickly.

"He wouldn't have felt the need, though, would he? Because I wouldn't be so starved of human companionship that I needed to have friends found for me." She argued back. He could see her point, but he refused to believe it was the case.

"Cain likes me, though. He would have managed it. I fail to believe that this world that suffers from a lack of the

108

public version of you doesn't still own your father, complete with all of his tyrannical tendencies. Cain would have dragged me along to a family dinner sooner or later." He theorised.

"I'll allow that." She grinned.

But he wasn't finished yet. "Also, Cain had this trip planned to include you from the start, no matter what. Even if your father hadn't been such a tyrant in imaginary world, you and I would still be here."

"I think you're probably right." She finally agreed.

The path came to an abrupt end. The river continued to flow, but a thick span of brush blocked the trail from view. A rather large tree had fallen, roots and all, and it seemed that it was going to be difficult to get around it.

"Crap!" She breathed. He looked at her quickly, not really sure she had said it at all. She caught his glance, and threw her head back with a short blast of laughter. "You're right, he'd throw a fit. I think I saw another path, just back there. C'mon, we're nearly there already."

He followed her as they retraced their steps a hundred yards. Sure enough, there was a trail, leading them a little more westerly than before. The trail looped around the brush, and eventually, they were back beside the river. Less than another 100 yards later, they were at the top of the waterfall.

The drop was about seven or eight feet into the lake below, which was large and clear. There was no path leading down, but a bank of rocks made a natural stairway. Vagan started down first, turning to offer her his hand. She wrapped her pale fingers around his, and he gently led her to the ground beside the pool.

"Beautiful." Her voice was little more than a whispered breeze. Her eyes peered across the surface of the water.

"Absolutely stunning." He agreed. He was glad she was looking at the water, because he was looking at *her*.

It took all of his concentration, and most of his self-control, to look away from her. He slipped the tripod bag off his shoulder, and with one swift movement, he pulled off the bag, and set it on the ground, positioning the top platform as high as it would go. He took the camera from the hard case, and fastened it to the tripod.

When he looked up again, Electra had removed her shoes, and was sitting on a rock, her feet skimming the water, toes barely puncturing the surface.

He took a moment to tear his attention away from Electra, and look at the space around them. The ground was dry and a little dusty where the summer heat had not completely been undone by the recent change in weather. The trees were beautiful, in shades of gold and red, the leaves not yet fallen. Although the immediate surround of the lake was dusty, there was grass around the outer space. The large boulder that Electra was sitting on was one of five or six on the land, whilst another couple peeked out from the surface of the lake. The waterfall was fairly wide, and sent a spray of fine mist into the air around it. It was exactly the kind of space he had been hoping for.

His project was to 'Capture Natural Beauty'; the kind of thing he would have expected from a high school class rather than college. He suspected that most of the others in his class, who were mostly arty females, would be concentrating on dolphins again, or maybe the seals on Seal Rocks. He was sure they were only in the course for the baby animal shots. The only other member of the group that had shown real promise, had dropped out halfway through the third week. The thing that disappointed him most was that because of the other class members, he was finding it hard to express his own talents, limited as he was by their lack of understanding, and their need for guidance.

Now, surrounded by this place of utter tranquillity, he found that natural beauty was not quite as easy when Electra was around. She threw everything else into pale relief around her. The way her hair fell, soft and warm in the sunlight, was more breathtaking to him than the waterfall, or the dappled sunlight under the shade of one of the towering redwoods. She leaned back, and her hair cascaded down her spine, contrasting brilliantly with the color of her dress. Her ivory skin, so pale and creamy, was translucent where it showed. He was trying hard to keep his breath slow and steady, knowing that now would not be the best time to give in to the thoughts that were crowding his brain.

"Dad hated it here. We came because mom loved it, and surprisingly enough, she used to like to spite him. She stopped that when they 'found' religion, which is a shame, because that's when dad got worse." She seemed to be talking to the whole lake, letting out a gentle sigh, then laughing gently. "Vagan, I hope you have better parents than mine."

"I think I do. They seem pretty good to me." He shrugged, adjusting his camera settings again. It was becoming like a nervous habit; it was totally unnecessary.

"What are they like, your parents?"

"Well, dad is hard working, and good. He may have been raised Jewish, but he really has lapsed pretty badly. They don't really do any of the things they're supposed to, which is why I'm not really worried by it. Mom is one of those all American apple pie type women. She fell in love with dad when they were in high school, and won him with brownies. They're older than your folks. Mom was 35 when I was born, dad closer to 40. They're getting close to wanting to retire, I guess. Mom was quite a beauty when she was younger, and I guess dad looked a lot like me, but they've both softened with time." He wasn't sure he had done them justice, but he would make sure that she knew that when she met them, eventually.

"You love them." It was obviously not a question. There was a note of envy in her tone. "I wish I could love mine. Cain has it so easy. At least he doesn't have to live with them. I wish *I* didn't have to. I'm so glad I'm in senior year, finally."

"You have big plans for the future?" He wanted to know where her plans were going to take her.

"I wish I did. Skating really isn't my life's ambition, but it's all I have. I'd like to travel, see the actual cities outside the hotel rooms. I fly to Paris soon, and all I'll see is the inside of a room, the inside of a taxi, and the inside of the arena. I won't even get to see the Eiffel tower, and it's only a five minute walk from where I'm staying. I want to see everything myself, instead of having to watch it on TV, or read about it in books.

"I guess I should have a career in mind, shouldn't I? I never took much time to choose where my life was going, where I was supposed to end up. I wish I had half as many options as you have." She leaned back even further, until her head touched the surface of the rock she sat on, and she lay her arm across her forehead, shielding her eyes from the sun. "Can I come and live on the farm with you?"

"Sure. If we go now, we wouldn't even have to tell your dad." He grinned, realising that the likelihood of it happening was slim. She laughed again, this time, a soft laugh, like the sound of piano keys being tapped gently. "I'll even make sure we get you a milking stool."

"Now you're being ridiculous!" She scolded gently. "Are you going to take some photographs, or did we just come here to talk?"

"I'm working on it." He grinned again, unfastening the camera without taking a single shot, and looping the strap around his neck. He moved under the shade of one of the trees, where the sunlight filtered through, dancing where the breeze rustled the leaves. He peered through the viewfinder, focusing the lens, and adjusting the settings for the third time in the past seven minutes. The image was captured – a swirl of golden leaves in pale light. He wasn't sure it was what the photography professor was looking for, but he decided it was definitely natural, and fairly beautiful, so it would do.

He turned back to the water, and moved to the edge. There was a dragonfly, buzzing happily in a small patch of reeds. He moved as close as possible to it, turning the shutter speed to as short as the light would allow with the aperture completely open, and snapped again, winding the film manually to the next shot.

"Can I ask you a favour?" He wasn't sure if this sudden thought was rather brave or rather foolish, but he decided to go ahead and ask.

"Fair is fair. I still owe you one, don't I?"

"Well, I would have been willing to call it quits, but yeah, I guess you do." He began, wondering how to phrase his request. "Would you, I mean, could you see your way to letting me....photograph you?"

"Like you needed my permission before!"

"Oh, well, yeah." He had guessed that Cain had made sure the picture went to her, but as she had made no mention of it, he hadn't liked to raise it. He could feel his face turning red, and tried to hide it from view. She turned onto her side, and he could feel her watching him.

"You know, I'm not sure. I'm not really model material. I always freeze with a stupid expression when I have to do those publicity shots." She responded, but he wasn't going to give up on the thought.

"You just need better instruction. I'll bet that most of the photographers you've ever met just told you to smile for the camera. All I'm going to tell you is to be yourself.

Be the you I've spent the last hour with, the confident, clever, talented, stunning creature I know you are." He pressed.

"You're trying to flatter me, aren't you?"

"Yeah, is it working?"

"I guess. What do I do?"

"Exactly what you're already doing."

He knelt on the ground next to the rock, and looked up at her, angling the lens so that it captured the side of her face, the shadows turning her ivory complexion to cream. The smile in her emerald eyes did not appear on her lips, but it was there, honest and open. He took the shot quickly, feeling his heart race as he looked through the lens into the depths of her eyes.

He reached across her, and took a lock of her hair between his fingers, letting it go so that it fell across the side of her face, and shot again. She turned onto her back, her hair spreading out across the boulder, and he climbed up so that he could photograph her from above. The smile reached her lips, and they parted, showing her teeth. He caught the image quickly.

"I told you you could do it."

For the next twenty minutes, he took shot after shot, until the roll was expended, replaced by another. Electra continued to surprise him, moving minutely in order to create a new view. When he paused to reattach to the tripod, she sat up, pulling her knees to her chest, wrapping her arms around them, laying her cheek on them. For the first time, her eyes looked sad, all trace of the smile gone. Finally, he realised there were tears in her eyes. He took the picture, then went back to kneel beside her. "What's wrong?"

"Sorry, it's foolish." She wiped her hand across her cheek. "I shouldn't take time to daydream, it always sets me off."

"What are you daydreaming about?"

"I'd rather not say, if you don't mind." She sniffed. "Sorry, I'll end up with red eyes, and I'll ruin your pictures."

"That's okay. C'mon, I'll show you something." He took her hand gently, and drew her up from the rock. She followed him as he moved back to the camera. "You press this one to take a picture, and move this arm – like this – to wind the film on. Take a couple of me, while I be you."

"You're nuts!" She laughed, her tears still not completely dry. He bent quickly to untie his boots, pulling them off quickly, then returning to the rock, and striking a pose like in the old men's wear catalogue his dad used to get – one hand shading his eyes, the other pointing to something that wasn't there. Electra was giggling, now. He heard the shutter clicking, and he changed the pose, jumping up and pretending to get ready to dive. "You really are nuts!"

"I know. Better?" He asked. She nodded. "Good."

"I promise, I won't get all sad again this weekend. I want to have fun, not dwell on my pitiful existence."

"I'll help however I can." He promised. She made her way back to the rock, and climbed up next to him. There was a suddenly mischievous look in her eyes. "What?"

She didn't say anything; she just grabbed his hand, and pulled him in with her as she jumped into the water.

It was a lot deeper than he would have guessed, the water just as clear beneath the surface as it had appeared to be. His head was well under the water level when his toes found the silt at the bottom. He forced his eyes to remain open against the pressure of the water, feeling her hand still wrapped around his own, and pulled her into his arms as they started to resurface. Once there, he held his left hand on the small of her back, using the right hand to help keep them afloat, treading water with his cold feet. She looped her arms around his neck, and he could feel her legs working, as well. It would have been so easy to find her lips with his own; he could almost taste them, again. As he looked into her eyes, he was sure he could feel the same thoughts within them, and he would have leaned in, given in to the urge, if not for the noise that disturbed them.

The sound of the shutter was not loud, but it was enough to make them both freeze momentarily. They both turned to look at the intruder.

"Sorry, couldn't resist." It was Devon, obviously out for a stroll in the woods. He had told them the day before, while they were on the road, that he had been photographer for his high-school newspaper. Vagan realised that this probably meant that the picture would at least be in focus, but he wouldn't hold his breath while he developed it.

Electra pulled her arms from his neck, letting a sigh escape, and swam to one of the large rocks that peeked out of the water. Vagan went the other way, swimming back to the edge of the pool, and pulled himself out. He shook his hands, trying to get rid of the excess moisture that clung to his skin.

"Where's Cain?" Electra asked, sounding distracted. He found that she had not taken her eyes from him.

"He was still asleep when I left twenty minutes ago. We didn't get much sleep. Those beds are really small." The other boy complained. "Well, I'll leave you to it, I guess."

Devon turned quickly, and strode off back into the trees. Vagan was suddenly very frustrated. He wasn't sure when he would get a chance to be that close, again. He wasn't sure whether or not he could depend on his own magnetism to impress her enough. She may still be looking at him now, but he was sure that wouldn't last for long.

Half an hour, and another roll of film, later, he was out of options. He hadn't expected to take so many pictures, but he had used three of the dozen rolls he had brought on the trip with him. The other nine were back in the van, on the top bunk where he had left them. He apologised that they would have to go back.

Electra had been lying on the grass in the shade, and now she leapt up and started to put her shoes back on. Vagan replaced his boots, before collapsing and re-bagging the tripod. When they were both ready, Vagan led the way back up the rock stairs.

"It's a shame Devon came along. I was just getting in to things." Electra commented. Vagan could feel his heart racing. "It kinda ruined the moment, I guess."

"Yeah, I guess." He agreed, having been thinking the same thing not long before.

"Umm, I think I'm going to go that way, if you don't mind." Her voice sounded strained, as if she was trying to control her emotions.

"Are you alright?" He asked, knowing that she was going to lie.

"Sure. I'll see you later." She whispered, and then disappeared quickly into the trees beside the trail. It took him all of a second to decide to put down his bag, and follow her.

There was a small clearing just the other side of the trees, where a fallen tree trunk made a natural bench. He found her sitting there, leaning forward, her face in her hands. He let the camera fall to the ground, knowing it wouldn't be damaged in the hard case, and stood in front of her.

"Stand up." He commanded her, surprised by the force of his voice, as she did as he asked. He had no more time to think; he didn't need it.

Once more, he placed his hand on the small of her back, and drew her in to him. For a moment, their eyes locked, searching each other's souls for the truth. The emerald eyes were filled once more with tears, but he didn't have time to worry about them, as he pulled her tighter into his arms, and his lips found hers.

Chapter twenty-three

She could feel her knees buckling beneath her. His lips were soft, urgent against hers, his arms warm and strong. His right hand was tracing up and down the base of her spine, his left hand tangled in her hair. She didn't want him to stop, and so crushed herself against him, letting her lips part enough for his tongue to caress hers. It had been worth the wait.

As the minutes passed, his lips left hers, tracing their way across her cheeks, kissing away the last of the tears in her eyes, moving down to her jaw, and the point where her throat began. He whispered her name, before returning to her lips once more.

Her knees were not going to take much more, but she had no desire to let him go. She twisted her hands around his neck, pulling his face closer to hers. Every inch of her body cried out for him, and she could no sooner explain it to herself than she could to anyone else.

"Electra." He gasped, pulling away from her for a brief moment.

"Please, don't stop." She whispered, begging, pleading. "Please."

"Shhh." He soothed, pressing his lips to hers once more, lightly as a breeze, twice more, gentle as a whisper. She could barely even recall now why she had been falling into the depression that normally only affected her when her father was close by. His lips had brushed all thoughts from her mind.

Even though the kiss came to an end, neither of them moved. She was unwilling to be anywhere but there, and so kept her hands around his neck, and nestled her head into his shoulder. His arms didn't seem to want to give up, either, and she could feel his right palm, strong and well formed, pressing into her skin through her damp dress.

It was a long time since she had felt so free, alive to the very centre of her being. She was more aware, suddenly, of the world around her, noticing, for what seemed to be the first time, the colour of the trees, the sound of the birds singing, the smell of the earth and moss; the feel of skin on skin.

"Are you okay?" He asked softly, his mouth only a hairs breadth from her ear. She nodded, afraid to speak in case it broke the spell. "You aren't sad, anymore?"

"I'm not sad." She told him, despite herself. "Was that wrong? Was I wrong?"

"No, that was...not wrong. Was *I* wrong?"

"No. Would you mind if I sat a moment? My legs are a little shaky." She apologised. Reluctantly, she withdrew her arms from his neck, as he untangled his from her hair. She caught it as he did so, wrapping her fingers around his, once more, and leading him back to the bench. "That was, well, that was nice."

"Nice?" He chuckled. She looked up, trying to think of the correct way to tell him what she really thought.

"That doesn't really cover it, I guess. Sorry, I'm not
really sure what I'm supposed to say. This is all new to
me." She apologised again.

"I know. Would you believe me if I told you that
it's new to me, too? I guess so." He sighed, his face turning
pink as he blushed.

"What do we do now?" She asked, praying that he
would want to see her again after the weekend was over.
The pain of not knowing was threatening to overtake her,
again, as it had done before, by the lake.

"Well, we hope that your father won't mind too
much that I'm Jewish." He was smiling, and she felt relief
wash through her. "I have a funny feeling he's not going to
like this much, is he?"

"No, he won't." Her voice was choked, sticking in
her throat as she thought about the prospect of telling him.
"Are you sure; do you really want to see me again?"

"Well, as I've pretty much been thinking about you
constantly since I met you, I guess so." His eyes flashed
across her face, and lingered when they met hers. The look
in them was so intense that she had to look away. "What
about you?"

"I guess that goes for me, too. I can't explain it, but
from the first moment I met you – no, from the moment I
saw you – all I thought about is you. When I close my eyes,
you're waiting there, behind my eyelids. When I sleep, I
dream of you. I want you, every part of you, and I don't
care what my father says, either. As soon as the Olympics
are done, I'll tell him everything. It may not make sense to
try and hide it, but it will be easier when he isn't on my
case all the time." She tried to clarify her own thoughts to
herself as much as to him. "Will you wait for me?"

"Even if it was until the end of the earth."

"Really? I mean, you really care enough? I never thought this would be so hard, because, well, I never thought this would be something I would be dealing with. When you said I could come and live on the farm, I thought I was going to cry, I was so happy. Then, I started to think it was just talk, and I *did* cry. Well, you saw that. I just want to be here, in this place, in this moment, and never have to think about anything else ever."

"That sounds good to me, but I think it may be a better idea to get back to the van, and get some dry clothes for you."

She hadn't realised that she was shivering. Her skin was goose pimpled, and the pool of water that had collected in her bra had turned to ice. She agreed it was a good idea, and he wrapped his left arm around her shoulder, stooping momentarily to pick up his camera, then again once they were past the trees to retrieve his tripod.

Electra's mind was racing, now, trying to decide what her best alternative was. Should she tell her father sooner? He would hit the roof whenever she decided to do it. Then, should she let Cain know? She was fairly sure that he probably already knew, but for some reason, she wanted to keep it to herself, at least for now. It was a long time since she had been able to conceal her thoughts from anyone; it was a long time since she had really needed to.

She wasn't cold anymore. Now that they were moving again, wandering through patches of dappled sunlight, and with Vagan's arm around her shoulders, there was no cell in her body that was not warm.

When they reached the camp clearing, they found the space deserted. Cain had obviously decided to go walking, too. Electra was glad. It would give her more time to think. Before they climbed back into the van, Vagan stroked the edge of her jaw with his fingertips, then tilted her chin up, and pressed his lips gently to hers once more, before releasing her from his arm.

She made her way through to the room at the end of the van, and proceeded to change out of the green dress. Every part of her clothing was wet, so as well as slipping the dress over her head, letting it drop to the floor in a pile of damp green, she slipped off her panties, replacing them quickly, then dropping her incredibly wet bra on the bed; she could cope without it for the rest of the day. She redressed quickly in a red sweater, and plain grey slacks, pulling on a pair of socks, before she made her way back out to the main seating area. She ducked into the small shower room quickly, peering into the mirror to check how much of a mess she looked. Her hair was tangled, so she pulled it back into a high ponytail, working her fingers through the roots to help it sit flat. Other than that, she was surprised to find that her skin seemed to be glowing, just ever so slightly. She smiled, and touched her lips with the tips of her fingers, recalling the pressure of his lips, and the way they tasted; sweet, but slightly salty, warm. They were so much better than she had imagined.

She carried on into the seating area, and found Cain and Vagan sitting at the table. Cain was telling Vagan a story of when they were kids, and they had been caught swimming in the lake by their father, who hadn't been at all impressed with them. She tried not to smile too much, but Vagan caught her eye, and she couldn't stop herself.

"Cain, don't be a bore." She scolded her brother playfully, then moved into the kitchen space. "Hungry?"

"Starved. All this country air sure gives me an appetite." Cain responded. "I could really murder a cheese sandwich."

"Vagan?"

"Sure. Can I help?"

"No, just sit there and tell one of your own tales." She requested, unwrapping the bread, and pulling a block of cheese out of the small fridge. She listened to the boys chatting, happy that the pair got on so well. It was going to make life a great deal easier for her when she finally decided it was time to tell her parents that she was falling in love.

Chapter twenty-four

So, there is no way that it was suicide or an accident." The coroner had finally finished delivering her verdict, again, to the gaunt, slightly balding, cop in charge of the investigation.

"Okay, okay, you've told me that before, but I need more than that. Have they figured out what the drugs were, yet?" He asked. He was starting to get tired of this one. If the girl hadn't been a minor celebrity, there was no way they would have spent so much time working on her case.

"Well, the morphine was easy. The other one has been harder, but the guys have managed to work out its properties, and synthesize it. If this is what is coming, then we have problems. It seems to be a mind-altering serum. You know how these things work – like LSD, it gives hallucinations, which thankfully appear to be fairly mild. But after that, it seems to completely eradicate any memory of what has happened from the mind. To say there has never been anything the same in the lab before is an understatement. It steals the voice of the person it is given to, so they can't make even the most simple of noises, which is not fair, because it also paralyses temporarily.

"Still, the victim, or whatever, can't remember anything later on. That is probably a blessing for them, but it does mean that proving anything is virtually impossible. When the heart keeps pumping, the serum is gone within two hours of the paralysis ending, leaving no trace that it was ever there in the first place. If this drug was administered by someone, then they are a truly disturbed individual, because they probably also created it in the first place," she paused to take a breath. "Other than that, there's only the hair."

"Tell me about that." He requested, still unsure of how they were so certain it was a useful clue.

"There was no tag on the end – no DNA available. That left us with little to go on. It appeared to be a dark hair, so we thought it may well belong to the girl, but on closer inspection, it became obvious it wasn't. Phaeomelanin levels were high, while eumelanin was low, which tells us the hair should have been red. Now, hair darkens when people get older, but to go from red, of any shade, to nearly black would take a very long life, and most people go grey before that point. There were no traces of any chemical on it, even shampoo, so it wasn't dyed. In fact, the only thing on it was a natural tallow, that hasn't even been used in soap for a few centuries. That hair was old, but it can't have possibly been *that* old. Hair is strong, and doesn't break up easily, which is why you find hair on mummies and things, but this hair had some life in it, of sorts. Even more importantly, when hair is old and dead, it turns reddish, which really doesn't help, I'm afraid, except that the hair that should be red just isn't. Unfortunately, I can't even begin to imagine how the hair became darkened, but whoever it belonged to was a red head once upon a time. I suggest you start there, and work your way out." She concluded. At least this seemed to be useful to the case. After all, there was one possibility when it came to the hair colour.

Originally, they had dismissed the possibility of any of the other skaters being involved. Perhaps it was now time to re-examine the suspects who really had something to gain from the death of Maggie Treat.

Chapter twenty-five

The whole van shook with the force of thunder. The day had been warm, but had ended with clouds moving in above the woodland. Now, there was a massive storm raging outside.

"All right, we've got beer, vodka, wine, and a small bottle of bourbon." Cain and Devon had declared it perfect drinking weather, and had started pulling out various bottles from several places in the kitchen. Now, Cain was acting as bartender.

Vagan wasn't a big drinker. He had avoided being invited to parties when he was in high school by doing his best to not fit in. Still, he was willing to try anything, once. Electra hadn't seemed too eager, either, but now, she seemed to be getting far more into the swing of things. Cain had been extra devious, and supplied her with large quantities of jelly worms and gummy bears. As she was normally made to avoid all types of carbs, the sugar was obviously going straight to her head, making her rather over excited, and a little giggly.

"I shall have a vodka, with orange juice, please, Cain." Electra told her brother, who didn't bat an eyelid at her.

"Vagan?" Cain asked.

"I'll take a beer." He replied, deciding that this was the safest option available. He wasn't about to bow out, now.

"And Devon will have some Bourbon, please." Devon told Cain, who handed the drinks out to their respective consumers, then sat back down with the others at the small table.

"No, don't get me wrong, Columbo is fun, but I much prefer Murder, She Wrote. I don't mind Perry Mason, at a push." Electra told them. Vagan wasn't sure how exactly the conversation had got round to TV detective shows, but he was rather pleased with Electra's choice.

"Why?" Devon asked. *Why not?* thought Vagan.

"Because I hate knowing who did it! What's the point? I know that Murder, She Wrote is cheesy, but to be honest, who wouldn't love it? Did you know, there's an episode where Seth Hazlitt curses? It's genius, I swear." Electra explained. Vagan grinned, recalling the episode without any problem.

"She's right." Vagan agreed. "Knowing who did it is just no fun. You can normally guess who it was, but there are those odd occasions where it makes no sense at all. And then, Perry Mason, you can guess, when he says that he wants to recall the witness later, that's normally the killer."

"But that's the good thing about Columbo. You get to see the culprit coming apart as they can't conceal what they did, anymore." Cain argued, draining his third glass.

Electra was on to her second, already, Devon on his fourth. Vagan was still nursing his first beer.

"Of course, Columbo has that glass eye." Devon commented.

"Does he?" Cain sounded doubtful.

"Yeah. Did you never notice?" Devon laughed. Cain shook his head no. "Observant, Cain; real observant."

Vagan tried for a moment to block out the sound of the conversation, and recall the memory of the kiss. He had never felt so much in such a short space of time before. He wanted to feel that way forever. He could still feel the warmth of her skin through the damp fabric, the way her hands had grasped him, the caress of her tongue. Her lips had tasted how he had imagined them, sweet yet sharply sour, like green apples swathed in chocolate. It was mingled with her salty tears, and it was a taste he would never forget. He blinked slowly, and saw her eyes behind his lids, brilliant as emeralds. The sound of thunder cracking in the sky close by brought him out of his reverie.

"Yeah, It's sad, I guess, but I don't get how a whole country can get so emotional. I mean, she wasn't exactly vital to the continuation of the human race, was she! Maybe I could understand it if she was still married to the prince, but I really don't get how *so many people* are all upset about it." He had missed the start of her rant, but he guessed that Electra was talking about Princess Di. "Did you see all those millions of flowers? And the people, all crying. They didn't know her!"

"Harsh, El." Cain commented.

"Maybe, but really, would anyone be that upset if the next president's ex-wife died? Worse than that, would half the people I *do* know react like that if I did?" Electra continued with her argument. Vagan could see her point, though.

"Well, we all would." Devon proclaimed

"I like you, Devon." Electra giggled. "What was I talking about?"

"You were telling us exactly what you think about the British and, in your view, their over reaction to the death of everyone's favourite princess." Cain informed her, and she looked rather sheepish for a moment. "We won't tell anyone, though, so don't worry."

"We should play a game!" Electra cried, inspired, no doubt, by the last time she had been on competition without her father watching her every movement.

"Sure, while I braid Devon's hair, and you get everything ready for the pillow fight." Cain mocked her playfully.

"I'll make s'mores." She said sarcastically, still showing enthusiasm for her prior suggestion. "I was thinking more like cards or something."

"What, strip poker?" Cain laughed. Finally, Vagan started to think about the possibilities involved with playing games, but decided it was probably not the best time to start down that thought path.

"Good idea." Devon sounded thoughtful. "But how about truth or dare, instead."

"Sure, but more drinks, first." Cain agreed quickly. This was what Vagan had been afraid of; that he would be expected to consume such quantities of liquor that he would be caught out. "Vagan, are you still on that beer?"

"Yeah." He admitted quietly.

"Come on, man, we have enough alcohol to last 'til Thanksgiving, here." Cain wasn't going to let him get away without at least another beer in him.

"Yeah, drink up, Vagan." Electra agreed with Cain quickly. He had decided that he was going to do what ever Electra asked him too, so he drank the rest of the bottle in one go, feeling afterwards that it may have been a very big mistake. It was replaced within seconds, and he started the nursing, again. "So, who's going first?"

"I have one, for Devon." Cain began. Vagan thought that this should be good, so tore his mind away from their meanderings, and focused on Electra's expression, instead. It didn't help much. "Truth or dare?"

"Truth." Devon sounded resigned, probably already knowing the question.

"Devon, name the first person you ever kissed." Cain demanded. Electra groaned, obviously believing the question to be of little relevance.

"Jack Williams, in the 9th grade, and he was fab-u-lous." Devon revealed, breaking the last word for further impact. Electra nearly choked, but Vagan was not surprised by anything, anymore. "Alright, I earn my go, so Vagan: have you ever been in love, and if so, when?"

"Only once." He could feel his cheeks burning, as he tried to divert his gaze unsuccessfully from the object of said love. "And I guess that that would be right about now." He finally managed to drop his eyes, and think for a moment. "Electra, truth or dare?"

"Truth, obviously." She was smiling when he looked up again.

"Alright, what do you fear most of all?"

"I fear everything, but if I had to pick just one thing, it would have to be a life without all this. I hate it, but it's all I know. If I didn't have skating, if I was just me, then who would I be? I may still have all of you, but I wouldn't be me, so I doubt that having you would make me as happy as it does. So, if I had to pick one thing to be truly afraid of, it would be not being in the game that I hate so much." She fell silent, and he thought about what she had said. Would she really be so much better off without all the pressure? Only time would tell on that score. "Cain, truth or dare?"

"Truth, El."

"Cain." Her voice was hesitant. "Are you gay?"

"What took you so long?" He smiled. Vagan had the feeling that the whole point of the game, and indeed the trip, had been to let Electra in on this particular secret.

"I'm not sure it did, I just wasn't sure how to ask." She shrugged, looking down at the glass in front of her. "I guess you aren't about to tell mom and dad, are you?"

"No, why?" He laughed.

"I just thought it might make it easier for me, is all. Oh well, I guess I have time." Her voice was light, but determined. He wondered if her thoughts had been returning to their conversation, and her request that they keep themselves quiet for the time being; he was pretty sure that Cain had guessed everything already, though.

"And you don't hate me?" Cain sounded weary.

"How could I ever hate you, stupid? Even if you weren't my favourite brother by default, you'd still be on the top of my favourite people list. I'm just glad you are who you are." She assured him. "Does this mean I get another brother, now?"

"Well, Devon's really more of a sister, but yeah." Cain grinned.

"Cool."

"Come on." Devon began, in an obvious attempt to remove attention from himself. "Is anyone up for a dare?"

"I'm not sure the game works that way, but I will." Electra accepted.

"Alright, Electra, I dare you to go and stand outside in the rain for 60 seconds." He challenged. Electra smiled, and drank the last of her vodka in one gulp. She stood up, climbing over Devon to get out of the bench seat, and crossed to the door. As she opened it, she pulled her hair up, then stepped gracefully out into the rain. "Now, please Vagan, I dare you to get out there and kiss her."

Vagan didn't even pause to think about it. He climbed out of his own seat, over Cain, and followed Electra into the night.

She was standing not far from the van, her arms raised into the air, rain falling hard against her upturned face. She dropped her arms, and pulled her sweater over her head, revealing her pale, unclothed skin. She hadn't seen him coming, and he surprised her by turning her, taking her in his arms once more. She smiled up at him, eyes flashing with anticipation.

"Devon dared me." He justified.

"Shut up and take that shirt off; you'll get hypothermia wearing those wet clothes." She commanded him. It made sense, and he did as she asked.

He could feel the rain in his hair, rolling down his bare back, and across his chest. Her skin was next to his, as he traced his finger along her spine, brushing his lips across her bare shoulder, up to the hollow of her neck, and along her jaw. He found her lips once more, as sweet as he had recalled, but far more intense. Her grasp was tighter, stronger, than before. She reached her hands around him, finding the slight hollows beneath his shoulder blades, pulling his flesh closer to hers.

His skin was freezing; by all rights, his entire body should be numb. Instead, every part of him felt alive, as if there was new blood running through his veins. He knew, standing there, feeling her heart beat next to his, that there was no choice for him now but to spend the rest of his days with her.

Chapter twenty-six

When the plane finally landed, Gideon felt relief wash through his veins. It was a long time since he had been so close to home. This would be his last pilgrimage, at least for the foreseeable future.

New Orleans International was the sort of place he despised. It was too bright, too full of people, all rushing to make connections or meet loved ones. He detested the mediocrity of the place. Even the music was wrong – off key to his oversensitive ears that heard everything in minute detail.

It was close to midnight when he reached the street where he had once lived. There was little left to show that he had ever been there. This was not what he had sought when he climbed on the plane. There was something more, something he needed.

The streets were dark, the air filled with the same heavy dampness he had known for his most formative years. His next stop would be the tomb where his family rested. The accident that had claimed the lives of most of those he loved was a long time behind him now. The most recent occupant was his wife. The tomb, shaped like a small house, held the remains of the De Montfort line, through countless generations. Only Gideon remained, now. He left the small wreath of daisies – his wife's favourite – and moved on.

He had booked a room at the Hilton. It was likely to be one of those generic places, where every room was painted in the same, inoffensive, shade of peach. The lobby was almost as bright as the airport had been, but rather less populated. The female on the desk smiled pleasantly at him. He didn't have the heart to point out why that was a bad idea. He could guess at what she was thinking; it was the same as most of the thoughts of those he met. It wasn't his fault he had a magnetic personality.

He rode the elevator, glad at last to be able to see all four walls around him, but slightly disturbed by the large mirror that covered one of them. He hated to catch his reflection unprepared. Now, though, he chanced a glance, and happily found that there were no shadows lurking in the dark recesses of his face.

The room was just as he expected, as chain like as any he had stayed in before. Still, there was a bed, and a private bathroom, and to be honest, he couldn't ask for much more. The mini bar was a useful addition, and he took the time to prepare himself a glass of whisky, poured from two boutique bottles over hollow tubes of ice. He drank, then placed the heavy bottomed tumbler on the table beside the bland easy chair, and tried to think through the past few hours. It was nearer to 3am when he finally managed to work through his current thoughts. It would be so much easier if he didn't have to be here, he guessed. But there was no escaping this; he had to be here, now.

For a while, he simply stared out of the window into the dark night, remembering how the world had felt when he last stood in the city. Things had changed; he had changed. Eventually, though, the sun began to rise, and as it did so, he pulled the drapes – fairly thick, which was a good thing – and climbed into the large, soft bed.

When he woke again, it was to the sound of the telephone ringing. He swore quietly, but reached out, taking the receiver from its cradle and putting it to his ear without opening his eyes.

"Gideon?" It was a voice he knew well, a voice he had known for a long time; soft, deadly, and French.

"Jacques; it didn't take you long to find me." He responded, slightly impressed that his friend had managed to find him, with absolutely no information to go on.

"Years of experience, old friend. I will meet you at the bar on Bourbon Street, at 7pm." Jacques did not wait for a response before hanging up. Gideon dropped the receiver, and forced his eyes to open. The room was mercifully dark.

The hotel had thoughtfully supplied a clock, and the hands were both pointing to the number 6. This didn't really help him, much, but the fact that he felt rested led him to assume it was pm rather than am. He confirmed this quickly by jumping out of the bed, and pulling back the drape, finding the fading light of dusk.

"Hell, Jacques, give a guy some warning!" Gideon scowled. He could get there in time, but it would take some effort, and he hated to expend any if he didn't have to.

He redressed quickly, pulling his boots on, wishing he'd brought some of his normal clothes with him, rather than those Jacques would be expecting. He left the room as quickly as he could, pulling the door closed behind him, and stowing the key in his pocket. He jogged along the hall, to the emergency staircase, and flew down them as quickly as he could. The lobby was far more crowded than it had been before, but he didn't pause to look at those who now inhabited it.

The streets of the French Quarter were bustling. He passed St Louis Cathedral, past the square, heading to the bar on Bourbon Street where he and Jacques had spent a number of hours every few months when they were younger, and less troubled by the world. Gideon was surprised, not for the first time, that he felt so much more at ease than he did anywhere else.

His friend was instantly recognizable. His pale, silver blond hair stood out amongst the other heads in the crowd, his pale blue eyes raking over the swarm as eagerly as ever. As soon as Gideon saw Jacques, he felt the old pull. There were few who had this effect on him, anymore.

"Gideon." Jacques' voice stood out amongst those around him, although it was quieter than the rowdy ones that created a din in the air. They had always joked that he was probably the only Frenchman living in the Quarter anymore. "Welcome home."

"Is that what this place is? I was beginning to think I didn't really have one of those anymore." Gideon greeted, sitting down at the small round table. The bar was the kind of place where the girls went to pick up all and sundry now, the kind of place where the guys drank large quantities of alcohol. It hadn't always been that way. When they were younger, it had been rather more sophisticated, the type of place where the women were well dressed, or, at the very least, well paid. "How did you know I was in town?"

"I smelt you." The Frenchman laughed heartily. He was eyeing one of those girls (the all and sundry type), and making sure that the girl was perfectly aware of him, while

Gideon tried his hardest to relax. "It was time, monsieur De Montfort, for us to meet. I'm glad you came."

"Of course. I have been waiting for the right time. I'm starting to get tired, Jacques. The world doesn't hold much interest for me, anymore." He sighed, taking a drink from the glass that his friend had put in front of him.

"Did you find what you were looking for there?" His companion asked. Gideon had feared this question, because he wasn't sure of what the answer was; he wasn't sure what he had been looking for, yet.

"Perhaps." He tried to stall. "Did you find what you wanted in Hawaii, other than a tan?"

"Perhaps. You must have found something, though. What of this girl? I am sure that she must be a neat addition to your family." Jacques suggested.

"The girl?" He was worried now. Jacques shouldn't know this. Still, what Jacques *should* know, and what Jacques *did* know had never been the same thing.

"The red head. You are not the only one who knows how to avoid being seen, Gideon." Jacques reminded him. "Or had you forgotten that it was *I* who taught *you?*"

"Of course not." Gideon resented the fact that his friend knew him so well, and knew the subject would not be dropped until he was satisfied. "Electra. She's my . . . cousin, I would guess you could refer to her as. She's been very – helpful – to me lately."

"You know the risk, of course. Or do I have to remind you of Amy?" Jacques' voice was dangerous. Gideon felt a ripple of anger down his spine, annoyance that Jacques had spoken the name of the girl from his past.

"Is that why you decided on here, Notré? Is that why I am back in this place that makes me want to run and hide from the world, again?" Gideon asked, agitated.

"Be calm, Gideon. There are too many people here for you to lose your temper right now." Jacques chided. "Why don't you choose one of these pretty things, and we'll head upstairs."

"Not now, Jacques. I haven't the time or the energy for your games tonight."

"But you've been asleep all day, correct? I can see yes. You're the one that gives us a bad name, you know? Even hiding away from the sun like that! You have no idea how easy it is when the skin is warm beneath your lips, how the pulses quicken at the thrill of heat, sun, sea airs. You should try it sometime. You'd be welcome to come on the next trip, taste the local flavours. But of course you won't, afraid of your own shadow as you are. How do you manage to keep existing when you won't act like you own the world? "

"I don't own it, anymore."

"So, live a little, friend. Come, I'll help you out a little."

Gideon watched as Jacques motioned to a couple of the all and sundry girls, who blushed and giggled as if they had no idea what he wanted. One of them - tall, pretty, and blond - eyed Jacques with interest, while the other – shorter, but far better formed, with glistening black hair and dark blue eyes – looked a little worried by the attention of the two. But the blond was already on her way over, dragging her unwilling companion behind her.

"Bon Soir, ladies. How are you enjoying the nightlife?" The blond giggled at Jacques' accent; Gideon thought that was brave. Jacques smiled, menacing as ever. "I am Sebastian Notré, and this is a friend, Lucian De Montfort. We were wondering if you would like to join us upstairs."

"I'm Cecilia, and this is Jennipher, with a p.h., and we'd love to." The blond greeted. Gideon was still feeling frustration that Jacques had given his real name. It made no difference if he wanted to expose himself, but did he have to drag Gideon down, too? The dark girl, close up, was even prettier than she had appeared, though, and now they were this close, she had relaxed, obviously under the influence of Jacques' careful gaze. "Are you from France?"

"Oui, mon ami. Is that okay?" Jacques gave his most gentle, fluid laugh, as the girl took a seat at the table.

"Sure; what about him?" She asked.

"I've been to France, but this place is home." Gideon tried not to get too interested. *This* was dangerous. "Jennipher, please sit."

The dark girl had hesitated, obviously less at ease than she appeared to be, but then sat in the fourth chair, beside her friend. He could now smell her, over the fragrance of stale beer and vodka. She was young, and fairly innocent; not as much a whore as she had looked from a distance. She was wearing a pale blush coloured blouse, which was wrong against her skin – too non-distinct – and her body smelt like musk and white roses. This was what he had feared. Now, there was no way he could deny that she appealed to him.

Jacques wasn't wasting any time. His lips were at the ear of the blond, whispering softly what he would like to do with her. She didn't even seem to be shocked by this, as his words flowed in his sweet French accent. It was clear that the girl would succumb to his gentle persuasion. Before he knew it, Jacques was on his feet, the girl following, and heading up to the dark recesses of the upper bar, where they had taken many girls in the past.

"Should we go, too?" Jennipher asked.

"Would you like to?" Gideon was willing to give the girl a choice. He couldn't help but think he might have had a very different life if he had been offered one.

"I can't leave her on her own." The girl was trying to decide whether her friend's safety was more important than her own; rather admirable, he thought. She'd decided, though, and stood to follow. Now, the choice was his, or rather he wished it were, because with Jacques around, neither of them stood a chance. He could only hope they would never know what hit them.

Chapter twenty-seven

She couldn't remember ever having felt worse. Her head pounded, and her tongue felt furry. There was a pain in the back of her neck from sleeping awkwardly, and her legs felt stiff and unused. She tried to get up, but couldn't get her eyes to focus, and hit her head. Then she realised she was in a bunk bed, the top one.

Reaching out her hand, she felt for the figure she knew was beside her. Her fingers traced the smooth outline of Vagan's profile. She turned and looked down at him. He was still asleep, and seemed so peaceful, that she would do almost anything to keep him that way, but her selfishness got in the way, because his lips were far too inviting; she bent and kissed him.

"I love you." She whispered, not wanting to break the spell of being so close to him, and drew back. She gazed at him as his eyes began to open. "Hi."

"Hi." He smiled back at her dreamily. "Where are we?"

"In the top bunk of a tiny room on a huge RV in the middle of the woods, together." She told him, shivering slightly. She looked down, and realised she was only wearing slacks and a bra. This was doubly confusing, as she could recall taking the bra off after their swimming session, but had no memory of putting it back on. "How did I get my bra back on? I wasn't wearing it last night."

"Well, we got a bit wet, and you refused to put on any clothes, or go to your own bed, so I was a gentleman, and put it on you. I think that may be a first." He laughed. "How much *do* you remember?"

"Umm, there was vodka, and gummy bears, truth or dare, getting very wet while I was rather shockingly naked, and kissing you again. Oh, and I think my brother came out to me." She recounted. "Did you know about that?"

"Yeah. He doesn't keep it quiet when he's not at home. The first time I saw Cain he was at a party with Devon, and it was really obvious." He admitted. "Are you annoyed that *I* didn't tell you?"

"Totally. In fact, I may never forgive you." She told him playfully. "Nah; it was his secret. I guess I'm more than just a little relieved. I think I always had an idea, but you don't mention them in homes like mine. Dad is going to be furious when he finds out, though. It's the whole 'mortal sins' thing. If I wasn't totally convinced that I could keep this a secret, I'd probably have to run away from home now, because when he finds out, it may turn in to World War whatever. Of course, I could always take the heat off him, and tell him I slept with you last night."

"Didn't I say I was a gentleman?" Vagan grimaced, and she laughed.

"Yes, you did. That's not really the point, though. Believe me, dad would find some passage in the Bible that said that sharing a bed, even without doing anything whilst sharing said bed, is wrong." She assured him, then remembered something. "I seem to recollect there may have been some kissing. Plus, you touched me."

"Only accidentally." He blushed wildly at the accusation.

"That's okay." She reassured him. "I guess I should get up."

"You don't have to, if you don't want to. I'm rather comfortable." Now it was *his* turn to sound mischievous. She felt a sigh gather in the back of her throat, letting it escape, and slipped off the bunk, feet landing gently on the floor of the van, feeling the carpet under her toes. "Okay, but we may not get this chance again."

"Sure we will." She grinned, and grabbed his hand, pulling him behind her, out into the seating area. The space was empty, and pale sunlight was filtering through the windows beside the table.

"There's frost!" Vagan exclaimed. She followed his gaze, and saw the thick covering of ice on the ground, seriously unexpected after the heavy rains the night before.

"I hadn't realised it was so cold. Ah, excellent, my sweater." She shivered, and pulled the sweater on. It was still slightly damp, but she decided she could cope with that. "I wasn't at all cold last night."

"Funny, that."

"Ugh, my hair's a mess! Do I look dreadful?"

"Honestly? You look amazing, as always."

"Thank you." She rose on to her toes, and kissed him on the corner of his mouth. "Breakfast?"

"Shouldn't we wait for the others?"

"No chance. I'll feed my man, Cain can feed his."

"I like that."

"Yeah?"

"Yeah. I've never been someone's man before. I feel like a grown up."

Electra laughed. It felt so easy, being with him. She had started to think she could probably tell him anything, and that he would understand. She felt serene when he was close to her, and everything felt *natural*.

She made pancakes, taking great care in the small kitchen area not to set light to something. Vagan made appreciative sounds from behind her, and she wasn't completely sure if they were for the pancakes, or for her. Every now and then, she looked across at him, and felt a thrill run through her that he was gazing back at her, the look in his eyes so full of affection.

"Ummmmmm, she's cooking." The sound of Cain's voice carried from the end of the van, and the door into the largest bedroom. "El, you know you can't eat that."

"No chance, Cain. I already overdosed on carbs last night. What's the point in stopping now?" She called to him, flipping another pancake onto the stack on the plate. She offered it to Vagan, who took it and sat at the table. "Cain, if you promise that you won't tell, I could see my way to making you some."

"I swear." He held up his hand as if pledging his allegiance. Devon, who had walked up behind him, rolled his eyes. "Besides, if I told on you, you might tell on me. It would get us nowhere."

"But isn't all fair in love and war?" She smiled, giving him a gentle nudge as she mixed some more batter.

"What kind of sportsman are you, Philips?" Cain shook his head in mock disbelief. She took a playful swat at him with the dishcloth, and Cain surrendered, taking a seat opposite Vagan, helping himself to three from the stack. "We need to hit the road by nine if we have to be back by midnight."

"Screw that." Electra muttered, and felt the glare of the three sets of eyes behind her. "Well, I felt like saying it!"

"That's fine. But dad'll have a search party out for us by 12:02, you know." Cain reminded her.

"Okay, so what I meant to say was screw *him*! We'll tell him we got a flat or something. I don't have school tomrrow, and I'm not at practice 'til one. So screw him!" She repeated, rather louder than was necessary. "I can't really be bothered with training, either, except I *am* a little stiff from not exercising yesterday. Plus, all those gummy bears really took their toll; the vodka didn't help."

"I'm sure Vagan will help you stretch." Devon commented. She was growing very fond of him, very quickly. Now that she knew the story, she couldn't believe she hadn't guessed sooner that Devon was gay. He wasn't overtly flamboyant, like many of the residents of Castro were, but there was something in his mannerisms which, when pointed out, became obvious.

"Maybe I'll just go for a long walk, and a swim." She decided, taking her seat at the table, and a well sized portion of breakfast for herself.

They chattered happily for the duration of the meal, then went their separate ways. Cain and Devon went walking in one direction, whilst Vagan walked with Electra to the lake. While she swam happily in the cold water for several hours, he continued to photograph the wildlife. She couldn't remember the last time she had felt so free, diving down through the clear waters, and surfacing under the waterfall. Every now and then, she would pause to look at Vagan, and most times, she found that he was glancing back at her.

Eventually, the sun went behind the trees, and the water, that had started to warm in the sun, turned icy again. Reluctantly, Electra pulled herself from the pool, wrapping a towel around her shoulders, which was rapidly replaced by Vagan's arms. Every now and then, as they walked back to the camp, she felt his lips brushing gently across her cheeks, the top of her shoulders, and the small space at the bottom of her left ear lobe.

The afternoon sped past, and before they knew it, the sky outside was darkening. Electra was surprised when Cain cooked up a feast, and then they sat around another fire, this time that she helped Vagan to build. They spent a few hours, sitting there, talking and telling the usual campfire stories.

They hit the road shortly before 11pm, joining the interstate quickly, and heading back to the city. The roads were fairly well deserted, and Cain drove a little faster than was really necessary. By midnight, they were back within the city limits, and at 12:14, Electra kissed Vagan quickly, then bounded up the steps to the house, turning to wave to them as they drove away.

The sound of classical music filtered through the hallway from the den as she unlocked the door, and stepped back in to everyday life. She groaned, knowing instantly that her father was waiting for her, and that there was no way she was going to get away with not showing herself. She pushed the door open, and stepped into the pool of light the television made.

"Hi, dad. Sorry, we got a flat tyre." She apologised to him, hoping that she was convincing.

"Okay. Get to bed. You have practice tomorrow." He reminded her. She was surprised he had accepted her excuse so quickly, but did not hang around to find out why. She raced up the stairs as fast as she could, dropped her bags inside the door of her bedroom, pushing it shut behind her, and flung herself across the bed, pulling the photograph of herself out of the back of her nightstand drawer. She held it close to her face, and whispered to her own image.

"I think I love him."

Chapter twenty-eight

Dylan wasn't quite sure what he was supposed to do next. He had pinpointed the location where The Old Man lived. He even had a picture in his mind of what he wanted to happen in the end. The problem was, he had spent so long holding on to the vision of what it would be like afterward, he had never bothered to search for the way he was supposed to end it. Perhaps, if he had taken his original path in life, he may have had an idea, but as soon as he had decided to abandon it, the knowledge that it would have brought abandoned *him*.

He had spent the last few days watching the house when he could. As soon as he managed to get out of the school building, which could have taken longer had he not been so good at managing time and space, he made his way to the quiet street, where the tall, magnificent houses stood as testament to a bygone era. He had come to the conclusion that there was very little chance that anyone else inhabited the house, which was so obviously occupied, although no one really ever came or went, least of all in the daylight. It was always with relief that Dylan said farewell to the sun, greeting the moon as she rose gracefully above the city. The shadows had been his friends for longer than he would normally care to mention.

What he really needed was to see Electra, but she was on leave for the next two weeks because of an upcoming championship tournament. He would have given anything to be able to speak to her, because he had realised that she was going to be very instrumental to the positive outcome of the final battle. The only vision he *had* managed to have of the situation in the recent past was of Electra, surrounded by rather a lot of flames. It disturbed him to know that he would have to send her in to them.

There had to be a way to find her. He sat very still for five minutes, searching the atmosphere for her. She wasn't at home, he knew instantly; neither was she at the rink, although he suspected she should be sometime soon. If he wasn't careful, Mr. Spring would get back from his appointment before he found her, and that would be a problem. It wasn't the first time he had left his shadow at work while he went out for a while, but he was sure to be required to take some dictation, or something, after the school board meeting, and he wasn't sure if the shadow could cope with that. He almost wished he had left one of those electronic voice recorders, just in case.

He was trying to decide whether or not to cut his losses when he sensed her, finally; she was close by, too. He got up as quickly as was possible, and sprinted to the corner, spotting her red hair across the street. He checked the traffic, and dodged his way toward her, narrowly avoiding a pink Toyota – obviously not an original colour – headed straight at him.

"Hi, Electra." He greeted her before she had a chance to disappear again, and take with her any chance he had to get what he needed.

"Oh, hey, Dylan. What are you doing here? Doesn't Mr. Spring keep you locked up during school hours?" She smiled up at him. He would have to remember to keep this short.

"Early lunch." He responded quickly. "How's the training going?"

"Not bad. I still have tons to do before I head to Paris next week. I fly out on Monday, if you can call 2am Monday, and back on Thursday. I'm not sure dad believes in jet lag." She was grinning, and he nodded his agreement. He wasn't about to let on that he had never suffered jet lag, even though he had been around the globe many times; it would only make her feel worse.

"Paris?" Now he really *did* care what she had going on in her life. The city where he had spent so much of his youth had changed a lot during his time. There was no longer a Bohemian atmosphere running through large areas. Almost all of that had died out with the wars, but just a mention of the city brought back floods of memories that would have overwhelmed most.

"I'm not getting too excited. I won't get to see much of it." She complained. He already had an image, though. The room was very like the interior of the Café he had lived above for a couple of cold winters after the death of his parents.

"Well, I'm sure you'll see enough. May I make a recommendation or two?" He requested, wishing as he did so that she may just get the chance to act on them, even if it was futile. She nodded, though, so he went on. "I assume you won't have much free time. However, if you do, I would like to suggest the Rodin museum, on Rue Varenne. It's an intimate setting for some of the great man's compelling work, and some of them could almost be you. If by any chance you get to visit a restaurant, try La Cremaillere, in Montmartre – you'll appreciate the décor. Ignore the Louvre; it's too big, and La Gioconda, the Mona Lisa, has nothing on you. Avoid the street kids, who'll try to sell you trinkets, which are better suited to the brash and brainless."

"How long is it since you were there?" She asked.

"A while." He smiled, recalling the last time he had been there, visiting a friend in 1971, whom he had not seen since the early days of the First World War. He would have told her as much, if only to see her reaction, because he was fairly sure that Electra was the first person he had met in a long time who had enough energy to accept the truth. "But that's another story, and not one for today."

"With dad on duty, I'll be lucky to get to look out the windows of the cab on the way to the arena." She scowled. Dylan laughed, finding that she was more right than she had intended to be.

"Eventually, though, you will get to see all those things. I don't think you're going to have to wait too long, either." He assured her, not completely able to rid his voice of laughter, as the image of her flickered though his mind.

"If only." She sighed.

"Anyway, what are you practicing today?" He asked, hoping to get the conversation back to the present, so that he could concentrate on what he needed to ask her.

"Speed. I've been working really hard on the quad; I'd love to be the first female to land a quad toe-loop in competition. You know, it would put me in at least one of those dull old history books." She grinned. "It's tough, but now that I have my secret weapon, I should be fine."

"Secret weapon?" He probed.

"Vagan. He's, well. . . I guess you would call him my boyfriend, now. He's a very fast skater, and I need more speed going in to my take off. As my coach is *not* going to be at my practice session today, we're taking the opportunity to cheat a little bit." Electra responded.

This threw Dylan. He hadn't expected this; he hadn't sensed it. There were no new people in her life, other than her cousin, that he could tell. Was this Vagan someone she had known for a while? He had to know.

"How long have you been sneaking around?" He asked, letting her know he realised her situation.

"I guess I met him about a month ago, and it was pretty clear where we were headed as soon as I did, but the sneaking around mostly started last weekend. We went off into the woods together, with my brother and his – friend. It just sort of happened." She shrugged. "I don't remember when I was last so happy."

"I'm glad." Was the only response he could come up with. He wasn't sure how this was even possible. He couldn't remember the last time he had been unable to sense all the connections within a life. The only thing he could think of was when all his own had disappeared. But this wasn't the same. It couldn't be.

As they had been talking, they had wandered slowly down the street, and now came to a stop at the corner to let a cable car rattle past. As it shuffled past them, Dylan caught sight of someone he recognised; the boy was standing on the sidewalk opposite them, and the smile on his face mirrored Electra's so well, that without any acknowledgement of the fact, Dylan knew that this was the new person in her life.

"Vagan." She sighed, and Dylan watched as the beautiful young male crossed the road, and folded his arms around her, tilting her head to kiss her gently. Instantly, Dylan felt the connection between them, knowing that this boy, the one that had been used for the past few months, was as important to his mission as Electra was.

Chapter twenty-nine

The Old Man knew that time was short, now. Someone was coming for him, he had known that much for a while. He knew exactly who it was going to be; he may have crossed a lot of people in his time, but this particular person had been the wrong choice. His fate had been sealed for a very long time.

Things weren't easy for him, right now, anyway. The boy was getting far too strong suddenly. He had never been fought against so hard without reason. He now seemed able to resist for far longer than he could just a few weeks earlier.

Perhaps coming to the city had been a mistake; he had only come because he was lonely. He had been alone for such a very long time now, that he was starting to crave companionship. He had managed to find a sort of solace in the people of San Francisco, and now that he had, he wasn't sure he was willing to give it up. If the time came, he *would* leave, if leaving was the right thing to do, but he wasn't giving up without a fight.

For now, as alone as he was, he felt very few regrets. He had always done what he had wanted, taken what he had needed. The world may not have wanted him, but that was of very little importance. What mattered most to him was that he be instantly gratified, and he would do what ever it took to be so. He really didn't care what the cost might be. Of course, his imminent demise had made him wonder what lay ahead for him in the next life, because he was sure it wouldn't be pleasant.

He sat silently in his tall chair, rotating an old silver dollar between his fingers. It had been given to him a long time ago, by a friend, when he felt he had no one, and that the world was against him. In all the years since it had come in to his possession, he had never been tempted to use it, seeing it not as money, but as luck. Many times, he had clung to it, hoping to stay the hand of fate a little longer. But it would not help him this time.

Chapter thirty

Your hands smell funny." Electra accused, giggling. Vagan smiled, lifting his right hand to his face and sniffing it tentatively.

"Sepia." He smiled. He had spent the morning in the darkroom developing the rolls of film from the weekend. He had been waiting all week to get the time, but his photography tutor had locked the darkroom and gone off for a few days. When she had finally returned, Vagan was the first to stake his claim on the space.

"Sorry, Dylan, this is Vagan, Vagan, Dylan." She introduced the young man to him. The other guy seemed vaguely familiar. Vagan shook his hand, and was surprised by the force he felt. It was almost like a pulse of electricity, shooting across his palm in a dull throb.

"Nice to meet you." Vagan tried to smile sincerely.

"Yes." The other boy responded. Something about his tone seemed dismissive, as if he would rather be anywhere but there. "Electra, I really should get back before Mr. Spring notices I'm not there."

"Sure, see you soon." She smiled, waving slightly, before turning back to Vagan. Dylan headed back to the office as speedily as he could, and replaced the shadow just in time for Mr. Spring to call him in to take notes. "Where were we?"

"I think you were telling me how bad I smell, and I was thinking how much I missed you all week." He responded, pulling her into his arms, and kissing her again.

"You don't smell bad, just funny. Do all photographers smell like that?" She giggled again as he kissed her jaw.

"Well, some of the chemicals smell pretty gross. I guess the ends justify the means though, because the brown and cream tones are so pretty when they're used properly." He tried not to get too carried away, but she didn't seem to mind all that much.

"Which is the worst?" She asked, sounding curious.

"Well, the stop bath smells of ammonia; it's pretty evil. Or there are the colour baths, especially the yellow tones, because of all the sulphur." He replied. He looked down at her as he spoke, and found that she was really listening, not just politely pretending. Most people couldn't care less when it came to his favourite subject, but Electra listened to everything intently. "Didn't I tell you I try never to be boring?"

"Yeah. You could never be boring, Vagan." Electra assured him. She slipped her arm around his waist, while he wrapped his around her shoulders, and he followed as she led them to the rink a couple of streets up from Haight.

The arena was just as bright now as it had been the last time he had entered it; this time, there were no other people around, though. The only person in the space was the guy on the Zamboni, whirring merrily across the surface that was already like glass.

"I've got the rink for a few hours, if you don't mind me being a bore." She apologised.

"If I'm allowed to be a bore, you certainly are." He promised as they climbed up into the bleachers.

"Thanks." She grinned, pushing him gently, then pulling him down beside her on the old wooden seat. "As soon as he gets to that side," she indicated the left of the ice, "I will go get my skates, and you can wait while I warm up. After that, I want more of that speed of yours."

"What do I do while you warm up?"

"You watch, and think about how wonderful I am."

"That guy, before, Dylan, how do you know him?" He was just curious, he hoped she realised.

"He works at my school. He's my God father's secretary. He seems to be quite the hot property, but not my type. I go for the dull farm boy type."

"That's nice."

The guy on the Zamboni was circling back, now, and before he had the chance to say anything else, Electra was on her feet, heading for the changing rooms where she apparently stored her practice skates in a locker. When she reappeared a few minutes later, she had changed out of the jeans and sweater she had been wearing, and was now clothed in a one-piece pantsuit the same colour as her eyes.

He watched her as she stepped on to the ice, just as the heavy machinery left it. For a few minutes, she simply skated slowly in small circles across the perfectly smooth ice. After that, she began to pull her limbs, stretching her left leg, then her right, high above her head.

"Vagan, you need skates." She called to him. He nodded, and made his way to the office where he had borrowed skates the night they met. It took him a minute to find a pair the right size, then lace them tightly over his thick socks. He knew from experience that hire skates could be problematic when it came to blisters.

He made his way back, slowly walking on his blade guards, and managed the steps without too much effort. He wasn't sure why, but he was suddenly feeling nervous, again. He should be over this by now, he thought, but obviously he still had a couple of issues to work on.

"What kept you?" She called, moving quickly to the barrier, and standing on her toe picks to better reach him as he bent to kiss her again, washing away all of his nerves instantly. "I missed you."

"Sorry, it took me ages to find these things. Half of them were blunt." He apologised, and stepped through the gap in the barrier, onto the ice. "Can you remember what I showed you the last time?"

"Yeah, but I wasn't sure how I was supposed to do it by myself. Or maybe I just didn't want to do it alone. I thought it was going to be easy, but I was wrong." Her lips pouted slightly, and he found her even more beautiful for it.

"It *is* easy. Trust me." He vowed. "Here, take my hand."

He led her into the centre of the ice, all the while holding onto her hand, and then began to draw his feet back and forth across the surface.

"Just try to let go of all thoughts." He whispered. "Feel nothing but the moment, forget what comes next."

"Vagan, I….."She started to protest, but he put a finger to her lips, smiling, and shook his head.

"Don't over think it, just feel it." He whispered again.

And then they were moving. The speed was exhila-rating, whipping an airless, freezing, breeze around them, which bit at their skin as they moved faster and faster.

"But how do I do this when you're not there?" She cried over the velocity.

"Easy, pretend that I am. I'm pretty sure I always will be." He called back. "Now, let go of my hand, but keep going. Don't hesitate, or you'll lose it."

He felt her fingers slipping out of his hand, and started to slow, hoping that she would be able to keep going. She had the last time he had shown her this. Why should this time be any different?

As he reached the barrier, he turned to watch her without leaving the ice. Her body moved so gracefully that he doubted there was any other creature that could compare to her. She continued to move with speed, radiating energy, positioning herself before swinging into the air and rotating four times before landing on one foot, the other swinging out to counter balance her. But she went on, tagging what he thought was a triple Lutz on the end.

"Keep going." He urged her gently. There was something about the way she moved that he found hypnotic. If he never did anything else in his life because of it, he would watch her forever.

She seemed to use the speed, practicing most of the moves she was known to perform at lower tempos. A triple Salchow, a few camel spins, twizzles, sit spins, step sequences. Seven times, she landed the quad toe-loop perfectly. Finally, she came into a Biellmann spin, lifting first her right then her left leg high above her head, her skate practically touching her chest as she leaned her head back. As her foot returned to the ice, she spun, her arms above her head, like a blur of scarlet and emerald, before coming to a stop, no more than a foot away from him.

"Sorry, I got carried away." She panted slightly, skating into his open arms. For a moment, she melted against him, laughing, as she breathed in and out rapidly.

"I forgive you." He told her, feeling her heart beating against his chest. He held her tightly, feeling her slide a little as she gave into her temporary exhaustion. She regained her composure quickly, finding her toe-picks, and righting herself. "Better?"

"I don't know how I coped without the speed before. That just made everything so much easier. Of course, it means I'll have to work out my times, because I'll be done too quickly for my music if I'm not careful. Of course, that's if I can do it again by myself." The comment seemed to be aimed back internally, rather than to him. "I should try, shouldn't I?"

"Go ahead." He encouraged her, reluctantly withdrawing his arms from her. Within moments, she was flying again, possibly even a fraction faster than she had been before.

"I'll have to tell Alderton I had a breakthrough. She'll never believe me, of course. And she'll have to figure out how to pack my routine a bit, too." She called to him, spinning from one foot to the other.

Somehow, he had managed to find this girl. For some reason, she liked him. It was a new sensation for him. He was far more used to being ignored by the opposite gender. The smile she wore now was directed at him, and he returned it with more enthusiasm than he had ever experienced in the past.

"Vagan?" She called again from the far side of the rink

"Yes?" He called back.

"Do you want to dance with me?" She asked, beckoning him with her left index finger. He pushed away from the barrier, and reached her side in less than a second.

He wasn't sure how, but there suddenly seemed to be music playing quietly from somewhere. He pulled her hand to his chest, and wrapped his arm around her waist.

For a moment, they merely swayed, as if slow dancing on the most slippery dance floor in the world. But the music started to build, getting faster, like their pulses racing, and before he knew it, they were crossing the rink, perfectly in harmony with each other. He lifted her, holding her in his hands, as she flipped over, landing lightly on her left foot.

For what seemed like an age, they twisted and turned, feeling the ice grow wet beneath their skates. He was exhausted before he was willing to stop, and he could hear her breathing getting heavier, but she wasn't stopping, either. Faster and faster, they pushed on, until the sound of a voice on the P.A system halted them.

"Electra Philips to the office please, Electra Philips." The nasal feminine voice called from somewhere above them.

"What now?" She groaned, releasing his hand, and speeding away from him. He waited, feeling impatient for her to return. He glanced at the large clock on the wall, realising that the time had slipped away faster than he'd thought, and that it was now late afternoon.

For a few minutes, he occupied himself with a few basic manoeuvres, things that his mother had shown him when he was still young and willing to learn from her. Now he wished he had paid more attention, wishing that he had even an ounce of the talent Electra had.

"We have to go." Her voice was urgent as she came back through the door to the barrier.

"What's wrong?" He asked, puzzled by her expression. She seemed scared.

"Dad called." She responded. He felt his grimace as she said the words. "It's okay, they didn't tell him I was with someone. Nancy, the girl in the office, she's cool. But, I still have to go. Apparently, there are some cops who have come up from LA to talk to me, about Maggie. Did I tell you, they think she was murdered? I guess not, but they do, and for some reason, they think I have some idea who did it. I have to get home, like now. I'm really sorry."

"That's okay. But why do they think you had something to do with it?" He was getting more puzzled by the moment.

"Apparently, I had something to gain from her death. Of course, Maggie was just *so* brilliant that there was no chance of any of us beating her on our own merits. It gets me down that they think that way." She shrugged, sitting down and starting to unlace her boots rather absentmindedly. He stepped through, and sat next to her, doing the same. "Sorry."

"Why?"

"Because we were having fun, and now I don't know when I'll see you again." She complained, sadly.

"Well, I'll walk you most of the way home, if that helps. Of course, if you were feeling brave, I'd walk you to the door and kiss you good bye, but then again, I'm not feeling so brave, myself." He grinned, and was surprised when she threw her arms around him, nestling her head into his shoulder.

"I don't know if I'll ever be brave enough, Vagan. I'm terrified of my own shadow at the moment." She was whispering, now, into his shoulder, and he squeezed her gently in his arms.

"We'll figure it out, I promise." He assured her. "Come on, before my bravery completely disappears."

No more than fifteen minutes later, Vagan found himself on the corner of Steiner street, watching her as she headed for the light blue Queen Anne that he had memorised, now. Her shoulders were slightly slumped, but she held her head high, red hair hanging around her shoulders, seeming defiant as she returned to face her father, and whatever the police had in store for her.

Chapter thirty-one

Glad you've decided to join us, young lady." Were the first words she heard as she came through the door. She groaned as quietly as she could manage, and hung her jacket on a hook by the door. It had been no more than twenty minutes since she had spoken to him. How had he managed to get his pants in such a twist in that time? "In here, please."

She followed him silently into the living room at the back of the house, where her mother was already seated on one of the large white sofas, opposite the two male police officers. They were both dressed in business suits, so it was not immediately obvious that that was what they were, but there was something about their manners that exuded their authority. He steered her toward the sofa where her mother sat, and pushed her gently down onto the seat.

"Ms. Philips," the older of the two men started. She wanted to correct him to Miss, but her father would surely have a problem with that. "We have reason to believe more strongly now that Maggie Treat was murdered. We aren't accusing anyone of anything at the moment, but we are hoping to find out some more information in the mean time."

"Okay." She could feel her heart beating rapidly, although she knew she had nothing to hide from them.

"There are anomalies surrounding Maggie's death, such as the two small puncture marks on the inside of her wrist, under the cut marks." The other guy informed them. "Also, there was a rather high level of morphine, and a chemical we have never seen before, in her blood stream. What blood there was left, that is."

"What do you mean *'what blood there was left'*?" Electra asked, looking from one of the men to the other.

"Well, normally, when someone cuts their wrists, there would be a lot of blood. To begin with, we assumed it was diluted by the bath water, but the concentration was wrong for that. In the end, we had to conclude that she was killed elsewhere, before being moved to the tub." The younger of the two explained. The image that filled her mind was more vivid than she would have thought possible. "There was only a very small amount of blood left in her body, which is unusual for someone whose heart stopped beating naturally."

"What has that got to do with our daughter?" Her mother asked.

"Well, that's the thing. We haven't found any real evidence pointing to *any* individual, so we are looking at anyone who had contact with the victim this year, hoping to find some clue or other that will help us." The first one went on. "Is there anything you can tell us about Ms. Treat?"

"I didn't really know her that well. We had met a few times, in competition, but she really kept herself to

166

herself. She didn't join in with us that much, and to be honest, I doubt anyone will notice she isn't there. For whatever it's worth, I liked her more than I had reason to. I should have hated her after the trick she pulled last season, but it isn't in my nature to hate people, I guess." She responded.

"What about others? Did any of the other competitors have a problem with her?" The younger cop probed.

"I don't think so. Besides, Maggie was one of those people who didn't put herself in danger. She played everything so safe, even her routines. She didn't take risks, anymore. The rest of us respected her for her achievements, but she was reaching the end of her career. I'd heard rumours of her retirement at the end of this season.

"I don't know what else to say. I really don't know why anyone would want to hurt her…"Electra trailed off as she noticed the expression on their faces; it was blatant disbelief. "I'm sorry, but is there something you aren't telling me?"

The two men exchanged looks, seeming to decide whether or not they should tell the Philips' what was really going on. The hesitation was too much for her father, apparently, and she could see the twitch in his left temple that showed his temper flaring.

"Look, if you're not going to tell us what's going on, I think this interview is over. Electra needs to mentally prepare for her next tournament, and I can't have her stressed before hand." He said firmly, his eyes tightening slightly. It was an expression she knew, from experience, meant for others to be wary. Another quick glance between them showed that they had come to a decision.

"Okay, here's the thing. When Maggie was first found, we thought it was suicide…" The older man started.

"We knew that." Mr. Philips interrupted.

"It was well published as such." He continued. "When we couldn't find a suicide note, we knew there must be something wrong. Plus, the way she was found, it was just wrong. That's why we looked further into the situation. The post mortem proved that there was foul play. We need to know what happened, and we need to speak to every single person she knew in order to do that."

"But, surely you must have some clues or something? I've seen Murder, She Wrote, I know there must be finger prints or *something*." Electra argued, frantic now that they were pushing for more.

"Unfortunately, there was nothing. It wasn't a case of them being wiped down. . . they were never there in the first place." The older cop informed her. She felt her stomach churn, reminding her of the way she had felt when she first heard about the death.

"But everybody has finger prints." Mrs. Philips said.

"Yes, they do. Unfortunately, if the perpetrator happened to be wearing gloves, that leaves us with nothing." He replied, as if he were speaking to a child.

"I think that that's quite enough. As Electra has stated, she really didn't know Maggie all that well. I see no reason to carry on this conversation any longer." Mr. Philips snapped, standing quickly, and moving to the doorway.

"Well, thank you for your time. And please, if you think of anything, call us. We can have someone here to take further information within a few hours." The younger officer told them, standing also. The older man hesitated for a moment, then sighed and moved slowly to follow his colleague to the door.

Electra could feel the questions coming before her father even returned. They were no doubt as confused as she was, but obviously thought that she would have more information than she did. This was what hell must be like, she thought, being pushed to answer questions she didn't have the answers for.

"What are you hiding, Electra?" Her father's voice boomed from the hallway a moment after the front door closed loudly. She could think of a couple of things, but none that related to Maggie Treat in particular.

"Dad, I know as much as you do. They didn't really tell us much. I'm as in the dark as you are." She responded, bewildered by how he could react so violently to things beyond her control.

"There is certainly more to the story than they were letting on. I cannot believe that no one knows what happened, and I cannot believe that you know nothing." He was not happy. The dark look in his eyes was harsher than she had ever seen it.

"I really don't know *anything*, dad. What am I supposed to know? Maggie died in LA, I haven't seen her since March, and to be perfectly honest, I really didn't know her all that well, anyway, as I keep having to tell every single person who asks me about her. She was a loner. I would have been less surprised if she really *had* killed herself, because she didn't know anyone well enough for them to want to kill her. I have no idea what you want me to say, dad, because I don't know any more than you do. I was busy, practicing, when I had to drop what I was doing and come home to deal with all this, and now I'm not sure I can remember where it was that I got to, other than the fact that I have just spent a few hours perfecting the quad. So, if I could please be excused, I could do with going and writing down all the technical details before they disappear from my head entirely." Electra felt her anger pulse through her, pouring out in a tirade that normally would have her running for cover. But she had reached the limit of her temper for the day, and she was not in the mood to sit and listen to him for another minute. She ran from the room, and made her way to the stairs, pausing only long enough to grab her bag, and then run upstairs.

Her room was normally her only sanctuary, but today, even there she felt trapped. Something about the atmosphere in the room was too oppressive for her liking. Perhaps it was left over from the words that had been spoken downstairs. She hoped that was the case, and flicked on the radio.

It was still early, and the station was playing melodic tunes that weren't really heavy enough for her mood, but Bobby Dee would be taking over in an hour or so, so Electra occupied herself with making some notes. She had finally figured out what made the speed so easy, not that she could put the actions into words, because it was more about emotions. It was about the feeling of being free – something that had been missing from her life for far too long, had possibly never been there in the first place. Perhaps there was also something about being in Vagan's arms, being with him when no one else was there, and feeling safe with him.

She had been sitting at her desk, making notes, for five minutes before she felt the breeze coming from the open window. She rarely opened it, because the wind whipped up from the bay too quickly, and whistled through it like a teakettle boiling. She turned to look at it, and was sure she saw a shadow pass across the bed, quickly ducking out the window.

Now that she was looking, she noticed the small, pale green velvet box resting on the comforter. There was an envelope there, as well, and she was curious enough that she crossed the room to investigate.

The envelope was merely labelled '*Electra*', but she looked at it for a moment, perhaps trying to find enlightenment on the white space. She turned it over, hoping there might be more on the back, but there was nothing there except the sealed flap. She slipped her finger underneath, and yanked at the top, pulling the opening apart. Inside, a further sheet of white greeted her, and she read it several times before she could understand what it meant:

Electra, I need for you to do something for me.
I would have asked before, but I was in a hurry.
In the box, you will find a symbol that will keep you safe.
I can't explain what from, but I need you to trust me.
Wear the chain and the symbol as much as possible.
It will protect you when I cannot.
Have fun in Paris, and take care.
I will let you know when I need it back.
Dylan Horatio Adams.

She concluded that it meant that Dylan had somehow been in her room, because there was no way her mother would have forgotten to mention a strange young man leaving boxes and letters for her. Her curiosity was now far greater ignited, and she lifted the green box. It was old, she knew instantly, but had been expensive when it was new. She lifted the lid, and looked for a long moment at the pendant inside. It appeared to be silver and crystal, shaped like a crescent moon, resting on the pale eau d'nil satin. A fine silver thread of chain snaked around it.

She wasn't sure what Dylan was up to, but something about him made her do as the note had requested, and she put the chain around her throat instantly. The pendant sat squarely between her collar bones, nestling into the gentle hollow, there. The crystal was cold against her skin, and although it had seemed heavy before she had put it on, it now felt weightless. What surprised her most, though, was the sudden sense of well being that flooded through her, nullifying the tension that she had experienced before. It was as if the past hour had not happened, and she had only just left Vagan, feeling again the safety she felt when he was with her.

"Electra?" The voice was so gentle, she almost didn't recognise it as her father on the other side of the closed door.

"Come in, dad." She called back, quickly shoving the note and the box under her pillow, and tucking the pendant behind her sweater.

"I'm sorry, Electra, that was uncalled for." He apologised. She had never heard him do that before, and her mouth dropped open with surprise. She closed it quickly, and tried to understand where this had come from. Surely the pendant couldn't really protect her, could it? And if so, how could it protect her from her father? She pushed the idea from her mind, because it really *wasn't* plausible.

"It's okay, dad, I understand that you have to be hard on me – I have to keep my head in the game, right?" She sighed, wishing she could just accept his apology with good grace and without comment.

"Yes, but sometimes, you have a right to be a teenager, and to keep your thoughts to yourself." He responded. Okay, there was no way that *this* was normal.

"Dad, if I *did* know anything, I would've said so." She assured him.

"So, how was practice?" He asked casually. She was still waiting for his wrath, or some sort of ordinary response, but she decided to lie nonetheless, refusing to believe that this relaxed version of her father could possibly extend to her boyfriend, or her brother for that matter.

"Good, dad. I think I really have got the quad down cold, now. As long as the Russians still have all their hopes pinned on the guys, I should be fine." She shrugged, pulling gently on the collar of her sweater to make sure the pendant remained out of sight. This was the closest they had come to a normal conversation in a very long time.

"You just have to try. I know you can do this. I have no doubt that you can win this thing, now." He was still speaking gently, and now she was getting scared. He couldn't possibly keep this up for long. "I know I've been hard on you recently, but I just don't want your potential to go to waste."

"It's okay, dad." She repeated.

"Okay. Your mother and I are headed to the Springs' for dinner in a while, but she's left some casserole in the refrigerator for you. We won't be late tonight." He was walking away now. She had forgotten that they were going out. That left her with an evening to herself.

He had pulled the door closed as he went, so now that she was alone, she went to the mirror to look at the pendant again. There was something about it that seemed instantly familiar, but she could not pinpoint what it was. Perhaps the shape, lying against her throat, depicting the waning moon that currently hung in the night air. Or perhaps it was the colour, which had appeared to be absent when she had first looked at it, but now it had a gentle pink glow to it. But then again, perhaps it was to do with the strange warmth that was radiating from it, sending shivers of heat through her being, despite the fact that it was still cold against her skin.

At 7:20pm precisely, her parents left the house to travel the three blocks to her God father's house. Electra waited for them to go, before grabbing up the phone, and calling her brother.

"Hello?" He answered quickly on the third ring, and she could hear giggling in the background.

"Cain, it's me." She smiled into the receiver. "Mom and dad just went out. Something weird is going on with dad – he was talking to me calmly! I don't know what's come over him."

"Did you get him drunk? Because that might just work, you know." Cain called back from the other end of the line. "What can I do for you this fine evening?"

"I was wondering if you could get the boy over here for me. I still have no way to get hold of him, you know. I guess it would just be easier to get a courier pigeon, but where would I keep it?" She laughed.

"Sure, I'll go whack something hard against his door. No, not that, Devon." Her brother seemed a little distracted when he spoke. "I'll even get him put in a cab and sent right over. Of course, you can't keep him for long, because he'll turn into a pumpkin if dad catches him there – or some other type of vegetable, I guess. No, Devon, calm down."

"I don't want to know what he's doing, do I?" She asked.

"No, you really don't. Give him half an hour, and if I don't speak to you again, have fun in Paris." Cain replied before hanging up on her.

The doorbell rang twenty-three minutes later, and Electra pulled it open, eager to see the face that stood behind it. In the few hours that they had been apart, she had barely thought of anything other than him.

"Long time no see." She greeted him, grabbing his hand, and pulling him through to the den. "Sit a while. Can I get you something to drink at all?"

"Coffee would be nice." He smiled at her enthusiastically, and took a seat on the pink couch, sinking a little into the deep cushions. She left him, returning as quickly as possible after the drinks were made. He was waiting for her, smiling to himself as he looked at the screen of the TV that was not switched on. She handed him the cup. "Thanks."

"I can't believe I have to leave you for nearly a wee-

k. You have no idea how much I wish I didn't have to go to the stupid championships in France. I hate to leave for even a minute, you know." She sighed, sitting down beside him, and resting her head against his shoulder. "How is it fair that I have to go all that way without you?"

"You'll be fine, but I'll miss you." He assured her.

"You know, the police really *do* think I know something about Maggie's death." She told him.

"I still don't get it. Why do they think you would want to kill Maggie Treat? It's not like you couldn't beat her blindfolded and handcuffed to an elephant. Do they actually think that you couldn't stand her that much?"

"I have no idea."

There was no way of knowing what they were trying to prove by questioning her, because there was nothing that she really knew. But now, sitting with Vagan, she was no longer worried about any of it. She had no way of knowing that the crystal that hung around her neck was slowly emitting its power over her, the protection that Dylan had promised in his letter. She had no way of knowing that as each hour passed, the shape of the stone was changing so slightly that she would barely notice it. She had no way of knowing that the attraction she was feeling was completely beyond her control, but that it would be a part of her from now until the day she died. And she had no way of knowing what was to come.

Chapter thirty-two

Gideon's conscience was not as clear as he would like. The image of the dark haired girl, the look of fear on her face, and the cry of anguish as she realised what was happening was too much for him to simply let slip from his memory. It had been a long time since he had been forced to do things against his better judgment.

It was Jacques' fault, he decided quickly. He was the one who had decided they should meet there, where they had taken advantage of far too many pretty young things. And then, worst of all, to mention his *wife*.

How dare he? Gideon was fairly furious about that, because it was Jacques' fault she was no longer with him. He had played the game to extremes, and had destroyed the lives Gideon and Amy had finally managed to build, despite the horrors they had witnessed during their time together.

Now, safely back in his house in San Francisco, it was easy to try and pretend that none of it had happened, that it was all just a nightmare, drifting away when he woke. Still, when he closed his eyes, he could picture all too clearly the blond girl who had sealed her own fate by being herself.

Who would believe him? If he told any of what he had seen and done during his life, would they think him sane? Too many things for most to know. And yet, if it were his choice, he would have done none of those things that had shaped him again. He would never have married Amy, would never have travelled to Europe, would have dismissed Jacques the first time they met.

He could feel the shadows waiting out in the city to catch him, should he choose to leave the sanctuary of his home. He didn't think the likelihood of that was too great in the near future. He could cope for a week or so without having to go out.

There wasn't much he could do about his fears, now. They had been a part of him for so long, he just tried to exist around them. He had always disliked crowds, which is what had led him to hide away in the country for so long, leaving the French Quarter, where the nightlife heaved for most of the year. Had he known that San Francisco was going to be so similar in places, he would have kept to the country. Then, of course, there was his distaste for light. More difficult to overcome than his fear of people, this was so deeply rooted in him that there seemed no possibility that it would simply fade. It was this that kept him asleep through the day, had led him further and further north, where the sun was harder to find, and the nights were blissfully longer. Jacques was welcome to his new life, his trips to Hawaii, and all that sunburn. Of course, his worst fear was of his own past.

Amy had made the fears go away, most of the time, any way. She had been the one to insist they leave France and head back to New Orleans. She liked the name of the city; it reminded her of where they had first met. She had been such a sweet girl, afraid of her future as he was of his past. She had been beautiful, with thick, dark hair – he'd always favoured brunettes – and brown eyes to match. She was travelling with a relative, stopped for the night, at a small inn on the roads between the north and the south. The relative, an uncle, had invited Gideon and his new friend, Jacques, to join them. It was as if fate had led them to that place, had brought Amy and Gideon together. When the uncle had disappeared out side with some local girl, Gideon and Amy spent hours talking, watching the flames in the fireplace as they dwindled, until the dawn had shattered across the sky, and he had fallen hopelessly for her.

The uncle's disappearance did not come to an end, and eventually, after three days of waiting, Amy continued on her journey toward the south. Gideon went also.

They were married in the spring, and spent several happy years together, first in the small hilltop village just north of Grasse, then returning to New Orleans. But that was where their story had ended.

Now, it was all just a memory. Amy was in the cold tomb in the cemetery that was now hung with daises. Not that any one would look at them, not that anyone cared. Perhaps a tourist might make note of them, as they made their tour of the cities of the dead.

Watching the quiet street outside his window, he could not fault his choice of housing. Even so, he longed for peace, and he had come to the conclusion that he would have it, no matter what the price may be.

Chapter thirty-three

Millions of lights were twinkling all across the city, helping it live up to it's reputation as the City of Lights. And in the centre of it all, the huge metal tower stood proudly, illuminated brightly by thousands of bulbs. The cool breeze coming up from the river was welcome after the excruciatingly long flight, first to Minneapolis, then to Paris Charles de Gaulle, and then the ride in a stuffy cab the size of a horse, and about as fast at times.

The city had flashed past her window, the sights and sounds cut off by the thin pane of glass next to her. She had been made to listen to her father, telling her once more what was required of her. The effects of the crystal didn't seem to be long lasting when it came to him. It still hung around her neck, though.

She leaned out the window, resting her elbows on the railing. It was the first thing she had done when her father left to head down stairs. She was confined to the room, but there was no way she would give up the view. The wrought iron shutters matched the railing, and although they were highly decorative, they would cut out about as much light as a light bulb. They were full of curves, whipping back on themselves before twisting onwards. According to the information pack the hotel had so thoughtfully left in the room, the railing and the shutters were original Hector Guimard works, and had been in place since the hotel was first opened in 1902.

The room was almost as beautiful. The walls were pale green, the same colour as the box Dylan had left the necklace in. A large double bed occupied a portion of the room, solidly built from a wood that had the texture of satin that came with age. The legs and headboard echoed the same lines as those of the shutters, and matched perfectly the huge mirrored dressing table, made from the same wood. The closet matched, too.

Through one of the three doorways, there was a bathroom, with an old, ornate tub, and a ceramic wash stand. Electra had never dreamed that she would be staying in such luxury. The only draw back was that one of the remaining two doors led to her father's room.

He would no doubt be back soon. It had been at least ten minutes since he had left, and it wouldn't take long to leave a message for her mother. There was no way she wanted to give up her peace, though.

She leant further through the window, inhaling the cool night air, and the many fragrances that swirled upon it. The smell of bread baking was the strongest. A small patisserie across the road was shut for the night, but fresh supplies were being baked inside. Next to that, an open window was allowing the aroma of crepes to waft her way, and she could almost taste them, warm and soft, covered in Nutella, with just a little crème Chantilly on top. Steak frites, with a rich pepper and brandy sauce lingered around the tables at a café two or three doors down from the hotel. Then there were the smells of the city, the river, and the cars. There was no where near as much grime here as there was in the other capital cities she had visited, especially London, where she had been permitted to travel on the underground, and had found that for days afterward, her skin never felt clean. She had heard tale of the Paris metro system smelling bad, but being clean. She doubted she'd get to find out.

It was all wonderful, and yet, it was some how – incomplete. It had not taken her long to realise what was missing. It had been obvious from the moment the plane had started taxiing away from the gate, and she had felt the dull ache of emptiness in her stomach. When he had left the house, slipping into the night before his presence was found out, she had missed him instantly. She could still feel the warmth of his lips against hers, the feel of his hands at her waist, pulling her tightly to him as if he wanted to make her a part of him. The gentle words he had whispered to her replayed in her mind, assuring her that he would be there when she returned home on Thursday, wishing her luck while letting her know she didn't really need it.

It was these thoughts that she knew would get her through the following day's tiresome events. It would be a day filled with long waits, and short periods of exhaustive action. The first day of competition was always the same, and the compulsory programme was her least favourite of all. At least the short programme was more her own style, while the final, long routine that she would perform on Thursday afternoon was all about the freedom of her abilities. She was saving the quad for that.

She supposed she should be tired, but the truth was, the flight may have been long, but she had got a lot of rest, making sure she avoided the speech through the flight by sleeping most of the way. It was almost midnight. The tower would be turned off for the night, soon, but for now, she watched the beam of the search light beacon flash across the sky as it swung around once more.

She turned from the window, looking at the bed, where her old case was sitting, open, its contents spilling over the pale green satin sheets. The color matched the walls almost perfectly, and she found it very inviting, especially when paired with the four plump pillows, the covers embroidered with swirls of pale peachy golden flowers. Unfortunately, the contents of her case clashed with everything in the room. Bright fuchsia sequins and acid green sparkles glinted brightly. She was almost as sick of having to wear the ridiculous outfits as she was of the life that went with them.

Still, another day was starting. At home, it was Thanksgiving week, but she would spend the whole of Thursday first on the ice, and then in the sky. As the beacon swung round once more, she tore herself from the breeze, and started to unpack the dreaded clothes, hanging the monstrosities in the closet, where they could no longer afflict her eyes with their hideousness. The other clothes were jeans, shirts, a sweater, the clothes she wore when she was not forced in to a uniform of some type. It didn't take long to straighten everything, and before long, she was ready for bed, hoping to slip into a sleep filled with dreams of the day when she would be back here, with Vagan's arms around her as he whispered kisses into her ear.

Chapter thirty-four

He could feel the energy flowing through him. As Dylan stood motionlessly on the bay bridge, he could sense the power of those that had forgotten The Old Man, power they had no idea existed. It was the first time he had tried to call the powers to him, although he had known it was possible for a long time.

In the days when he had followed the old man around, he had felt their energies, forces they could not conceal. When each had died, and been reborn to a younger version of themselves, all memories of The Old Man had been wiped from their minds. Dylan was the one exception to this, though. He had gone on living, choosing to forestall his own death when he had decided to pause his aging, before The Old Man had even touched his life. The energy they had been given lasted through out their days, impossible to hide from those who could recognise its purpose. Unlike the energy of the new boy, which Dylan had failed to feel. This boy was different, but Dylan could not tell why. Perhaps it was because of this that he had been chosen by The Old Man, because Dylan could not see that much promise in his future right now. Or perhaps The Old Man was doing this. But that seemed unlikely, unless The Old Man knew something that Dylan didn't.

Better than the power he could feel, though, was the sensation he was getting form the crystal, as far away as it was, right now. He could smell the air, taste it on the tip of his tongue, sweet as he remembered it to be; the air in Paris. He couldn't describe the flood of memories that filled his mind, because no one would ever believe it if he did. Still, he took a moment, standing there as still as he could, and found himself lost in a dream of his own past, like another lifetime, one not entirely his own. Not that this one was either, but it was infinitely more enjoyable.

Their names were Amennette and Maria, the girls at the café where he had spent that winter, so cold and un-friendly after the death of his parents. Had he another c-hoice, he would have left the city, but he'd nowhere else to go. So, the café had been his refuge.

It was the kind of place where the wine flowed freely, and the food was basic. It did a good trade, catering to the artists who dwelt locally in their studios, unable to afford rooms for living, as well. Only a few had enough talent to make names for themselves, and now those names were still recalled by some. Perhaps if The Old Man had been paying attention, he would have chosen one of them, instead.

As the winter had progressed, it became more and more clear that the older girl, Amennette had grown fond of him. He hadn't the heart to tell her he was well over a century older than she. Whilst the girls huddled together in a single bed night after night, her thoughts betrayed the fact that she would rather be huddled with him. It hardly seemed fair that he should still have the magnetism, even when he had managed to get away from The Old Man, but he knew it was what drew her to him, what still drew the girls, even after all this time.

The proprietor of the establishment had been mean, and while he allowed them all to live in the tiny rooms above the café, he would not give them fuel to keep warm. Dylan had done what he'd had to in efforts to keep them alive.

It seemed so long ago, now. He could taste it, feel it, almost touch it; but it was not real. He missed who he had been then, longed for the life he had given up the following summer, when he had gone in search of justice, stopping first in London, before travelling to the Americas, to where he had sensed The Old Man had fled. The long months had given him the strength he needed to maintain his power levels.

The last time he had been back, it was to attend a funeral. The life he had foreseen for Amennette had flourished, and her family had grown. The ceremony had been well attended, and she had been welcomed into the tomb of her husband's family, in the old cemetery in Montmartre. It was now her great grand daughter who kept up communications with Dylan, writing long letters to whom she thought was a relative of a friend of a relative.

It had been easy to maintain his secrecy from them. It was nothing to do with his own talent, but more that they were not concerned by the truth. Unfortunately, it had not been so simple to conceal his being from The Old Man. The fact that he had managed to take back his own life was a miracle. As far as he could tell, he was the only one to ever take back their own liberty. It had not been easy. His parents' self sacrifice had helped him grow stronger, but it had still taken all of that strength and more to rip himself from that tenacious grip, and slip away unseen.

Time had given him both patience and perspective. He no longer cared who knew what he was. It hadn't been easy being the good guy in silence for so long. It had started to make him a little reckless. It wasn't really his fault. The problem was the power. As time had passed, he had discovered all his abilities, and the most recently discovered ones had allowed him to move with such ease, and as invisibly as the wind, that he could afford to be anywhere he liked, whenever he wanted. Unfortunately, there was a high probability it was going to get him in trouble sooner or later.

"Dylan, I need that file, please." The voice on the intercom was loud enough to bring him back, breaking into his tranquillity. He arrived back at his desk silently, and carried the correct file into the office, handing it to the principal. "Thank you, Dylan. Oh, and I forgot to mention, we'll be expecting the head of the school board at 3pm rather than 2."

"Certainly, sir." He nodded, and knew he was dismissed to return to his own pursuits.

Chapter thirty-five

The pain was back, stronger than he had felt in a long time, squarely between his shoulder blades. The weeks he had spent growing closer and closer to Electra seemed to have separated him from the pain. Now, though, he could feel the throbbing, so violent that it threatened to pull him under.

Vagan knew that the only way to get around it was to head for the shack, and hope that the place would work its magic as always. If only he could figure out what it meant, he was sure he could get past it. But for now, he couldn't see another option.

The air was cold; late November air. It was too early for that, though. He had expected the weather to be warmer, here. Perhaps it was because he felt so alone, knowing that Electra was so far away.

He had watched her on TV, finally grateful for the expensive sports channel package Billy had insisted they get. As she had spun effortlessly in her acid green dress, he had felt thrilled. Then, as she had leapt into the air, revolving four times before landing perfectly, he had felt his breath catch in his throat. After the free programme had finished, she had sat in the kiss and cry, waving and blowing kisses to who every one must assume would be family and friends, but he knew was him. She had promised him that every one would be for him, and he really wanted to believe that was true.

She would be home in a few hours. He had to be himself again before that. He had to figure out what was happening.

"Vagan! Hey, Vagan, where are you going?" The voice was as familiar as it was unwelcome.

"Hey, Billy, what's wrong?" He sighed, turning to look at his roommate.

"I was hoping you'd do me a favour. You remember that girl Gigi, the girl I brought back a few weeks ago?" Billy asked. Vagan groaned internally.

"Which one was she?" He responded, unable to recall precisely.

"The one with the dark hair and the well stacked rack." Billy grinned. The description didn't really help; it described half the girls Billy brought back. The other half were blond.

"Sure, what about her?" Vagan sighed again, feeling another wave of pain.

"Well, I promised I'd take her out, but then I got a call from a girl I know, and she's only in town one night. I was hoping you might tag along, play the extra date for us."

"Oh, Billy, I don't think that's a great idea. I'm seeing someone, and I think it might be serious, so I should stay away from well stacked racks wherever possible." Vagan protested, and felt another pang in his shoulders, almost as if someone had hit him.

"It's not like I expect you to sleep with either of them. Just come to the bar, and chat with one while I chat with the other." Billy was trying to be persuasive, but Vagan was not going to give in that easily.

"I really have to be somewhere, Billy." Vagan objected further, and started to walk away.

"Look, just think about it, buddy. We'll be at the bar from ten." Billy called after him, but Vagan wasn't stopping as he headed for the shack that had seemed so familiar to him a while ago, but which he had not seen in weeks.

CX∂O

Time must have passed. He could feel the cold had increased, grown damp, like the hours before dawn. He opened his eyes, despite his better judgment, and found the shack in all its glory.

The pain in his shoulders had subsided, though the dull echo of the it remained. He tried to sit up, but his limbs were stiff, his legs tender as if he had been hiking up mountains all day. The taste of rusty copper lingered in the back of his throat.

He tried hard to remember what he had been doing for the past few hours. He glanced at his watch, and realised it was 3am. Electra would be home, soon, and he had promised her he would be waiting for her, across the street, where her father wouldn't notice him.

He pulled himself off the ground, rubbing his calf muscles in hopes that he might be able to run most of the way. The sky outside was still dark, as he slipped out of the wooden door, and started running.

The city was quiet across the bridge, but cars still sped past him as he followed his feet. It was a long way to

Steiner Street, but there was no way he wasn't going to make it, even if he had to push his legs to the limit. He could feel the muscles in his lower legs protesting, his shins felt like they were splitting, but still he pushed on. He was desperate to see her.

The pale blue house was imprinted in his memory. It was there, just as he knew it would be, lit well from the front porch light, and the windows of the front living room. He could see the outline of a woman behind the sheer lace that was pulled across them, a hint of the pale, strawberry blond hair revealing her identity. From here, it looked as if she had a cigarette between her fingers, the glow of the lit tobacco only faint in the brighter light. He was surprised to see it, believing that Electra's father would no doubt disapprove of the habit.

The sound of a diesel-powered car signalled their return. He could have told she was on her way, though. He could feel her coming, like a force that he was tuned to, the approach of a fragrance on the air. He turned to look at the car, seeing the older man sitting beside the driver first. He pulled back into the shadows, watching Mr. Philips as he climbed out of the car, waiting while the cab driver took the cases from the trunk, then following him up the front walkway. Then, there she was, standing on the sidewalk, looking at him as he stepped forward quickly, kissed her briefly on the forehead, then stepped back. She smiled, her lips parting sweetly, reminding him of their taste.

"I missed you." She whispered to him, then turned to look at the man who was standing on the porch, looking tired but stern as he counted the bills he was handing to the driver. "I'll see you tomorrow."

"Early." He agreed. She smiled again, running her hand under her jacket, revealing the gentle glint of her shiny, golden medal.

Chapter thirty-six

It had been so easy to call on the boy. He'd almost forgotten how sweet it was when he was answered so quickly. He had no idea what had changed, and didn't really care. The boy had come, bringing a beauty of minor proportions to him.

He could still taste her, even though he had let he go so quickly. He preferred when he had a little time to play with them, first. Unfortunately, this one would be missed far too quickly, and he couldn't risk the boy being caught.

Still, even while her scent lingered in his throat, he wanted more. He could go in search of it himself, but it was too late for that, right now. He would have to wait until the lights were lower, when the beautiful creatures came out to play, and the ones who *wouldn't* be missed were far easier to find.

For now, at least, he could feel his heart pumping, its slow, steady rhythm like a song remembered from the past. It was one of the few sounds he missed when it stopped, which it would soon. The blood that flowed through it was not his to keep. He craved more, anything to keep that sound a little longer. Perhaps he should call the boy again? He thought of it, but decided no. He had to have patience, now. Surely he had managed to acquire that during his very long, very dark life.

But no, he hadn't. Like the blood that coursed through his veins, now, it was not a part of him. He was used to having what he wanted, when he wanted it. If he needed to keep his heart pumping backwards as it did, then it was up to him to get what it took to do it. There would be plenty for him to choose from, when the world fell asleep, and the whores came out again.

Chapter thirty-seven

The sun was barely up when she stepped out into the morning. She had slept for only a few hours, sure that she should be more disoriented than she was. The little yard at the back of the house was starting to shut down in anticipation of the colder months to come; her mother's tiny weed garden was almost devoid of life all ready.

Along the back of the yard, there was a tall fence. During the summer, it was home to several climbing plants, but they were also hiding, now. The gate in the middle of the fence was metal, painted red, as if a warning to any who might wish to take the time to stop and look, or try to trespass within. But the red was starting to fade a now, and no longer held such sway over possible intruders.

Electra could feel every muscle in her stomach complain. It had been a long flight with nothing but some celery, and the meat from a sandwich, to eat. The peanuts had been snatched away from her quicker than she could refuse them. The look on the flight attendant's face had been one she recognised; pity, mingled with a little fear, and a lot of annoyance.

She settled on the swing seat, feeling the gentle sway caused by her own breathing, and pulled her knees up to her chin, humming softly the songs she had heard from her hotel room window. She wondered how much the whole package had cost, the flights and the hotel, knowing that her father would never have spent that much by himself. The hotel had been too well appointed to be cheap.

"Is it safe?" The voice came from beyond the gate. It was like a great weight had been lifted from her, and she felt the tension, and the hunger, ebb quickly away. She jumped up from the seat, and crossed to the gate in seconds, closing the space between them as quickly as she could manage. "Good morning."

"Hi." She sighed as he handed her a wild flower through the gate. "I missed you."

He laughed, leaning to the gate, fitting his face into a gap in the metal. She reached her other hand through, and stroked his cheek, leaning toward him to press her lips to his. Where she had felt at ease before, she now felt elation, knowing that his lips would be hers for as long as she wanted them. She unlatched the hook, and allowed the gate to swing open, taking his hand, and walking out into the small passage that led round to the front of the house.

"How are you going to explain your absence to him?" Vagan asked, holding her hand to his face, and kissing her fingertips.

"I'll just tell him I went running. Why else d'you think I'm wearing sneakers?" She told him, pulling his arm around her shoulders, her own across her chest so that their fingers remained locked together. "He knows how I love to run when I should have jet lag."

"Most people stay in bed all day." He laughed again, gently but with sincerity. She couldn't remember ever having been so blissfully happy, knowing that she was becoming more and more attached to Vagan with each passing moment.

"But I'm not most people, don't you know? I happen to have managed to sleep for the entire 8 hours to Minneapolis, and then it really wasn't that much further. I am very well rested, and don't think I could sleep another minute. Of course, it helps that I'm still dreaming."

"About me?" He asked, sounding surprised.

"Of course of you." She tugged his arm gently, and he kissed the side of her face, just below the temple. "You know, I was just in what is supposed to be the most beautiful city in the world, but it was nothing compared to right here, right now."

"It's nice here." He agreed, and she looked around her at the ally way between her house and the one next to it. The ground was dusty, void of life except for a few weeds poking their way through the cracks. The blue house on one side was well painted, having been recoated in the spring, but the pale yellow one next door was looking slightly dilapidated. But the ally was short, and they walked out onto Steiner Street, where the view was far more appealing.

"It's not so bad." She grinned. "How was your week?"

"Lonely; and long, very long," he sighed, kissing her again. She was starting to really enjoy having him in her life. "When are you leaving again?"

"Not 'til after Christmas, now. The finals are a while off, then obviously I have the trip to Japan to contend with. How about you? Are you leaving for the holidays?"

"I'm not going anywhere."

They continued to walk, heading down Steiner Street, toward the still sleeping Haight-Ashbury region. It was still early, and the city would not start opening for a couple of hours, yet. The only places open were the early morning coffee spots, and the newsstands that were offering the early morning editions. The area may have been quiet, but it still held the aura of its history, filled with the ghosts of its hippy past that refused to be silenced. Electra would have been happy, then, living in a world that was free, where she would not be the first to rebel against her father.

There was some sort of delivery going on outside one of the small store fronts, and neither of them looked too closely at what the delivery consisted of; the shop window display made it fairly obvious. Across the street, an early vendor was taking advantage of the clear pavement to set up her blanket, pulling lengths of thread in various glorious shades from a carpetbag, along with pictures to illustrate her proficiency for braiding hair. Once her display was complete, she sat on the blanket, her legs crossed, and began to meditate loudly, the volume of her 'om' carrying it down the street.

Eventually, they entered the Golden Gate Park, where the sun was making everything warmer for the day ahead. It was still chilly, though, probably no more than 51°f, if that. They walked happily past the children's play park, void of the usual laughter of five year olds, and the planetarium, where a guy was sweeping the step, looking rather bored. Finally, they came to the Tea Gardens, and came to rest on a bench overlooking the koi pond. A couple of large fish were at the surface, sucking in air along with a few insects that had landed on the surface, believing it to be solid.

"So you didn't fall in love with Paris, then?" Vagan asked after a while, looking at her with curiosity.

"No, unfortunately, it was missing one vital thing. Besides, I'm not sure it's possible for me to love anything else right now." She smiled, leaning toward him, resting her head against his shoulder. "You know, though, it was weird without Maggie. I don't think I really noticed at Skate America, what with Jo being back, and all the excitement of first tournament of the season, but it seemed really quiet this time. I guess because Paris was Maggie's favourite comp. She always made a big deal of it, new routines, new outfits. She always went that little bit further than the rest of us for this one. I think it had something to do with her Grandmother being a French Can-Can dancer or something. I know there was some weird story, any way."

"French Can-Can? That sounds like a bad storyline for a soap." He laughed.

"I know." She agreed. "But it was like no one wanted to talk about her. I guess that everyone knows about her death now, that it was murder, I mean. I thought there would be more gossip, but no one was really talking about anything. I've never known it be like that. Jo and I were the only people talking to each other. It was kinda depressing."

"Have they questioned her?"

"Yeah, made her feel like she had something to hide, too. I don't get it. Jo lives in Georgia. It's not like she was even in the same state! I really don't have anything to hide, but they made me feel like a criminal when they came to talk to me."

"They still think you would have something to gain?"

"Obviously. Of course, the perfect quad I landed yesterday should prove my point, shouldn't it?"

"I think so. What does your father think?"

"For some reason, he thinks I'm as guilty as sin."

They lapsed into silence, as Electra pondered the fact that she felt accused of something that she had nothing to do with. The fish that had been sucking up the insects turned on each other momentarily, the larger one latching on to the smaller.

The only possibility she had come up with was that they thought she had managed to get someone to harm Maggie for her. It was an idea she never would have entertained, had it not been for the same thought Jo Fox had voiced only a couple of days earlier, reminding her of the incident only a few years earlier, when one skater had been so desperate to win, she had had her boyfriend smash the knee caps of her opponent. Of course, it had backfired on that occasion. But this was worse. Maggie was dead, not able to heal from this. If it weren't for the fact that Electra *knew* she had nothing to hide, she would have felt some guilt over the event. Still, there was something happening, and although she could not pinpoint what they were searching for, she felt sure that there was no end in sight for their probing.

There was a chance, though, that they had something to tie any one of them to the crime. She couldn't think what that might be. If they had stated what they thought she knew, she may stand a chance to defend herself against their accusations. But they were unwilling to share, so she had no clue as to what she was meant to be hiding.

Time passed faster when they were together, and after what seemed only minutes, but was closer to an hour, it became necessary for them to make their way back to the blue house. Slipping once more between the houses, Vagan walked her back to the gate. A quick peek told her the space was still empty, so she wrapped her arms around Vagan's neck, pulling him close as she pressed her lips against his, feeling once again the uncontrollable pull that became apparent whenever he was near to her, the pull that seemed to have them bound together, with little chance that she would ever want to give him up.

Chapter thirty-eight

There was an atmosphere of hope in the air. It was something that he had come to recognise over time, as the approaching holidays offered joy and peace. When he had been part of a family, he had enjoyed the sensation, but now it reminded him that he was alone.

The past two weeks had passed quietly, while Dylan continued his vigil outside the house, watching and waiting for the chance to make his move. It had, however, become clearer over that time, that he was going to need Electra's assistance far more than he had previously thought.

During the short periods he had managed to sleep, he had been dreaming more, and had seen the way things were. Her strength was growing, and the crystal was working to protect her, especially now that it had once more waxed toward completion. She would not have noticed it, so far, but it would become apparent soon enough.

His sight had shown her amongst the flames, but standing proud, not falling under the spell of The Old Man. He feared now only for the fact that she was so connected to the boy, who would also be there when the final battle came to pass. If the boy was in danger, she may not be willing to leave him.

It would not stop the fight, though. The others would come in to play soon enough. They had as much to gain from The Old Man's demise as Dylan did. Of course, they would not know that they were gaining anything. When the time came, he would call on them, knowing that they would come quickly.

"This is going to be so simple." He laughed, gently, as he stood on the front walk of The Old Man's house, invisible as air, silent as a whisper, watching the sky grow darker as a storm began to roll in across the bay.

"Sorry, sir, but if I could take your order. My boss is really harsh when I take too long." The voice of the waitress broke his concentration, pulling him back to the diner on Montgomery Street. He looked at the girl, dressed in a uniform that had seen better days, and seemed to have shrunk at some point, because it was clearly too small for her.

"I'll take the hamburger platter, thanks." He smiled at her, handing the yellow menu back, and watching her walk away.

There were only a handful of days left until the end of the semester, when the halls would empty for Christmas, and he would have plenty of time to make sure that The Old Man felt *everything*.

Chapter thirty-nine

Not now," Gideon mumbled as he reached for the telephone receiver. "Hello?"

"Hey, Gideon, are you okay, you don't sound so good?" His cousin's voice responded. He was starting to agree with Jacques; it had been a mistake seeking out family.

"I'm fine, Cher, just a little busy. How can I help you this morning?"

"I'm in need of a little assistance tonight. Could I come over, say 6:30?" She asked. He groaned internally, but it did not escape to betray him.

"I'm going to be busy, until 8 or so. You could come over later, though." He tried to hide his disdain. He wasn't sure he succeeded.

"Are you sure you're alright?" She asked again, and he found that it was not completely true that he was fine.

"Of course. I'll see you this evening. Bye, Cher."
He hung up before she could speak again, rolling over once
more to close his eyes.

Ever since his return from New Orleans, he'd had
the feeling he was being watched. It was, no doubt, part of
the extended paranoia that had begun to spread through
his veins recently. The shadows seemed to be moving in on
him, trapping him within their darkness. He would have
been happy to retreat into their depths, of not for the fact
that these were no ordinary shadows. They were filled
with fear and danger, and while they had gathered around
him for a long time now, they had only recently become so
forceful.

His throat was dry, void of the sensation of liquid
trickling between his lips. He could still taste the warm,
salty flesh of the brunette that Jacques had insisted he play
with, but the thought of her filled him with remorse. He
wasn't sure he would ever be able to forget her face, not
even if he lived a very long time. He grasped for the glass
of whisky on the nightstand, feeling the burn as it coursed
through his system, draining the glass, and hoping that
sleep would return quickly. But it was a vain hope, and he
would have to wait a while.

He lay across his bed, staring at the ceiling, feeling
the soft sheets against his skin. It was certainly more
pleasant to sleep in a well dressed bed than it was to try
and rest in a rough cot, which he had in a past version of
himself.

A shaft of light was managing to leak through the
heavy drapes, along the tops, where they had started to sag
under their own weight. The brightness ran in a long V
across the ceiling, and he watched as a spider scuttled
through the space, making its way home to the web it had
spun in the corner of the dark red walls.

Finally, he found himself drifting into a restless sleep, where nightmares waited. The same as it ever was – the darkness that enveloped him, stealing away his reason for living.

The demise of Amilie De Montfort had been the turning point for him, the catalyst that had lead him to run away and hide in the small village high in the Rockies, where he had been seen and known until it had become apparent that he needed to move on. The nightmares had continued, even though he had tried to outrun them, returning whenever he felt the shadows around him once more.

When he finally re-woke, there was something different in the room. He could feel it. No longer was it mere shadow. This was tangible, almost solid compared with the usual sensation. It was overwhelmingly powerful.

"Leave me alone." He whispered, knowing that it had worked before. But the feeling grew stronger still. This time, he screamed it "LEAVE ME ALONE!"

He had to get out of the house, get into the open for a while, as much as the thought filled him with dread. He glanced at the clock, and found it worse than he had imagined. It was still light outside.

He pulled on a pair of blue jeans, and an old grey shirt that had seen better days, pausing a moment to throw a sweater over the top. The stairs were taken two at a time, as he raced to leave the house.

His old boots sat just outside the door, warm from the sun, and he shoved his feet in to them forcefully. The bright sunlight that greeted him on the outside was as bad as he had feared, but he could not take the time to pause, now.

"I'm photophobic, for Christ's sake." He muttered to himself. "I want my dark, I want my bed. I don't want to be out here."

Unfortunately, the house did not seem to be listening, and now, he could feel it outside, as well. He didn't linger, but ran down the front walk, and started to wander, heading for nowhere in particular.

Although he had told Electra that he was fine, he was starting to feel old. He was too strong for the exhaustion that he was experiencing, too fast to slow down to a pace more appropriate to his age. His body may show no signs of wear, but his soul was tattered and torn.

The city was one big hill, steeper than the mountains even. His legs were quick, and he did not worry about them, though, as he walked further and further, seeking refuge. Perhaps if he could walk quickly enough, he would manage to outrun the shadows, lose them in the streets.

It didn't take him long to conclude he had no idea where he was going. He had not explored the city, at least not while it was still light. He paused at an intersection, looking around him at the brightly painted houses, feeling ill, wishing that he could return to his dark sanctuary.

He walked on, up and down hills, past the Golden Gate Park, before tuning back on himself, and onto Market Street. Finally, he found himself in the financial district, where the buildings were closer together, and he could slink into the dank alleyways between them, where no one would look for him. His breath came more easily, here, and he inhaled the dampness. He could easily appreciate this side of the city.

Eventually, darkness descended above the city, and with twilight fading, he left his new haunt, and started back to the main thoroughfares of the city, where the bright lights invited people to take the time to spend what little they had on needless items.

Christmas was in the air, fragrant as ever. Cinnamon, cloves, and nutmeg lingered around a bakery, its window filled with holiday cookies, commemorating the birth of a child who had, in his opinion, never existed. But plenty of people still believed it, and were happy to spend all their money on gifts for people, giving in to the commercialised theories that had become more and more commonplace over the years.

The other shop windows were filled to brimming point with useless things – scarves with large holes in them, jeans with torn patches, winter coats with no sleeves. He decided that the times of people dressing appropriately had been over taken by these new styles more concerned with fashion than sense. He'd seen enough trends come and go to realise that fashion was fickle.

Further on, he passed gift shops and a department store, its windows decorated in candy colours and rich golds, invoking the past, richness and power. There seemed to be a theme, possibly an homage to 'Arabian Nights', or some fairytale being depicted in royal blue, deep purple, rich crimson and a shade of pink that could only be described as shocking, with silks and velvets tumbling across deep piled carpets and high backed chairs. One of the windows was filled with toys, wooden trains and tin cars sitting next to baby dolls in ornate cribs. Then, of course, the omnipresent Barbie and GI Joe dolls, in their respective vehicles. He would have preferred to see the Barbie in the tank, but never mind.

Walking past all of this, Gideon recalled his past Christmases, when he had been happy, when Amy had been by his side, and there had seemed a real possibility that their family could grow. He had thought it would be nice to have a youngster around, and would have enjoyed decorating the tree, wrapping all the gifts. But that had never come to pass, and he had stored the thoughts away with his memories of Amy. Going home had made him think of them again recently, but soon his thoughts would go back to sleep until the next trip.

Now, thinking about his past, he thought about his present, and Electra, his saving grace, the person who had pulled him back from the darkness for a time. It had been enough to get him settled in the city. He wanted to repay her for all she had done for him, and for being short with her when all she had wanted was to talk with him. He knew he wouldn't be around for long, now, realising that the shadows that he thought he had left behind had caught up with him. Soon, he would have no choice but to leave in order to save his own sanity. When that time came, he wanted to be remembered by the beautiful creature who had given her time to him so willingly. He would achieve this remembrance no matter what he had to do.

Perhaps a gift, he thought, something that would keep him in her mind when he was gone. There were plenty of shops around him, selling whatever any person could need. Surely he could find something here. He hunted through the windows, hoping to glimpse something that reminded him of her. Finally, he spotted it, in the window of a small jewellery store, glittering in the bright lights. It was old, which made him think of how he felt currently, and striking, which reminded him of Electra. He smiled to himself as he pushed the door open, and looked at the elderly man behind the counter.

"I'd like the pin, in the window." Gideon told the man, gesturing toward the front of the store.

"Yes, sir, a very fine piece." The older gentleman bustled, pulling up the end of the counter, and flipping through his keys to find the match for the lock. The whole of the wall seemed to swing open, allowing the shop keeper to access the window display. It only took him a moment to choose the right item, and hold it up for Gideon to view at closer range. "This was first made in 1912, in Paris of course, by the house of Cartier. It was owned originally by a French dancer from the Follies Berger, who married a wealthy diplomat. It has excellent provenance to the fact."

"How interesting." Gideon could smell this man's affection for his business, and found it rather an appealing scent.

"The diamonds are not large, but there is a total carat weight of 3.6. They are set in platinum, with a backing of gold. This is very fine jewellery. It would be nice to have it worn again." He held it against the light, and the stones refracted the beams, sending thousands of rainbows dancing across the room.

"It's perfect. I'll take it." Gideon smiled.

"Very good, sir. I'll wrap it."

Gideon waited while the other man retrieved the red and gold box from the window display, fitting the pin into the box that was made for it. Then, the box was wrapped in fine tissue paper, before it was placed in a small red bag. Finally, a ribbon was tied through the top of the bag, finished with a bow. The shop keeper looked very pleased with himself. Gideon paid the man, then took his life.

Chapter forty

The same nightmare, again and again. The dark room, hard bed, rotting wooden chair. No light found its way in, the window painted black. Standing at the door to begin with, pounding fists against the wood. Then, cowering in the corner, knowing that there was no escape.

Finally, the door swinging open, and The Old Man coming slowly in, his face hideous, fingers curled out to take her. She could feel his hands on her skin, cold and harsh, pulling her from the floor, dragging her to the other room, where candles flickered in a breeze, and The Old Man sat in his tall backed chair, holding her across his body as he drank from her throat.

This was the point at which Geena Du Pré woke every time she slept, feeling once again the pain in her shoulders, tasting the warm, metallic flavour of her own blood in the back of her mouth. Her sobs came in ragged bursts, scaring her as much as the nightmare had.

She could no longer leave her room without checking she had her pepper spray, although she wasn't convinced it would save her from whatever The Old Man was. It was hard to leave her bed, most of the time. She hadn't looked at her reflection in a mirror for weeks, terrified of what she might see in her own face. She knew she was a mess.

She walked the city, desperate to find answers. But they weren't there. Her energy was waning, and she felt alone; lost. Finally, when she was sure she could take no more, she felt a flicker of remembrance at the house in front of her. She wasn't sure it was the same house. She wasn't sure of anything, anymore. Still, she waited, watching, hoping that somehow, she would find what she was looking for.

Chapter forty-one

W ow, it's beautiful." Electra exclaimed, stroking the glistening surface with the tip of her finger. She wasn't sure she had ever seen anything quite so perfect.

"You like it?" Asked the man beside her. Although she didn't look up, she was sure he would be smiling. She nodded, stroking his image on the sheet again. "I didn't take it, of course."

"Obviously, otherwise you wouldn't be in the picture with me." She grinned, finally turning to look at him. He was holding her close as they sat on a bench in the Presidio, and she was wishing the weather were warmer so that she could feel his skin next to hers.

"He knows his camera stuff. I'm glad about that, because I think it turned out well. It's a shame I can't use it for my project; I doubt I'd get away with it." He told her, resting his cheek on the top of her head.

"Oh, the `Natural Beauty' thing. How did the rest turn out?" She asked, curious about the dozens of shots he had taken of her.

"Well, you beat the seals that everyone else took snaps of. I have to say, if I didn't have to use my scholarship here, I'd be off to some other college some place. Of course, I'd have to take you with me. I'm not sure what your dad would say about that." He replied.

"He'd get over it." She murmured, wishing that there were some way, any way, that she could run away with him. "I'm going to get this one framed, I think."

"That might be just as risky."

He had a point. Whilst there was nothing improper in their poses, there was still the promise of what would have come had Devon not disturbed them, what came eventually that day. She could feel that stare, again, looking into Vagan's eyes, seeing her face reflected there, feeling his arms wrapped around her, wanting to be with him as long as he was willing to hold her. She had seen the longing in his face, too, felt the anticipation as he moved to kiss her. Though the moment had been shattered it was now held forever in this image. She leaned her face to his throat, kissing him gently.

"I didn't say where I was going to put it, did I?" She giggled, kissing him again.

"Let me guess, in your bathroom?"

"No, I was thinking of above my bed, on the ceiling." She kissed him again, moving her lips to the underside of his chin.

"That's a bit distracting, you know." He told her lightly. She grinned again, pressing her lips to the tip of his chin this time. "I'm not complaining, though."

"Good, because there is something about your skin that just makes me want to taste it." She confessed. "You taste like cream and cinnamon, and kinda eggy, but in a good way."

"Thanks, I think."

"No, really. I wish you could taste what I do right now." She insisted.

"Well, how about I get to taste you? Because you taste like bitter chocolate and green apples." He told her, pulling his head back, and lifting her chin gently with his index finger. The way she felt when he kissed her had not changed since the first time. The intensity of his lips, their warmth, as they responded to her own, was unlike anything else she had ever known. She wanted to be with him forever, and knew that if he asked her to marry him right now, she wouldn't refuse.

When they were finally out of breath, they sat again in silence for a while. She was beginning to wonder how she was going to ask her cousin to help her. She would have asked Cain, but she had the feeling that it was better not to turn to him too often, lest her parents grow suspicious of her true motives. If she could get Gideon to agree to be her cover story once a week, she would get twice as much time with Vagan as she did now. It was an appealing prospect.

"What are you thinking?" He asked, kissing the top of her head.

"Hmmmm, I was just thinking that this would be so much easier for us if I didn't have parents." She sighed. "How do we get on with this if we can't be together?"

"We can be. Think about it – you have all the practice time you need, right, because your dad thinks it will help. But you and I both know that you don't need anymore practice, because, well, you're perfect. So just keep telling him you're there, and I'll be where ever you are."

"Really, you will?"

"Where else would I want to be?"

"With friends?"

"Friends!" He snorted. "Firstly, I would require some friends, then I would have to get over the fact that you fill 99% of my thoughts, and the fact that I seem to be falling rather heavily in love with you."

"Are you? That's a relief." She breathed, feeling less anxious suddenly.

"Am I what?"

"Falling in love with me?" The anxiety was back.

"Yes, as long as you are falling too, because other wise I'm just falling in love *for* you, which is nowhere near as interesting a prospect." He responded quickly, and she managed to breathe evenly again.

"I don't think you need to worry about my side of things. I think that falling in love with you was as inevitable as the sun setting. I have no idea what it is that I find so – enticing – about you, but there is something that just makes me want to be with you every moment that I can, every second I'm awake, and most of the ones where I'm not. You've filled my senses with so much warmth and passion, I can't begin to describe what I feel when I'm with you, or worse, how I feel when I'm not. Of course I love you. How could I not?" She admitted, feeling her face grow warm. She had known for a while that she loved him, but the relief of telling him was as immense as knowing he felt at least partially the same.

As her confession had been made, she had seen in his face the tranquillity that she felt expand to encompass him. Now, he was gazing into her eyes once more, his lips curving into a smile.

For far too long, Electra had put up with all the stress and pressure her life had inflicted upon her. For a long while, it had made her depressed, although she had hidden it well, never revealing just how bitter her feelings were toward her father for pushing her so hard. It was this same depression that had reared up when she was allowing Vagan to take her photograph. She would never admit to the fact that it had been such a large part of her for so long. The only person who had even the slightest idea was Jo Fox, who had been through just as much as she had. Still, even in her darkest moments, she had never considered that there might be some magical answer to it. Now, she realised once more that Vagan was the only answer she had ever needed.

It was dark, and the start of a rain shower was upon them, lightly dusting them with icy droplets. Electra pulled her coat tighter around herself, and tried to lean closer to Vagan, which was difficult as she was already pressed against his body. She shivered, and though he rubbed her arm with his hand, she was still cold. She supposed it was time they moved, before she lost interest in doing anything other than sitting.

"Do you mind coming to Gideon's place with me?" She asked, looking at her watch. It was 7:45 now, which meant that they would be there sometime after eight. She had asked him earlier, but wanted to confirm he was still happy to accompany her there.

"Where ever you want to go, I'll come." He assured her once more. She felt his arms loosen, as he stood up, holding his hand out to her. She took it eagerly, and allowed him to lead her to the street, heading back across town. The rain came more heavily after a while, so Vagan hailed them a cab for the dozen or so blocks remaining. When the cab stopped, Vagan paid the driver, and they started across the sidewalk.

She didn't see the pale blond girl at first, huddled in a corner by the front steps. The sound of her crying was lost in the gentle pitter-patter of rain. As they approached, the girl looked at them, her eyes quickly switching between the two. More troubling was that Vagan had stopped walking, and was looking at this girl with recognition.

"What's wrong?" Electra asked, turning her gaze back to the girl, but addressing Vagan.

"I...I'm not sure. Geena, what are you doing here?" Vagan asked the girl, who was struggling to her feet.

"I need to know what happened." She cried. "I need to know why you brought me here, what that *thing* did to me when you left me here."

"I've never been here, Geena." He eyed the house with doubt.

"So what, you just happen to be passing? And what about this girl? Is she next? Well?" The blond demanded.

"I'm sorry, I seem to have missed something. I'm Electra, and I'm here because my cousin lives here. Vagan is here because he and I are a pair, and I barely go any where without him. A better question would be who you are, and what the *hell* you are doing here." Electra demanded in return, looking at the girl, trying to identify the emotions that were present on her face, and deciding it was best described as terror, but also massive exhaustion.

"He hasn't told you? Those looks that make you feel special, but which he uses to lure you away, and then you wake up a day later, no idea where you've been, but filled with the nightmare that won't go away. He did this to me. He brought me to this hellhole, and left me in the grasp of a . . a . .*demon*. I have no other word for it, but that creature, he did things to me, and Vagan is to blame. How can you trust him? How can you not feel the way he pulls you in? You have to get away from here, *from him*, before it's too late." The girl cried pitifully, and Electra would have been willing to comfort her, had she not just accused Vagan of being in league with a monster.

"You expect me to believe any of that?" Electra laughed, but felt harsh doing so. The girl needed help, obviously, because she was no doubt disturbed mentally.

"I expect him to tell you the truth! He must be having the nightmares, too. Why won't you tell her?" She was pleading, begging Vagan to speak, but when Electra looked at him, his face was confused, but guilt free. Either this girl had everything wrong, or Vagan felt nothing over his actions if they were a reality. Electra hoped fervently that the latter was wrong, and wanted to be sure that the girl got the help she required. "Don't go in there, please? Get away from here while you still can. If you have any sense of personal safety, then you'll run, now."

"I'm sorry, but I've had enough of this. Come on, Vagan." She turned from them, and continued up the walkway to the tall house. The shades in the living room were wide open, and she could see her cousin there, looking thoughtful as he watched the conversation continue out side his home.

"Go home, Geena." Vagan was telling the girl, now, and following Electra. The blond looked at them one more time, before turning away, running down the street, her sobs echoing in the still, damp air.

Now that the girl was gone, Gideon had turned his attention to her, instead. The thoughtful expression changed quickly, breaking into a smile that was unfamiliar on his face. Within moments, and quicker than Vagan could join her at the door, Gideon was pulling it open, the smile still in place.

"Hi, come in." He greeted her, kissing her lightly on the cheek, then waving to Vagan, who was still walking, slowly, looking over his shoulder a couple of times. She followed her cousin, leaving the door open for Vagan to use when he eventually got to it. "I'm in such a good mood, right now." Gideon was leading her back in to the living room, and she was finding this version of her cousin rather unsettling. "Sit down, I'll get you a drink. Vagan, come on in, I'll get you a drink."

Electra sat on the old love seat, waiting for Vagan to join her, and Gideon left the room. She could hear him whistling in the kitchen at the back of the house.

"I think he's gone mad." Electra whispered as Vagan sat. "Maybe there was some outbreak of crazyitus on the street, and they both got it."

"Sorry, I think she must have a screw loose. She goes to college, she was in my psyche. class at the start of the semester, but she went all weird and dropped the class." Vagan told her.

"You have no idea what she was on about?" She asked, starting to wonder whether he *was* hiding something from her.

"No. Before she went weird, though, she went missing for a day. I *had* seen her the afternoon before she disappeared. Maybe she just put the two events together." He shrugged. "And I guess the house is a little weird looking from the outside."

"I guess that makes sense." She nodded, trying to be satisfied with his reasoning, but finding herself unconvinced. She didn't have time to press the issue, though, because Gideon came back, carrying a tray with three glasses.

"I'm so glad you came!" His enthusiasm had not waned while he had been in the kitchen. He handed them each a glass, filled with dark red, warm liquid. "Mulled wine. I made it myself. Don't worry, all the alcohol is gone. It burns off with the heat."

"Thanks." Electra sipped from her glass, tasting the wine, filled with citrus peel, cloves, cinnamon, and nutmeg. It was warm and sweet, and reminded her of Christmas.

"Did that strange girl go away?" Gideon asked, drinking from his own beverage. "She's been out there for over an hour."

"She went." Electra assured him. "You seem – happy, tonight, Gideon."

"You know, I've had an excellent day. I went out, and took a long walk around the city, which I haven't done in a while, and remembered how much fun it is to window shop. San Francisco is amazing, if you just wander around looking at things." He informed them.

"I know." She responded. "I've lived here a while."

"I never realised the city was so pretty. I must explore it more often."

"Gideon, are you drunk or something?" She questioned, hoping to find some answer to this strange attitude to everything he suddenly seemed to have.

"Nope. I might have had a little too much sugar, though." He was nodding rapidly, and Electra was reminded of the way she had felt after the gummy bears. "Oh, and I found something, that I want you to have. Wait there."

He left the room again, whistling the same tune from before, which Electra vaguely recognised from an old movie. She shook her head, hoping to dispel the thought that he might, in fact, be high, and looked at Vagan. He seemed just as perplexed, raising an eyebrow and shrugging.

"It was my grandmother's." He announced, coming back with a little package in one hand, presenting it to her carefully. "Go ahead, open it. I'm sure you'll like it."

She held it in her palm, weighing it. The box was red, embossed with gold. The age of it was apparent, and her curiosity was raging. She stroked the top, her finger tracing the gold line carefully, before pinching the top between her thumb and forefinger, and lifting the lid away. The pin inside was nestled into a space that was made for it, and her eyes nearly popped out of their sockets when she read the name of the makers, because that would have to confirm that the stones that were dazzling her had to be diamonds. The swirls and curves were a lot like the ones that had adorned her hotel room in Paris, and she knew that it was far too good for her to accept.

"I can't take this, Gideon." She told him, objecting to taking something that deserved to be owned by a great beauty, or at least someone with class.

"Of course you can. I demand you take it, and not think more on it. It reminds me of you so well." He insisted, pushing her hand toward her when she tried to pass it back to him. His enthusiasm was too much, and so finally, she closed the box, cupping it between her palms. "Good. Now, you wanted to ask me something?"

"Err, yeah." She tried to gather her thoughts back to some sort of order. "Well, I guess you could probably tell that Vagan and I are dating."

"Obviously." He agreed, nodding vigorously.

"But I haven't quite told my parents, yet." She cringed at the thought.

"And you want me to be your alibi?" He guessed. She hesitated, then nodded. "Of course, my dear girl, why would I not? Now, would anyone like some more mulled wine?"

"Sure." They both replied at the same time. Electra was eager to get him out of the room for a moment, so that she could speak to Vagan privately. She spoke quickly, quietly. "He is not right, this evening. This thing, it's Cartier. I don't care who it belonged to; it must be worth so much, thousands, big thousands. It's covered in diamonds, Vagan."

"Has he ever been right, though?" Vagan asked in whispers.

"Maybe not. He was strange with me on the 'phone this morning, then this. He seems so hyper. I think we should go before he does something." She felt suddenly worried by his actions, and wanted to be far away before his excitement wore off, and he became irritable, again.

"Well, he agreed to cover for you, so you're alright. We'll go as soon as he comes back, or after we drink whatever this stuff is." Vagan looked at the glass in his hand, wincing. Electra drank some of her own, and had to agree, now that it was getting cold, because the cloves and cinnamon were sticking together. Still, being brave, she drank the rest of the contents quickly, feeling the spices burn her throat as it went. She placed the vessel on the small side table, and picked the small box up again, chancing another look at the pin, and finding her breath taken once more by the magnificence of it. She found no choice but to shut the box again quickly. The steadily growing volume of full out singing was indication that Gideon was coming back.

"Hmm, I was going to ask you something, but I've clean forgotten. Here, drinks." Gideon announced his return, handing them the new beverages. They both drank quickly, emptying their glasses in the time it took Gideon to sit down. He seemed to be concentrating hard, then all of a sudden, his head snapped up, and he clicked his fingers. "That girl, Vagan seemed to know her. Who was she? Other than strange, I mean."

"Her name is Geena. I know her from college." Vagan responded, echoing her own puzzlement at his interest.

"Geena? Hmm, she did seem a little familiar. I wonder if maybe she tried to sell me something. There has to be some reason she picked my house to sit before." Gideon shrugged.

"Yeah, well, Geena Du Pré is not worth worrying about. She's gone, now." Vagan assured them.

The sound of shattering glass filled the momentary silence. She wasn't sure what it meant, but Gideon's face had twisted, as if in sudden agony. From between his clenched fist, a torrent of red spilled, mixing wine and blood as they rained to the carpet that covered the otherwise bare floor. A shrill cry bled from his throat, tortured beyond recognition.

"What's wrong?" Electra asked, terrified by this strange reaction.

"Get away from here!" He yelled in response, not looking at them. "Leave now, while you still can, while you still breathe."

"What have we done wrong?" Electra begged, bewildered.

"Nothing." He whispered, now, holding his hands in front of his face, looking at the mess of splintered glass and wine mingled with his own blood. Finally, he looked at her, and the fury in his eyes was so plain, that she was instantly petrified by what she saw. The green of his eyes, so similar in colour to her own, had vanished, replaced by blackness, a void of bleak, dark thunder. "Please, please leave, Electra, before I do something that I really might regret."

Vagan stood quickly, and pulled her up behind him. They didn't pause, leaving the room as fast as their legs could carry them. Electra was still clasping the red box in her hand. She was tempted to drop it at the door, but she could not make her hand open to do so. Within moments, they were back on the street, and Vagan was walking away toward the brighter lights of the city. He stopped when he realised Electra was not following him.

"What's wrong?" He asked, turning back to her, finding her confused eyes filling with tears. He moved back to her, wrapping his arms around her, pulling her close to him. "Come on, we need to get away from here."

"What have I done?" She cried, trying to pull away, despite the warmth he was offering. "I have to make it right."

"You didn't do anything! I'm the one who said her name. That's what set him off, though I've no idea why." He soothed, gently rubbing his hand across her shoulder.

"I need to talk to him," she insisted, trying again to struggle free of his embrace. This time, he could feel her persistence, and released her, against his better judgment.

"Come on, Electra, we can come back soon," he was trying not to beg, but there was something in Gideon's reaction that scared him. Geena couldn't be right about The Old Man living in the house, but there was something familiar in his expression, filled with such wrath, that reminded Vagan of the dark dreams that had filled his nights for so many weeks, now. He wanted to be as far away from this place as he could get. If Electra was unwilling to go with him, he *would* go alone this time. "Please."

He held his hand to her, hoping that she would take it. She looked at him for a moment, the tears continuing to spill, then moved to accept it, slipping the red box in her pocket, where she could no longer look at it. Vagan led her home, through the rainy streets, leaving her a block from her house, kissing her gently before he went, assuring her as he did so that Gideon would be fine, if he had ever been fine in the first place. He would have stayed with her to the door, but the sudden pain that was filling his shoulder blades was more piercing than he had ever felt it before. He knew that it was pulling him away from her, that she needed him so much more than whatever it was that called to him, but he was unable to resist it.

He walked as quickly as he could, hoping that he would reach the shack before the pain dragged him under, but all hope was lost, when he was less than halfway across the bridge, and knew he had to turn back before his legs gave way entirely. He fell into a mound of leaves, garbage, and dirt, into unconsciousness, where he would remain until the pain went away.

Chapter forty-two

Sometimes, it is impossible to know what is happening. The pain would have worried most people, filling their minds with dread and questions that were too hard to comprehend the possible answers to. But Dylan knew what the pain meant. It had been a long time since he had felt the intense ripple of The Old Man's call, but it was as if once known, ever recalled.

It was hard to know how this had happened. Even when The Old Man had called on the others, over and over again, he had never felt the throb, had never had to remember the agony of the days he had spent in darkness. Something had allowed this intensity, and all Dylan could think was that The Old Man had finally become aware that he was stalking him, and that he only had a short time left to him.

For it was time to begin the end of The Old Man's existence. There would be no way for him to escape this time. Sitting within the protective circle that his mother had so many years ago taught him to cast, he pictured all those who had come to feel the pain in these few moments. The pain would not cease until The Old Man was gone, but by tapping into it, he could use it to his own device, calling them forth to the city, where their power, unknown by all of them, would merge, filling Dylan with the light of the lives they had regained when they had finally lived and died, reborn to be other existences that were as everlasting as he was.

Looking deep into the heart of the flickering candle flame, he called to the full moon that hung around Electra's throat, calling the power of his parents back across the years that had passed since their deaths. With one almighty shout, as quiet as a whisper, he called them to order. Then there was nothing to do but wait for them to come.

Chapter forty-three

The house was empty when she arrived. She could feel the void before she even opened the door, and felt for the first time in a while relief to be on her own, without even Vagan for company. She would never be able to explain it to him, but she needed time, hoping that with it would come some explanation for why she felt so wretched. It wasn't like it was her fault, even. She had no idea why Gideon had reacted to the girl's name the way he had. It was irrational to think there might have been anything she could have done about it.

At the same time, though, she knew that there was no way it would have happened had Vagan not been there. Other than anything else, Electra didn't know the girl, so could not have caused the reaction.

She shrugged out of her overcoat, hanging it on a hook by the front door, and headed for the kitchen, wishing that when she got there, she would find that her father had been magically replaced by someone who didn't care about her nutritional requirements, and would have stocked the cupboards with candy and cookies, and the ice box with ice cream. Unfortunately, it wasn't to be. She read the note pinned to the refrigerator with a banana shaped magnet, explaining that they were out, and would be for most of the evening. She sighed as she pulled the door open, and found a salad, ready prepared, with a side dish of steamed rice.

"Oh, joy." She mumbled to the kitchen table as she put it down, searching for a fork in the drawer by the light from the hallway.

She ate slowly, contemplating the coming winter, knowing that there had never been so much pressure on her to be what her father wanted her to be, that there was no choice but to go on, and that she had probably ruined her relationship with the only family member other than her brother to really care about the outcome of her life. Even her grandparents had never really been that interested, while they'd survived. She was fairly sure she had missed out on the vital things by not having a single grandmother who baked apple pies, or a grandfather who would have let her help in the tool shed once in a while. Both her sets of grandparents had been far more interested in their own pursuits to worry much about her or Cain.

Her meal eaten, she made her way upstairs, hoping that her room would feel safe and warm. She reached it slowly, wondering how hard it would be to lock the door and transport her whole room to some far off destination, where she could watch the world go by without any of the hassle coming to find her. It wasn't to be, though. Her bedroom door wouldn't lock, the key jammed every time she tried, where the wood around it had expanded over time.

She left the light off, flicking on the radio, and undressed slowly, taking the time to fold her shirt, placing her shoes squarely by the dresser, letting her pants drop around her ankles before folding them, too. She stood, naked and alone, in the darkness, suddenly aware of the voice of the DJ on the radio.

"Hey, people, this is Bobby Dee, and you are listening to KW-SFR. I've done this job for a long time, and I never tire of what I do, but once in a while, I have to ask myself whether there isn't something more. Life, love, passion and beauty; all these things and more lead me to believe that the world is great. But maybe I'm wrong. Still, some music could be nice, so to continue my recent trend, I'm bringing you one of my favourite tracks by the great Lloyd Cole, this is 'Butterfly'. Rock on, people."

The music started, and it took only moments for Electra to start moving. She twisted and turned, spinning on the spot, rotating her arms in the air. She knew that the world outside her window could probably see her, but she didn't care, as she became lost in the music and the moment. Nothing mattered when she was dancing. The way Gideon had reacted, the way she was trapped by her existence, the fact that although she wanted Vagan to be with her, she was scared that he was hiding something from her, all disappeared into the night.

The music was soft, the lyrics provocative. She closed her eyes, winding her hands through her hair, pretending that he *was* with her, how his hands would feel upon her skin. She didn't want to think that he was keeping things from her, but she had to admit that there was something going on, because he knew that girl, and he knew there was something she was troubled by. Whether it was to do with Gideon or not, it was to do with Vagan, and whilst she knew she loved him, she wasn't sure she could ever trust him if he would not tell her the truth.

The song came to an end, and Electra fell to the floor at the foot of the bed. Silence enveloped her, the radio apparently no longer willing to entertain her. She pulled her knees up to her chin, wiping at the tears that had sprung suddenly from her eyes, falling in streams like torrents of salt water, as the silence deepened.

"Sorry about that folks." A voice finally broke through. "We had a little technical hiccup, there, but we're back, now, ready to take you through the night. Hey, it may be raining out there, but people, go out, find someone to hold, find a roof top, dance 'til dawn, we'll keep you going."

She was laughing, uncontrollably, almost hysterically, knowing that she had only two options. Either she would have to talk with Vagan, get him to tell her the truth, or she would have to tell him good-bye. Her heart felt like it might crack when she came to the conclusion. Her stomach cramped painfully as a spasm of fear ripped through her entire being. She didn't want to tell him that she never wanted to see him again. She didn't want to give up the only thing she'd ever had in her life that wasn't dictated by her father or by anyone else.

Perhaps time would give her perspective. Maybe if she could sleep, she could dream, find a way to work through this negativity. All she could really tell was that she still wanted to feel his hands on her body, still wanted his lips against hers.

The sound of a telephone ringing snapped her out of her current emotion. She looked around, confused, because the sound was not coming from the private line in her own room. She pulled on her robe, and raced down the stairs, her heart beating fast.

"Hello?" She called into the receiver before it was even at her ear, hoping beyond all rationality that it would be Vagan, and that he was willing to come to her now. But she was disappointed to be greeted by nothing but static. "Hello?"

"Electra, can you feel it?" A voice asked. She wanted to recognise the male, but his voice was muffled, made unfamiliar by some method of disguise.

"Feel what? Who is this?" She demanded.

"A friend, Electra. The time is nearly here. You will know what to do when the time is right." The voice replied cryptically. The other end of the line disconnected before she could speak again, and she stood for a moment, her mouth open ready to continue. Instead, she looked at the receiver, willing it to tell her some part of the secret it held back from her. She replaced it slowly, looking around her at the dark room. There was a mirror over the fireplace, and the gentle glint of light reflecting off the crystal she wore around her neck caught her attention.

She stepped forward, into the shaft of light from the hallway, gazing at her reflection. She couldn't guess at why she had failed to notice the difference in the shape of the crystal. What had first looked like a pale crescent moon, was now as round as the full moon that currently hung in the sky. Yet it still felt so light, lighter than it should with such mass. Perhaps it was a trick of the light. She lifted her hand to touch it, finding its shape as round as it looked.

She dropped her hand, looking into her own eyes. The smile the reflection returned was not hers, and for a second, she was frightened. But it *was* her smile, despite the fact it wasn't on her own face, and it promised her peace to come. She ran a finger down the side of her face, stroking it from temple to jaw, proving that it was her face she was looking at. She felt power radiating through her flowing through her veins.

But there was something else running through them, too. It was something she had never experienced before. A pain rippled across her shoulders, down her spine. It didn't last for long, though, and she put it out of her mind, as she turned toward the hallway, heading back to her room and her bed.

Sleep came quickly, filled with dreams of fire and fear. All the while she slept, the pain grew steadily, although she did not feel it in her slumber.

Elsewhere in the city, Vagan was walking, unaware that he even moved. Had he been awake, he may have dwelt on the fact that he had witnessed the event that would potentially part him from the girl he loved. He had no idea how far he walked, free from the pain.

The Old Man was not worried, now. He had made the adjustments he needed in order to be ready for the final days of his life. He could feel all of them as they felt his power over them. They may not know who he was, but they could all feel him, now.

Chapter forty-four

Vagan woke up where he normally did. The small shack was filled with the dull light of a rainy morning. He had collapsed hours earlier, he knew, and far from the shack. He had no idea where he had been, or how he had ended up where he was.

Memories of the evening before started to play before his eyes, and he could clearly recall the reaction of Electra, the shout of Gideon, the scared expression of Geena. No matter what else may come, that series of events would never be erased.

Geena was the source of all the other reactions, he knew, but he was the reason for *hers*. If only he knew without any doubt what had happened when she had disappeared, perhaps he could tell her what she needed to know. But he didn't understand. The dreams that had haunted him since moving to the city, and all the time he had lost, the times when he had woken in the shack, all of these things were connected. He thought that if he could just unscramble all these things, put them in to some rational order, he could say what it was.

But it wasn't rational. There was no way to unscramble it all, because he was missing a piece, the piece that would throw all the others into light relief, obliterating the shadows that currently hid them so well. Perhaps, he thought, the key was the identity of The Old Man.

Geena knew that The Old Man was to blame as much as Vagan. But it was he whom she had confronted, because The Old Man seemed more like a myth than any reality.

He wanted to be brave. He wanted to go to Gideon, and ask him straight out what was going on, because he had to believe that he would not have reacted to Geena's name that way unless he knew something about her. Not only that, but he wanted to be brave enough to go to Electra, parents or not, and tell her the truth, that he had no idea what was going on, but that he was scared that he had done something very wrong, something he could not tell her about because he did not know *what* it was.

He was not brave, though. He was scared, and his mind was unwilling to listen to his heart.

He wanted to get out of the shack. It was reminding him of the darkness. He tried to stretch his legs, feeling the blood rush down them in millions of pinpricks. He put his arm out to raise himself up, and noticed the edges of a red stain on his sleeve. Looking down, he saw the extent of the large, rusty red patch, which could be nothing but blood. He knew without any doubt that it was not his own.

The nausiation rose in his throat so quickly, he had no time to stop himself from heaving, but his stomach was empty. This time, he could not hide the fact from himself that he had caused harm to someone. He gagged again, bile filling his mouth as he slid forwards to the floor.

"What have I done?" He asked the room, not convinced he wanted to be told.

He dragged himself from the floor, pulling the door open, and stumbling into the rain. The air was cold, but smelled sweeter than the air he had previously been inhaling. He breathed deeply, trying to fill his lungs with oxygen, because he thought he might have forgotten how to breathe while he had slept. It was like ice, freezing in his chest, but he was grateful to be feeling it.

The campus was fairly deserted when he arrived back. The large clock told him it was 5:15, early for a Saturday morning. The rain was falling heavily, now, rolling down his face and back in large rivulets, soaking his blood stained shirt, causing shivers through his torso. He hugged himself, pulling his arms around him in an attempt to block it out.

There was a man across the field, running to get somewhere, a damp newspaper held above his head. His brown wool suit looked heavy with rainwater. A couple of younger guys were conducting their business under the eaves of one of the buildings, looking around themselves to make sure there was no campus security about. Vagan hurried on, desperate to get back to his room, change out of his wet shirt, and avoid the countless questions Billy would ask if he got the chance. In his haste, he stumbled again, unable to right himself as he fell, hitting the ground with his right shoulder.

"Are you alright?" A concerned voice spoke from close to his face. He looked at the girl who had spoken. Her pale blue eyes were full of worry.

"Yeah, I'm fine, thanks." He responded. It wasn't totally true, because the ground was very cold and very hard. She knelt beside him, looking at him, then offered her hand to help him up.

"Hey, Paige." Another girl spoke. Vagan looked at her, now. "Paige, we should go."

"Just a sec, Gracie." The first girl, Paige, responded, then turned back to Vagan. "Did you realise your aura is all weird? It's all black and red. Hey, you're bleeding!"

"I'm fine. What d'you mean, my aura's weird?" Vagan asked, not really sure what an aura was. He struggled to his feet despite her assistance.

"Well, her aura," Paige said, indicating her friend. "Is kinda orange, which is good, cause it means she's generally happy and full of passion, with a bit of green, which means she's balanced. My aura is mostly purple, 'cause I understand my own spirituality. You aura, though, well, it's all black and red. The red isn't so bad; it just means that you are really, really in love, which is kinda nice. But the black? I've never seen anything so scary. Normally, aura's are sorta transparent, but this just hangs there, it's so *dense*."

"What does that mean?" He asked, wondering if this might be the answer he sought.

"Well, it means I think you should be really careful. I don't think it's your fault, and I don't think there's much you can do about it, but here, take my card. I give readings and cleansings." She told him, handing him a card with details printed on one side.

"Come *on*, Paige." The other girl pleaded.

"O-*kay*, Grace. Take care." The girl smiled weakly, then turned and walked away with her friend, huddled once again under a large, yellow umbrella.

"Paige Knightingale," he read aloud. "Aura cleansing and readings. (415) 555-42-73."

He wasn't sure why, but he slipped the card in his pocket, and continued to make his way to his dorm room, where it would be dry, at least. When he got there, he found Billy spread out across the couch, a girl wrapped around him, as usual. Vagan went straight into the room, stripped quickly, and climbed into bed, shivering uncontrollably.

"What the hell happened to you?" A voice broke through from somewhere in the distance.

"Hunh?" Vagan murmured through the dregs of sleep remaining in his head.

"Vagan, wake up. For Christ's sake, this place is a dump. What happened to you last night?" The voice continued. Vagan opened his eyes, fighting the light that filled the room. Billy stood beside his bed, holding the bloodstained shirt in his hand. "Did you have an accident or something?"

"What? Oh, yeah, I slipped on some wet grass, hit my nose." He lied, rubbing his finger over the bridge of his slightly crooked nose.

"So, where were you?" Billy demanded, although Vagan was fairly sure it was none of his business. "Hey, did you get lucky?"

"I may have been with a girl. I mentioned her, remember?" Vagan continued, spreading the truth thinly across his lies. He didn't care to try and explain things to this guy who he would never befriend voluntarily.

"Okay, well, I'm leaving this afternoon, so have fun. I'll see you in a couple weeks." Billy seemed satisfied, now. Vagan was confused, though.

"Leaving?" Vagan asked.

"For the holidays. Shit, man, you're really out of it, aren't you? I'm headed back to San Diego. Don't your folks want you home?"

"No, they don't celebrate Christmas. We're Jewish, not that we observe any Jewish festivals these days. Besides, I can't afford the bus fare right now." Vagan explained, propping himself up on his elbows.

"Okay, well, I'll see you later. Oh, and if Madison Brooks should come looking for me, tell her I'm real sorry, but I'm just not into that."

Billy left the room, dropping Vagan's shirt as he went. Vagan dropped back against the pillow. He was more tired now than he had been when he'd woken up in the shack.

Again, memories of the night before returned to him, of the house, of Geena's warning, and Gideon's reaction. And then there was the gift Gideon had given Electra. There was something about the pin that didn't seem right. Certainly it had been old, but Vagan found it hard to believe that Gideon had kept it for years, and had only just remembered that it existed. Other than anything else, it was probably worth a small fortune. Worse than the fact that it was given to her in such suspicious ways, was the fact that he could never hope to give her anything as glorious.

He knew that some day, he would present her with a ring, but at the rate he was going, it was more likely it would be made of plastic than gold. He did think it would be rather symbolic, but rather a let down to Electra, who deserved so much more. He knew she was the one he wanted to spend his life with, as long as she would forgive him when he finally told her everything.

Suddenly, his thoughts returned to the girl who had helped him that morning when he fell. She had truly believed what she had told him. She was a stranger, an unknown. She had had no reason to offer her assistance, but she had given it willingly. He would not have thought about her any longer had she not seen this thing that hung around him. If it was possible for this girl to see the darkness, then it really must be there. He wanted to find the answers, and thought he might accept the offer of aura cleansing. But then again, he probably would not.

As soon as he was able to speak to Electra, he would feel at ease, again. There was a pay phone out in the hallway. It wouldn't take much effort to call her. He could call her private line, and her father would never know. He scrambled out of bed, pulled on some clothes, not really noticing what they were, and made his way to the corridor. The phone was right there, waiting as if it had known he needed to make a call. He fed a couple of quarters into the slot, dialled, and waited. The other phone in Steiner Street rang fourteen times. He didn't wait for a fifteenth, as he replaced the receiver, then went back to his room to think.

Chapter forty-five

He was growing more and more frustrated as time passed. He hadn't waited almost a hundred years for it all to fall down around him now. He hadn't expended all this energy planning just to have it all go wrong.

He had known for a while now that the first boy had found him, was closing in on him. He had far too much strength. He wished now that he could have seen just how strong the line was in this wise man, a freak among freaks, who had been his most beautiful, charming, and magnetic servant. He had retained his memories, and was the only one who could possibly take away what he had gained over time.

It was all because of the boy's mother, of course, from a line so old it seemed impossible it was not sourced in the evolution of the earth. When it had combined with his father's line, it had been almost unstoppable, but The

Old Man had managed it. Now, the boy was as alone as him. All the friends and family he had ever really known were long since gone. There was still a branch of the family, somewhere, but the boy held very little personal contact with them anymore.

The Old Man didn't want the time to pass any more, but it had to. It would soon be time for him to move on, now. He would wait for the new year, though, convincing himself that it was better to wait it out, hope that the boy went away again. After all, the boy had as much time as he wanted. He would never have to worry about the passage of time unless he felt like it.

Sitting alone with his thoughts, The Old Man reflected on what had come and gone during his days, remembering the days were war and bloodshed meant he was never short of sustenance. Feeling the ghost of old blood running through his veins, he thought of the days where monarchs had lost their heads (he had watched as the blade fell on her, rattling in its wooden frame as it went), and the poor did away with the rich. They had not really tried to fight back. That was what made The Old Man different, he thought. The fact that he was willing to fight for his existence had to count for something, didn't it?

Chapter forty-six

So, what's the verdict, doc?" Electra was starting to worry now, but was determined not to let it show. The pain had not gone away. The only way she had found to dull the throb was to take off running every morning, yet it persisted. It had been a week, now, and her father had insisted she go see her physiotherapist about it.

"Well, I'd like to run a few more tests," the female doctor, Jess Munroe, responded, looking at Electra over the rim of her glasses. Doctor Munroe had been looking after Electra's well being for ten years, constantly having to put up with calls from Electra's father. Over that time, she had changed from a young, slightly green girl, into a mature and caring woman. Electra liked her, and respected her more than most of the other people she knew. "Physically, I can't find a thing wrong with you. You're in better shape right now than you have been in months. To be honest, I'm a little stumped."

"But there must be *something* wrong. The pain just won't go away. And you know how against medication my dad is." Electra complained, wishing she didn't sound quite so whiney.

"I know. I'd prescribe Percodan, but he'd hate that. Try some Tylenol, instead. It should take the edge off." The doctor responded, writing on her note pad quickly. She looked back at some of the earlier notes she had made, and then looked at Electra thoughtfully. "How are you dealing with the death of Maggie Treat?"

"Do I have to talk about her to *everyone*?" Electra asked, frustrated to have to describe her feelings on the subject once more as another wave of pain spread through her shoulders. "I barely knew her. I don't really care about what happened to her, and I am not depressed because of it, either."

"Are you having troubles any other way?" The woman probed, running a hand through her long, dark hair.

"How long do you have? No, not that I can't handle. Not that I haven't handled for the best part of my life so far." Electra dismissed the thought, but it was one that had started to worry her already since the pain had begun. Was this possibly a physical manifestation of the fear that she was not only unloved, but that she always would be? It was the fear that had plagued her for most of her teen years, although it was not until recently that she had come to understand what the brief periods of deep depression meant. How could she tell anyone this fear? Vagan had helped to dispel it, but now it reared its head, filling her with anxiety. The pain was secondary to the emotion.

"I'd believe that, if I hadn't known you so long." The doctor laughed lightly.

"I know. If it was anything that I thought you might be able to solve, I'd tell you. All I can say is boy trouble, not that that really explains much." Electra sighed, looking at Jess rather sheepishly.

"Ah, well, I can understand why you can't talk too much about that," she agreed, smiling and nodding. Dr Munroe was far more understanding than Electra ever thought to remember. "Still, I think it might help you to talk to someone, other than me, of course. You remember my sister, Liz, was studying to be a therapist? Well she recently took a practice in the city, and I think it might help you to talk with her. I promise, we won't tell your father, and it will be just between us."

"I don't know. Really, I just want to keep myself quiet for the moment. Dad mustn't have any clue about it, because he may well kill the two of us," Electra wanted to dismiss the idea, but couldn't quite do it altogether. The thought of having someone else to talk to was appealing. Maybe if she could do it without letting her father know, she might find some release in this avenue.

"Well, think about it. And here, if your father gives you any trouble about the Tylenol, show him this." The doctor concluded, handing her a brief note, explaining why she thought it a good idea that Electra take the painkillers. "Take care of yourself, and I'll see you next week. If you want to see Liz, give me a call, and I can make you an appointment."

Electra thanked the doctor, and started to make her way home. The office was not far from Steiner Street, but Electra took her time, stopping in a small drug store to pick up the tablets she had been advised to get, along with a bottle of water, taking three of them as soon as she left the shop.

It was raining again, and the streets were slick beneath her feet. She wasn't really paying attention to where she was going, just following her feet as they wore a path through puddles. She crossed the street with the flow of other pedestrians, feeling the sidewalk return beneath her soles rather than seeing it. She was so distracted that she didn't even see the young man standing in front of her until she walked in to him.

"Ouch, hey, oh, hi." She mumbled, looking up into Dylan's smiling face.

"Hi. Sorry, I thought you were going to walk right past me." He apologised.

"Sorry, I'm not paying any attention to the rest of the world, I'm afraid." Electra apologised in turn.

"What's wrong?" He asked, trying to feel her pain, knowing exactly what it meant when he did.

"Not so much." She laughed bitterly, as another shot ran through her. "I'm sorry, but I really need to sit down a moment."

She crumpled down on to the sidewalk, her feet on the blacktop, and rested her head against her knee. Dylan sat beside her, looking at her with concerned eyes. The sidewalk was wet, and the moisture seeped through her pants, making her legs cold. She shivered, and was surprised to feel Dylan's hand rubbing her shoulder blades, close to where the point of pain was worst.

"Come on, I'll get you home." He promised her, standing up, and then helping her to her feet. He led her along the streets, keeping her close to his side. She didn't think to wonder how he knew where she lived. All the way, he was silent, his hand still resting where the pain was most intense.

He waited while she unlocked the door, then followed her into the empty house. The kitchen was large, filled with the grey light that came with the rain. Electra told him to sit, and got some iced tea out of the fridge, pouring it in to tall glasses.

"How are you feeling?" He asked, still seeming concerned as she put the glass in front of him, and sat down across the table.

"Foolish. If I could figure out what's going on with me, I'd be fine. Don't pay any attention to me." She mumbled, then went on, angry with herself. "It's this stupid pain! I have no idea where it came from, or why it won't go away. All I know is it's driving me nuts! My physio says there's nothing wrong with me, but I'm fairly sure there is, and now she wants me to see a shrink."

"When did it start?" He sounded thoughtful, running his finger around the rim of his glass.

"Last Friday night." She responded dully, her fury dissipating as quickly as it had flared, and she put her head on the table. If he had never felt the pain, he might have thought she was overreacting, but he knew what it was like for short periods, and could only guess what it would be like for a week.

"And what happened before that?" He questioned her.

"Well, I was visiting my cousin. Remember, I told you about him, from New Orleans. Well, Vagan said something, and it set Gideon off. Maybe it's just stress." She moaned, lifting her head again.

"Maybe. What did Vagan say?"

"It was stupid. He said a girl's name. She was just some weirdo who was outside Gideon's house, but Vagan knew her, and I think he might have lied to me about her."

"You think he might be seeing someone else?"

"No, well, maybe. I don't want to think that way, but sometimes, he just gets a bit distant. He gets this weird look in his eyes. It only lasts a moment, but it scares me." She confessed.

"What about it scares you?" He probed.

"Oh, maybe I'm scared that I might end up alone after all, or because I really want to be with him, though I have no idea why. Maybe I'm scared that he might be bored by me before we've even started, and he's decided to take up with other girls instead. Or maybe it's because the girl was so *scared*, like she thought that Vagan had hurt her some how. If he hurt her, he could hurt me. What would there be to stop him?"

"Firstly, I have no doubt that Vagan cares for you. How could he not? Secondly, I also don't think he could hurt anyone; not intentionally, anyway. What about your cousin? Have you spoken to him since? Perhaps you wouldn't feel quite so badly if you did."

She was doubtful, because although she wanted to make right whatever small part of the incident she had caused, she wasn't ready to face the fact that she may have done him harm. She picked up her glass, unconsciously mirroring Dylan's action, but put it down without drinking. She was angry again, though not sure why. Dylan's reasoning made so much sense. His voice was soothing, tinged with the slightest of accents that she rarely noticed.

"I hate this!" She cried, as the pain rippled again. She had not yet connected the anger with the pain. Dylan knew that the best way to defuse it was to calm her.

"Please, Electra, call your cousin," he pressed. "And I must go. I shall see you soon."

She watched him stand, and walk out through the back door. She took a drink, trying to postpone the inevitable. Minutes passed, and eventually, she pulled herself from the kitchen chair, made her way down the hall, and to the living room, where the downstairs phone sat, looking at her with scorn. She picked it up, despite the animosity it radiated, and dialled the familiar number quickly. She counted the rings in her head: one, two, three, four, five.

"Hello?" The voice at the other end of the line was aggravated. She took a deep breath, then spoke.

"Gideon?" She asked, trying to keep from crying at the relief of hearing his voice.

"Cher! I'm so sorry, I think I over reacted the other day. I have to apologise." He spoke quickly, his accent distorted as he worked to get the jumble out quickly enough.

"It's alright, Gideon. I have to say sorry, too. I don't know what it was that I did, but I want to make it right." She responded feebly, sagging against the couch next to the telephone table.

"Cher, you did nothing. The fault was all mine, I swear. It was foolish, but it's all water under the bridge, now." He assured her. They spoke for only a minute longer, Gideon continuing to repent, while she continued to feel remorse for making him feel bad in the first place. When she replaced the receiver in its cradle, she felt somehow lighter, more able to handle the afternoon ahead.

Chapter forty-seven

Young Elvis spotted in San Francisco!" Cain read aloud, laughing. He was waiting for Devon to get dressed, but he was taking forever, as usual.

"But no one spots young, cute Elvis. They only ever spot old bloated Elvis." Devon called from the back of the closet. "Where was he?"

"Pier 39." Cain responded, scanning the article for the detail. "Where else do you expect him to be?"

"Of course." Devon came out of the closet, wearing nothing but a tight black t-shirt, and black sneakers. "I have nothing to wear."

"You have plenty." Cain groaned. It was not the first time they had had that particular conversation that week. Devon took up more closet space than most other people. In fact, one of the conditions he'd had when moving in with Cain was that he get the bigger half. That had been over a year ago, now. "Just put some clothes on, honey."

"You just don't care!" Devon threw his hands up in the air, but went back to the closet, and reappeared a minute later, having pulled on a floor length black skirt, and a red feather boa. "Okay, I'm dressed, and mostly presentable. Lets go."

"No boa." Cain objected. Devon's face fell, but he pulled it from around his neck, dropping it on the bed, then put his thick red sweater on over the t-shirt.

Fifteen minutes later, they were climbing out of Cain's pick-up in the parking area of the tree lot. It wasn't normally the ideal vehicle for his day-to-day life, but sometimes, it had its advantages. Christmas was one of those times.

The lot was filled to brimming with trees. All of them had their own characters, coloured in many shades of green, all lined up in neat rows, arranged by height and quality. The scent of pine was pungent, mixed with the inextricable fragrances of gingerbread and Christmas spice.

Devon went in search of a small tree, something that would fit in the corner, while Cain looked at the larger ones, dreaming of a day when he would have enough space for a majestic pine tree. He turned slowly, inhaling deeply, and then noticed a familiar figure close by, examining a huge Douglas fir. Her red hair was loose, flowing down her back, and her hand was stretched in front of her, stroking the branches. Cain couldn't resist, sneaking up behind her, slipping his hands over her eyes.

"Guess who." He whispered in her ear.

"There's only one person who would do that to me." She laughed, leaning gently against him, as he kissed the top of her head. He took his hands away, and she turned to look at him. "What are you doing here?"

"Hmmm, what would I possibly be doing on a tree lot?" He asked, holding his index finger across his lips, looking thoughtful. "Probably buying a tree."

"Shut up!" She grinned, pushing him gently. He was surprised to see her so happy, having been told by their mother about her recent problems.

"How are you?" He asked, looking at her for any signs of distress.

"I guess you've been talking to mom. I'm fine. How are you?"

"I'm good. Are *they* here?" He felt panic rising in his bones.

"Yes." Electra winced.

"Great; so is Devon. In a skirt." It was his turn to cringe. Electra laughed again, and put her arm around his shoulders. He hugged her back for a moment. "Hey, what exactly have you been doing to the boy? He's been in a bad mood for days."

"Oh, it was stupid. We went to see Gideon, and something happened. I have no way to get hold of him, and he hasn't called me. God, Cain, I love him! He might never speak to me again." She cried. He squeezed her again.

"I'll talk to him for you." Cain promised her, and began to lead her to where Devon was standing, debating the pros and cons of a potted spruce. "Hey, look who I found."

"Hey, little sister, how are you?" He grinned, kissing Electra on the cheek.

"Does everyone know?" Electra asked. "She should really take out an advertisement in the paper."

"Relax, honey. I enjoyed watching you perform. Where did your mother get all those lime green sparkles from?" Devon smiled, teasing her gently as if he had known her forever.

"I think she has a dealer; someone who supplies her on the black market." She joked back easily. "Did I mention I love the skirt, Devon?"

"I have style."

Cain scanned the lot, constantly aware that his parents might appear at any moment. Electra and Devon were bantering like old friends, and Cain was grateful that they were so at ease with each other. Until they had been away, Cain had constantly worried that his sister may be lost to him because of his sexuality. It had been such a relief when she had been so accepting. Now, he just had to hope that when he eventually told his parents, they would be as understanding. He didn't think it was likely. Still, he would not be mentioning it anytime soon, even though he had just spotted them heading their way.

"Ah, Cain, how nice." His father greeted, clapping him on the shoulder. His mother was looking at Devon, though, taking in his 5ft 10 frame, well-defined shape, and slightly long, dark hair. It was rare that Cain though of how Devon looked to others, because it was rare for them to meet people out side of their close group of friends.

"Hi, dad, mom. How are you?" He responded, his voice cracking a little.

"I'd be happier if they weren't charging so much for trees. $50 for a tree! It's daylight robbery." His father exclaimed, and then finally seemed to spot Devon. "Hello."

"Sorry, mom, dad, this is Devon, my, roommate." He struggled to get his words out coherently.

"Hi, Mr. Philips, Mrs. Philips, how do you do?" Devon asked, sounding far more masculine than was normal. "I share a suite with Cain and a freshman."

"How nice. That's an interesting outfit." His mother commented. Cain wished he could run for cover, but Electra spoke up.

"Well, you know there was that picture of Mel Gibson wearing a skirt in the paper a couple of weeks ago." She said quickly to her mother, knowing as well as Cain did that their mother had a soft spot for the actor. Their mother seemed impressed by the information.

"Dear, I really think we should look at the trees." His father commented. Perhaps his father was totally oblivious to the entire world, after all. But his mother did not seem interested in trees anymore. She was chatting with Devon, asking whether or not Cain had been seeing any nice girls recently. Devon said he was sure there were bound to be a few girls heartbroken when he settled down, but shot Cain a wink, which normally indicated his affection.

Eventually, his parents both wanted to make a move, and so they made parting comments. Devon picked up a tree, taking it to be wrapped by the sixteen year old girl with acne who was manning the electric bagger. Electra was still standing next to Cain when she suddenly looked far paler than normal. Her breathing changed, becoming fast and shallow. He watched her expression twist on her face, turning abruptly to terror. The noise that erupted from her was close to a scream, before she fell to the ground, and didn't get up.

Chapter forty-eight

They had been sitting in chairs for over an hour. Her husband periodically stood, paced across the space, then sat back down. No one was telling them anything, and that couldn't be a good sign. Cain had come with them to begin with, but he had disappeared a while later, and still hadn't returned, although he'd promised he would.

"What are they doing to her?" He demanded, asking no one in particular. It was like him to get aggravated for things beyond the control of any of them. Worse still, he had a tendency to push their daughter too far when all she wanted was a break. Not that she would ever tell him that she blamed him, of course, but she did.

"I'm sure they'll let us know what's happening when they know." She replied, soothing his temperament as well as she could.

"And where the hell did Cain get to?" He yelled, getting up and pacing again. All Cain had said was that he had to go and see someone, and that it was very important. They would not have to wait long to find out, though, because at that moment, Cain walked round the corner. "Where the hell have you been?"

"Calm down, dad. You aren't going to like this, but I had to bring him." Cain looked more scared than she had seen him in a long time. It wasn't until then that she noticed the young man standing behind her son. He was familiar, but only because they had met him once, a few months earlier.

"What? Why have you brought this boy here? Does he know something about Electra?" Her husband was angry, not willing to even appear curious.

"Well, that's why I said you wouldn't like it. Dad, Electra and Vagan have been dating in secret, for a couple months." Cain explained, bracing himself for the fury that was sure to ensue.

"And you knew about this?" His temper was like a small explosion. She had long known that he was the kind of man who could not control his rage. It had become clear before the birth of Cain, when he had become frustrated over the trivialities of their everyday lives. Thankfully, his temper was not accompanied by violence.

"Please, dad. That's not really the point right now. Yes, I did, but it won't change the fact just because you shout at me. Electra needs us. She needs to be surrounded by people who love her, and *he loves her*." Cain spoke softly, but firmly. His father's face was turning red.

"Love? They're kids, what do they know about love?" His voice was filling the place, now, his hands balled into tight fists. "I've never heard anything so ridiculous in my life!"

"Fine, dad, I get it. You think Electra has no idea about the real world, and maybe you're right. You've certainly done a good job of keeping her out of it. I want to stay, but if I have to deal with this crap, then I'm going." Cain turned, and started to leave, but she reached out her hand to stop him.

"Cain, wait," she paused, turning back to her husband. "He's right, Frank. You and I both believe that Electra needs us, and if she needs this boy, too, then she should have him here."

"Did you know about this, too?"

"Of course not." She snorted at him derisively.

"Mr. Philips, I'm sorry, I'll go." The young man spoke up, looking as if he knew far more about them than they knew of him.

"Nonsense, dear. Come, sit with me. Tell me about yourself." She insisted, trying to calm the situation. But she never got a chance to listen, because at that moment, the doctor came around the corner.

"Doctor, what's going on?" Frank Philips demanded of the male doctor who, despite his age and the time of day, seemed very tired.

"She's still unconscious. I have to be honest; we've no idea what the matter is. I understand she's been having some pain, and it seems possible that the two are connected. Other than that, we really have no clues.

"She's not in pain right now, as far as we can tell, but she is nowhere close to being awake. We ran tests, and we took a brain scan. Her brain activity is normal, and her blood work doesn't show anything except Tylenol. She was a bit dehydrated, so she's on fluids. I'm sorry, but there's not much more that we can find right now. All we can do is wait. She'll wake up in her own time." The doctor told them. Her husband sat heavily on one of the plastic chairs, while Cain came to her side, putting his arm around her shoulder. "It could help her if you talk to her, let her hear familiar voices."

The doctor walked away from them, and she sat down beside Frank, ready to break down. Her daughter was the most precious of her belongings. Although Cain was her eldest child, she had always been more devoted to Electra's well being, knowing that her life was more fraught with pressure and pain than anyone's should be. She also knew that her husband was far more over bearing than was ever going to be necessary. The thought that her daughter was now so far from her help scared her.

Cain had grown very pale, and was rubbing his forehead with the tips of his fingers. He seemed to be trying not to cry, and sniffed deeply. Vagan, on the other hand, was frozen for a moment, before his legs gave way, and he landed on the floor, sitting with his head buried in his hands. He made no effort to stop his sobs, which broke through the barrier of his hands.

"How can there be anything wrong with her? She's in peak condition. Doctor Munroe told me as much." Frank told them, rejecting the possibility that Electra was anything less than perfect.

She wanted to shout at him. She wanted to tell him that this was all his fault, and that if he had only stopped for a minute to think what he was doing to their daughter, she may not be in this position now. She wanted a cigarette, but didn't think it wise to leave her husband right now. She was proud of her children for everything they did, in every field, and not just in the open eye. But she couldn't show him that. She couldn't try to convince him of their true merits without risking her own existence.

More than she wanted to yell at her husband, she wanted to comfort the young man crying on the floor. If this was the one Electra loved, then he was as much a part of their family as any of them were.

"It won't help anything to shout, dear." She whispered, scared that her own tears were not far away. "I am going to sit with her. Cain, will you come, please?"

Her son followed her, as she made her way to the room indicated by the reception desk. The door was slightly open, and the sound of a heart monitor beeping was loud in the mostly empty corridor. She pushed the door wide, and looked at her child, pale and sleeping, surrounded by machines and tubes. Cain squeezed her hand, and they went in together, sitting by the bed in plastic easy chairs.

The room was bland, although some attempt had been made to enliven it, using plastic plants in bright orange containers. They seemed too cheerful for the room, and she wished they had saved themselves the effort.

"Your father doesn't understand, Cain." She sighed, stroking a stray lock of hair from Electra's forehead. "He thinks he can solve the world by shouting at it."

"I know, mom." Cain murmured, looking at one of the orange pots blindly.

"Just remember that I *do* understand." She continued, wishing that their lives could be easy, just for once.

They sat listening to the machine, talking about the weather, and plans for Christmas. She mentioned the new costume she had planned, which would be very different to the normal ones, and she was thinking of chiffon, maybe in green, tied with ribbons, decorated with pearls. It seemed so stupid to be thinking of such trivial things, when Electra was in no condition to be performing, but she thought it better to keep her thoughts focused on possibilities rather than realities.

Chapter forty-nine

Her skin was so pale that he was not even sure she was really alive; creamy and translucent, like a porcelain doll. Her long, soft red hair lay like a halo spread across the lumpy hospital pillow that supported her sleeping head.

It had been hours since he had arrived at the hospital. He had had to wait to see her until her parents had finally left to attend a church service of some kind. Cain had stayed with him for some time, but he'd apologised eventually, leaving because he wanted to be with Devon for a while. Still, Vagan had remained, sitting, staring at her, listening to the constant beep of the monitor.

He was angry with himself. Maybe if he hadn't been so stubborn, she wouldn't have been suffering alone. Cain said that she had been not only in pain, but also depressed. He felt to blame.

If only he could explain things to her now, but it was too late to make things right with her. If he lost her now, he had no one to blame but himself. Everyone else seemed to. Especially Mr. Philips, who had yelled when Mrs. Philips had disappeared with Cain to see her. His booming voice had reverberated around the waiting area, drawing scared glances from others. Eventually, a nurse had told him to calm down or be removed. He had chosen to be quiet.

He had watched the sun rise beyond the window, punctuating time as only it could. It was still early, but pale sunlight streamed through the window, painting the pale green walls with a glint of orange that was far more attarctive than the planters. During the night, there had been an electric light, filling the room with false brightness.

Every few minutes, he reached out to touch her, stroking her face, her hand, running his fingertips across her lips, tracing the shape of her breast beneath the thin blanket. She seemed so frail, so unlike the fiery woman he had come to expect.

"Please come back to me," he begged in a whisper, not for the first time. The doctors had said she could hear them, and he hoped that was true, because he wanted to tell her everything, to try and explain what he had done, and what he thought it all meant. "I have to tell you, well, everything. I should have told you before, but I didn't know how, didn't know what it was I had to say.

"First, regardless of anything I say, I want you to know that I love you. You may not want to see me ever again, but that's beyond my control, because nothing that I have done is because of my own design. If I knew who or what was making this happen, then I'd stop it, but I don't.

"So, here goes. Geena, the girl, I did something to her, but I don't know what. I took her somewhere, but I have no idea where. She went missing, and stayed missing, for seven hours or so. She blames me, and as I can't account for those hours, I blame me, too. I don't even remember talking to her. Worse than that, she's having the nightmares, not the same as mine, I don't think, but bad enough. Mine, well, they revolve around The Old Man, who may or may not exist, and fire. Still, I met you, and you pulled me out of the flames, and for a while, I was perfect.

"But then, I lose time, again. I wake up with no idea what I've done, nothing but a vague memory of being bad. I don't want to be bad, but I don't think I have a choice, because he calls, and I have to go.

"The pain. If I hadn't been so stupid, if I'd been there, I could have told you what was going on, because I've felt the pain. It goes away, but not until I do the bad things that I don't know about.

"So, it's all my fault, and I can't change that. I lied when I said I didn't know what Geena was on about. I knew exactly what she meant, because I did this. I'm going to try and fix it, because I did this to you, too. My world has leaked in to yours, infecting your bright brilliance with darkness. I need you, and I love you, and I *will* fix this." He fell silent as the door behind him swung open.

The young male nurse had been on duty most of the night, and now he looked as if he was reaching the end of his energy levels. He smiled at Vagan before starting to check the tubes on her drip, making sure that the fluid was continuing to flow properly.

"I think she's starting to pick up a little, but the docs would know better." The nurse was trying to sound reassuring, but Vagan just found it irritating. All he offered was a nod in response, waiting for the nurse to leave. When the sound of the door lock engaging in the frame made it clear he was gone, he spoke again.

"I'm sorry I stopped trying to call you. I did try a couple of times, but you didn't answer, and I kinda decided you didn't want to be reached in the end. I was a fool, and I'm sorry." He apologised again, resting his forehead on the side of the bed.

When he had first sat there, he had wanted to shout, throw things around, but it wouldn't have helped anything. Then, there had been points where he had been on the brink of crying again, but he had refused to give in to the urge. Now, it was almost as if his emotions had locked themselves away, leaving him numb.

"Vagan?"

He turned to look to the door, wondering who could have found him here. The male standing just inside the closed door was one he had met only once, and then he had been far more interested in Electra than him. Now, looking closely at him, Vagan saw a face that was more familiar than it should have been.

"Vagan, you and I have a lot in common. I would normally try and spin this out, because I rather enjoy theatricality, but to be honest, I've waited long enough for this day. Unfortunately, we need to wait until dark, so I'll give you some time to get used to the idea." The young male told him.

"Sorry, who are you?" Vagan asked, struggling to recall whom Electra had introduced him as.

"Dylan, Dylan Adams. My story could have been a bit like yours, except I made choices along the line. I'm far too old to be doing this, you know." He responded, smiling gently, crossing the room to the bed. "The reason I came now is that it's going to take some time to get her released."

"She can't go anywhere. She's been unconscious since yesterday afternoon." Vagan muttered, but Dylan wasn't paying attention.

"I know, and I'm sorry about that. I should have been keeping a better eye on things than I was, and I shouldn't have made that attempt without thinking through the consequences first. I should have thought about his anger and its effect on the pain I am a little rash at times, I suppose. That comes from living a very long life, I've found. Still, it won't be a problem. Her parents will need to see her awake, which she will be soon." Dylan assured him, putting his hand in his pocket, and pulling out a small brown bottle. "Hmmm, a couple of adjustments on the crystal, I think." He murmured absentmindedly, and unscrewed the top of the bottle, shaking several drops of liquid from it. The fragrance was pungent; sweet but earthy. He rubbed his hands together, then ran them over her face, not quite touching her skin, and began to whisper unfamiliar words. "Athena, protectress, *riportila, faccia il suo libero, portila vicina e lascila essere.*"

"Now what?" Vagan asked dubiously.

"You wait, but not for long, because it'll start working in a minute." He replied, and leant closer to her. "Electra, can you hear me? It's Dylan. I know you can hear, because I know a lot of things. I need you to wake up, now, because I need your help. When you wake, you'll be here, in the hospital, and you'll have to stay a while, but Vagan is here, and he'll stay with you."

Dylan stood back, watching her breath rise and fall in her chest rhythmically. Moments passed. He would have worried had he not foreseen what was to come for them. Finally, her eyelids started to flicker, as she began to wake. Vagan looked into her eyes, filled with relief because she had woken. She smiled, and he kissed her gently, feeling her lips move. She tried to put her hand to his face, but the IV tube in her arm wouldn't let her.

"I have to go." Dylan said quietly. "I'll be back at sunset, to speak to the doctors."

He left as silently as he had come. Vagan pressed the call button, and the male nurse returned. Eventually, doctors joined the party, and finally, family members returned. Through out the day, Vagan remained with her, not even leaving to eat or drink, merely relieved to be with her again.

Chapter fifty

She had no idea where they were going, or what was happening. She had been surprised when Dylan had appeared, shortly after the sun had started to fall. She hadn't expected him, even though he'd said he would come.

It had taken a couple of hours to convince the doctor that she was fit to leave, and even then she suspected it was because of some power that Dylan had that they'd managed it. Now, she sat behind him, Vagan next to her, in the dark interior of an old car. They sped through the streets, listening to Dylan singing cheerfully from the front seat, in French.

Electra was mystified. She hadn't even realised that Dylan could drive. When he appeared, it was normally on foot. He hadn't explained anything, except that they had to go.

Vagan sat beside her, holding her hand. Just as Dylan had promised, he had been with her all day, and had not even gone when her parents had arrived. She had expected her father to be angry, but when he had finally come in to her room, he had been perfectly calm, and she had been reminded of the first time she had put the crystal necklace on, and he had spoken to her rationally for the first time in many years.

The day had been long, and frustrating. All the while she had been in bed, she had been waiting to go, knowing that something needed to be done, without any real clue what that was. Now, she was still in the dark.

"Dylan, where are we going?" She asked again, when he was between verses. She was starting to get frustrated with his lack of communication on the subject.

"We'll be there soon." He repeated for the fourth time since they had climbed into the car, and continued with his song. This time, however, he was telling the truth, because as he turned the corner, he started to slow, pulling up in front of a house at the curb. "See, told you we'd be here soon."

"Here?" She looked up at the house, recognising the dark building without any trouble. "Why here?"

"Because this is where it will all end. I'm sorry, I have to be cryptic sometimes; you may be the first in a while to get used to that. Anyway, I need for you both to go in there. I'm glad you're wearing that coat, Electra. There's something in the pocket that you will need." He told them, cutting the engine.

"Aren't you coming?" She was scared, although she had no real reason to be.

"Not just yet. He knows I'm here, but he needs to see you, first." He assured her, opening the door and climbing out of his seat. Electra followed his move, pulling Vagan out behind her. "I wish I could see his face when he realises that you have come for him. I also wish that Vagan could be more helpful to you once he does. Go, now, and don't look back. You need to head for the basement."

Electra decided it was not the right time to ask any further questions, but led Vagan up the walkway. He seemed reluctant, but she continued to tow him behind her.

The door was slightly open, as if the occupant had known they were coming. The lights were all extinguished, bare bulbs hanging blankly from the ceilings. Through the house, though, there was a dull, orange glow, leaking up from the doorway to the basement. She walked toward it, feeling anxious, recalling her nightmare of the flames, and Vagan sitting amongst them. She could feel her heart hammering inside her chest, and was only then aware that the pain between her shoulder blades, which had been so strong only minutes before, had disappeared altogether.

"Where is he? He's normally here by now." Vagan spoke from behind her, still hesitant.

"Dylan said we needed to go to the basement," she whispered, not ready to think about the answer to his question. They were at the door, now, and she found she didn't want to go down anymore than he did. But then again, she knew instinctively that Dylan would not let any harm come to her, so carried on regardless.

The candles were radiating heat, flickering wildly in a non-existent breeze. The room would have been pitch black without them, as there was no chink of light coming in from the street. But the candles cast their glow on the darkly painted walls, illuminating The Old Man who sat at the end of the room, and the familiar face in the painting beside his tall chair.

"Good of you to come, boy." He sneered at Vagan, who was suddenly still beside her, no longer struggling, no longer really there at all. The Old Man laughed, and reached out his hand, beckoning Vagan forward. He seemed to be in a trance, and there was nothing she could do to stop him, as he walked forward, and sat on the floor beside the chair.

"What have you done to him?" She cried, terrified for his safety. The Old Man laughed again, as his expression, his face, began twisting, changing.

"I'm sorry, Cher, but he was mine before he was yours." He told her, his voice low and exotic. "I may let him go someday, but by then, you may not want him anymore."

"I don't understand." She wept, looking at the face of her family twisted into something new and sinister. He was no longer a man, but evil incarnate, a demon, just as the girl had said.

"Well, of course you don't. You didn't want to see me, I suppose, but this is me, the real me, the only me there's been for a long time, now. I wear a pretty face, but inside, I am Hell. I guess you know already that your daddy was right about me," he smiled. "Didn't you?"

"I would have told the world otherwise, Gideon. I would have staked my life on you being good." She wanted her memories to be true, not this vision in front of her now.

"It's a long time since I was good. I've been bad for centuries, but oh, I've had such fun! You have no idea what it has been like, watching the world turn, knowing that it could never hold me. Taking all the beauties I wanted, leaving those that didn't meet my standards. Oh, the pleasure of a life enjoyed, the way it tastes, just so sweet. Like that little old man, so full of sugar I thought it would take forever to wear off. He was divine. Or that girl, who thought that the world revolved around her. I took her away from her family, proving the world still turns." His dark words flowed quickly, filling her head with images.

"You've killed people?" Her anguish was no longer for the loss of her cousin, but for the loss of those lives.

"Many. But not all of them. Some of them lived on, got over themselves. I don't get out much anymore, but Vagan has been very helpful to me these last months. Besides, the last two were in your honour, Cher."

"I don't want you to kill people!"

"But they had it coming. The little old man was far too cheerful, but I'm sure you liked the gift I got from him before his demise. And that girl! Oh, that girl. Competition? I don't think so. Winning things because she'd been around so long. It doesn't give you the right to take what isn't yours."

"You killed Maggie" Realisation spread through her so quickly it threatened to overpower her. She had no doubt that this was the truth that everyone had been trying to get from her over the last weeks.

"It was so easy to do it. I snuck out in the middle of the night, and took her. I love to confuse the authorities. It used to be quite a game for Jacques and I, back in the old days. Then I married that girl, and the fun was better, for a while, at least. Urgh, love. I'd never do *that*, again. Still, I did think that coming here would be better for me than this. You made me soft, again, and that is not acceptable," he chided her. "You made me soft, and the shadows came back."

"I'm sorry." She felt guilty, although she knew it was irrational to feel any remorse for this creature's actions.

"You're sorry!" He chuckled darkly. "Who are you sorry for? The pointless women who I drank, or the children they never had? They were as worthless as the sun at night time. Or maybe you feel sorry for the ones who had possibilities, the ones who thought they were better than I? If that is the case, your grief is misguided.

Take my advice, girl, get over yourself, before you get an ego."

"I was sent here, and I don't know why, but I know I don't want to see you again, Gideon. You're not who I thought you were."

"Sent? What do you mean, *sent*?" He demanded. "No one knows me! Who could have sent you?"

"Dylan. He told me that I had to start what he would finish. He has protected me from you, although I didn't know he was doing it." She was defiant, standing her ground against him. "Dylan knows who you are, what you are, and he sent me."

"You know *him*? He won't stand a chance against me. He didn't then, and he won't now. His weakness made it all too easy." He sneered. She wanted to run, wanted to escape the thoughts that now filled her mind. She tried to hold her emotions together, fighting back the tears for her lost cousin, and her stolen love. She patted the pocket of her overcoat, hoping there might be a tissue concealed in it.

The hard, square box was not what she had expected to find, though. For a moment, she took her eyes from the scene in front of her, looking instead at the shape of her pocket, reaching her hand inside, and withdrawing the expensive box slowly. She held it in front of her face, remembering what Dylan had said about her needing it, and laughed, feeling suddenly stronger.

"What is it? What have you got there?"

"Something I never should have taken." She lifted the lid, looking once more at the incredible pin inside. She snapped it shut again, and was glad that her hand-eye co-ordination was so good. As she pulled back her arm, she kissed the box, thinking how much she wanted for Vagan to be standing beside her. With all her thoughts wishing her back to the safety of her bedroom, and the predictability of her life filled with pressure, she swung her arm back, releasing the box, and watching as it flew through the air, hitting Gideon in the face before falling amongst his long robes.

His cry of anguish was instant; loud and piercing. Electra felt more powerful in that moment than she ever had before. Gideon's face crumpled in pain, but as it did so, he threw his arms out. The candles either side of him flickered madly, then started to topple, one after another, setting fire to the ground, the fabric hanging beside him, the painting that was almost as old as he was. The flames danced wildly, spreading quickly to encompass Vagan. This was the scene from her dream, and she couldn't bear to look. She stepped forward, trying to get to Vagan, but he was so deep within the fire that she could not reach him.

"You must run, Electra." The words were soft inside her head, but she recognised the voice. "It's alright, he'll be fine, but *you must run!*"

She didn't pause to think, spinning on her heel, and sprinting back up the stairs. The kitchen was no longer dark, filled with the light of the flames, and she headed for the back door, but it was locked, unmovable. She turned to the front of the house, hoping to reach the front door, but the hallway ran directly above the basement, and the flames were already eating into the floor. She could hear the maniacal laughter through the roar they made. She only had one other choice, and ran up to the second storey of the building.

She was unfamiliar with the layout of the upstairs of the house, and started trying the doors that branched off the landing. The first would not open, and the second was a bathroom. Another door lead to an attic, but that would be a really bad choice, she thought. The smoke was getting thicker, now, and threatened to choke her. Finally, she pushed a door open, finding a bedroom, sparsely furnished, but with possibilities. She shut the door behind her, remembering her fire safety, and slipping off her overcoat, wedging it in the gap under the door.

Again, the urge to cry threatened to overwhelm her, but she fought against it, rushing to the blacked out window, and tried to pull it open. Like the back door, it would not move, even though it was loose in the frame. She didn't know how to fight it anymore, and threw herself onto the bed, sobbing uncontrollably, not only for herself, but also for the future she had wanted, and the man she had planned to spend it with. She pulled her knees up to her chest, rocking slightly as she did so.

But crying wasn't helping either of them, and she pushed herself away from the bed, finally looking around her self at the room. It may have been sparse, but there was one thing she could use. As the heat beneath her feet intensified, a new urgency came to her, and she picked up the mouldering chair, hoping she was strong enough. She chucked the chair, and was gratified by the noise of glass shattering.

She leapt toward the open air, gulping it in, cold as it was. Beneath her, a tiny back yard was covered in brown grass. There was a small, pitched roof, and she heaved herself onto the ledge, lowering herself to the edge. The pitched roof was on an open porch, and she hung from the gutter, swinging her legs back and forth, imagining herself back in her gym class, as she launched herself backward, spinning in the air, and landing on the dirty ground. But she didn't look back at the house. She ran forward, pushing through the gate at the side of the house, feeling the heat radiating from the building. She ignored it, and pushed onward to the front of the house, tripping as she went.

Dylan was waiting. He sat cross-legged on the roof of the car, where he had watched the happenings within the basement through the crystal.

"Dylan! Vagan, he's still in there!" She cried, breathless with panic.

"It's okay. I'll bring him back for you," he promised, touching her shoulder gently. "Get the car a couple of blocks down, just in case the house starts to go, and I'll be back soon."

He handed her the keys, and she watched as he made his way up to the house. She looked at the key for a second, and when she looked up again, he was gone. She did as he had asked, climbing into the car, starting it up, and putting it into drive. She was nearly at the corner when the sound of the roof of the house falling in crashed behind her, and she felt her heart break.

Chapter fifty-one

The past ninety years had been leading him to this. As he had placed his hand on her shoulder, he had felt the force of her emotions, and knew that they would give him the strength to fight, now.

He slipped through the door, finding the flames he had expected. The heat would have been too much, had he been mortal, but he knew how to deal with it, allowing the cool air from the outside to touch him, instead. He moved quickly and silently, finding the stairway with ease. The fire was more intense here, empowered by De Montfort's anger, but he continued, feeling not only his emotions, but also the pain of his own kind from so many years before. It was a long time since these senses had been so strong in him. The last time, he had been a very long way from San Francisco, in a world where the present was only a distant dream for the future.

The flames burned orange and yellow in front of his eyes, but in his mind, he saw the pale blue driftwood fires his mother had burnt when he really *was* young, before he had committed his life to this path, and frozen his existence 200 years earlier. He had no regrets in that choice, though.

Lucien Gideon De Montfort was exactly what he appeared to be; bitter, twisted, old, and damned to hell for all he had ever done. As the flames danced around him, and all fell in tatters at his feet, Dylan Horatio Adams smiled silently.

"Boy!" The Old Man growled at him; still Dylan smiled.

"It's been a while. I'm surprised you remember me, Old Man. The years appear to have been kinder to me than they have been to you." He laughed. The boy who sat beside The Old Man now was not as expendable as Dylan had once thought he would be. Vagan didn't have any idea what was happening to him, but Dylan had foreseen his importance, now, and was not willing to risk it. His future sparkled with not only his own talent, but also with Electra's.

"This was not the future that was so promising, boy. You should not be here." The Old Man hissed.

"Neither should you, Old Man." Dylan threw back. "At least I made the choice that kept me here. I knew what I was doing, and I knew the risks. But when all is said and done, when I am finally taken back to the beginning, I will be welcomed back by my family, into the arms of those I love, and who loved me."

"Ah, but was it all worth it? Was it worth watching lives turn to ash while you remained?" The Old Man pressed, eager to find fault, no doubt.

"Yes, every minute of it. I have enjoyed my life, and I know that when I die, I will move on, as my parents did, and as their parents did. Perhaps that future, the one you saw, that drew you to me in the first place, would have been filled with glories. But if it was up to me to do again,

I'd choose the same, De Montfort." Dylan was happy to oblige the man with answers, thoughts that had filled his mind for far too many years. "And you?"

"Your future was the sweetest. You were going to give so much to the world. It was all going to be yours – mine – for the taking. You were a fool to throw it all away." His opponent scolded, not answering his question. Dylan had known, though, what he was giving up, and exactly why it would hurt The Old Man so badly. Dylan chuckled, expanding his shadow out toward his enemy. He drew back, shrinking against his chair. "I know why you came here, magician, and you will have a fight on your hands."

"That may have been true ten minutes ago, but your integrity is starting to fail. She has quite a right arm, that girl. And I knew that you knew I was coming. After all, how could you not? I'll assume you enjoyed my little visit last week. I've made my peace with the world for its results, but it was so nice to see you." Dylan laughed, recalling how easy it had been to send his shadow creeping through the house while Gideon had slept. "I've waited a long time for this, so very patiently. I'd worry about monologuing, but you barely have enough strength to stand up, and most of that is going in to keeping that boy in a trance. Now that I have the flames under control, I'd rather like this to be a slow process, thank you.

"How I've imagined this moment. That coldest of cold winters, when the Seine froze, and I had to steal coal to keep my girls warm and alive, the one thing that kept me focused was knowing that this moment existed. I saw war, knowing that you got more from it than any other dark human might, and when the rest of the world was damned, only you and I were made to withstand the horror, not counting the cockroaches, of course. Then, I had to put up with that bloody Beatle mania! What were my countrymen thinking of when they did *that*? Really, it was not called for. But through it all, I trusted that we would both be here, now, and that this would come to an end.

"It was brave of you, Lucien, to come here and seek out blood ties of your own. I suppose you never let on exactly how distant a relative you were. She will have sensed it, of course, not that she will have known what it was. She has more energy than most. The boy was a brave choice, and I'm not sure what you thought you would gain from him. His singular future isn't spectacular. He can't take your picture, after all; not unless you want the world to see that shadow behind you. Best not to look at it. No, there won't be that much money, and Vagan won't be special without Electra. Together, though, they shine. I've seen that for myself.

"So, here we are, in a city where peace and freedom abound. I couldn't have planned the location any better. It will be a pleasure destroying you."

"Are you going to reach your point anytime soon, boy?" The Old Man interrupted him.

"Yes." Dylan smiled again, stirring the air with his fingers, sending out ripples of power, watching the robed figure squirm in his chair as they reached him, his shadow creeping around the chair, closing in on Gideon. "You have been allowed to exist for far too long. You have haunted the lives and dreams of women, children, men, lovers and virgins. You have led people into lives of desperation without caring. You became the voice of my father after you had drunk him dry. My mother was heart broken, but not for long, because then you devoured her, leaving me to be comforted by your *wife*. I see you turned on her quickly enough, when you realised she was better than you. I didn't even get to mourn them, because I was still held in your power. You killed my world, and ripped it out from under me. Then you deserted me.

"And I grew strong. I had my mother's power, and my father's strength. I found peace, I met many people, who taught me many things. I have humanity, and humility, and now, I am sending you back to where you belong." His voice grew stronger, finding force from his memory, and from his ancestors.

The shadow was now directly behind the chair, wrapping itself around the fading figure sitting there. Dylan watched as the shadow pushed its way through Gideon's body, revealing the ages upon him. The lives he had taken were locked within him, and now they took their revenge, painting themselves across his face. He had spent many years ravaging whole families, and now their mortal souls were finally able to fight for their freedom, erupting from within him. Without them to support his body, Gideon began to decay.

As he did so, the last of his true power began to fail, and Vagan was released from his trance like state. Dylan drew him out through the flames, turning them blue as he did so. The fire of his mother's ritual was now his own, and it did what was necessary.

The decay was slow, but harsh, as it spread through Gideon's body. Beside Dylan, Vagan watched with curiosity. Dylan watched with satisfaction, as minute by minute another part of Gideon lost form, until nothing remained but the robes he had been wearing.

"Vagan, we should really go." Dylan said to the boy beside him.

"How do we get past the flames?" Vagan asked. Dylan didn't respond. He had heard the sound of sirens approaching, and he was sure there would be questions if they just walked out of the burning building. He sighed, and brought his shadow to heel. He placed his hand on Vagan's shoulder, whispering a few choice words under his breath.

The shape of the room whirled around them, distorting the blue flames. The house was already devastated, so Dylan felt no remorse at bringing down the rest of it, as they were invisibly ejected from the house, landing safely by the car, where Electra had parked it a safe distance from the house on Prescott that had just fallen down.

Chapter fifty-two

Electra was sitting in the car, huddled in the back seat, crying uncontrollably. The three fire trucks that had sped past her, followed by a police patrol car and an ambulance, had led her sobs to become even more frenzied. She couldn't bear to look at the house, fearing for lives that were more important to her than her own.

She was rocking slightly, hoping that the pain could be rocked away, hugging her knees. The tap on the glass shocked her, bringing her out of her state of fear. She looked up, and the wave of relief that flooded her emotions was more powerful than anything she had ever felt before.

Vagan pulled the door open, and she sprang into his arms, inhaling his scent, feeling her way across his shoulders to make sure he was real, and alive. Beside them, Dylan Adams laughed gently, as Vagan kissed her tenderly.

"I was so scared." She whispered against his chest.

"I told you he'd be fine," Dylan reminded her. She pulled back her head to look at him, and not for the first time, wondered exactly why Dylan seemed to know so much. He seemed so happy, it radiated from him, as if a weight had been lifted from his world.

"What happened?" She asked him, looking into his eyes, and seeing there the timeless wisdom of the stars.

"Magic. He won't be hurting anyone ever again. He's gone, because of you. All that time, I thought I couldn't get to him because I was weak, but it was more because I wasn't tied to him well enough. It took your blood tie to him to make it possible. You did well, Electra. Thank-you." He replied.

"So, can you please tell me what the hell he was?" Vagan requested. She had wondered herself, but knew only that he was something that shouldn't exist.

"He was the very worst of his kind, one of the worst to ever live. He was born a very long time ago, when the world was younger, and this land was still a mystery to most of it." Dylan began. "He was a spiteful child, or so I have come to understand, and he grew up a menace to those around him. He was 27 when he met Jacques Sebastian Notré, who was already turned. Together they carved a path through half the known world, until Gideon met Amilie, the pretty thing who was running from the revolution, fleeing Paris for the south. Gideon and Jacques went their separate ways, and eventually, Gideon returned to New Orleans, where he had spent some years.

"I crossed paths with him 90 years ago, and he turned my world inside out, leaving me as much in the dark as Vagan has been these past months. We were both used by him to bring what he needed. He was always partial to pretty girls, and yes, a number of them died in my time, when he didn't have to be quite so careful about the numbers he consumed. It wasn't our faults, though, Vagan.

He would have got what he wanted without us, and he did on occasion. A week ago, for instance. I knew what he had done when I felt the pain. His anger was more intense than I'd felt in a very long time. I suppose you know what that was about?"

"A name; Geena Du Pré." Vagan shrugged.

"Well, that would have done it. That would be the blond girl, I assume." Dylan commented. Electra and Vagan both nodded. "Amilie carried the family name Du Pré. She was a terrifying woman. Attractive, but vicious."

"So, what *were* they?" Electra asked again.

"Blood drinkers. There have been many names for them in the past, but the most common would be vampire, these days. He was very good at his job. Those who died didn't feel anything, and those who survived rarely knew what had happened to them. There is an enzyme in their saliva, it works on the body to subdue and erase. I'm afraid that Geena is one of the exceptions to the rule, but I'll make sure she gets past this." He assured them. "And then there was Maggie, of course. Don't feel guilt for her death, Electra. I know that it is there, but the thought will fade. If it hadn't been for that hair, they would not have even thought to look at you. It is a shame, but De Montfort was once a red head, you know. For some reason, his hair changed colour when he was remade. It may have been as a defence from persecution. Red hair was once seen as a sign of working with the devil, especially common in myths of witchcraft and vampirism. Thankfully, things have changed, and we are no longer persecuted for things beyond our controls. Besides, as far as I know there are no redheads in my family tree. I always wondered why they thought that, anyway. Things to muse on, but not worry over for too long."

"So, what do we do, now?" Vagan asked.

"Go home. I can go back to work for a while, at least until the end of the school year. I can't stay much past that, because people will start to ask questions. Maybe I might get another year, but I'll see how it goes. I won't be far, though. Vagan, you need to stick it out on that course of yours, because there is going to come a time when your participation in the class will make a difference. Besides, you can't go anywhere until the both of you head to Utah. That's where the world will gratefully watch Electra dance, because although you will be awarded well in Japan, you will be more happy to go to Salt Lake City. Then, when you dance together, the whole world will hold its breath for the beauty of it. I'll be there, because I can't wait to see it again." Dylan paused, and smiled. "After that, I'm not really sure, because the future gets harder to see the further away it is."

"I'll miss you, Dylan." Electra told him, feeling suddenly that her life was going to move her away from the life she had known, toward the life she had always hoped for.

"I'll always be somewhere. As long as you wear that crystal, I'll know if you need me." He promised her. She suppressed a yawn, not ready to be tired when there were still things she wanted to know. Dylan would still be working at the school, but talking to him would never be this easy again.

"I have to know, did Gideon sleep all day because of the sun?" She questioned.

"No, he was just a bit weird. He gave all the rest a bad name, you know. He was afraid of the light, and open spaces, and people; not the best combination when you depend on those things for easy hunting." Dylan chuckled.

"So he wouldn't burn up?" She pressed.

"No. That myth was invented by Mr. Stoker, and friends, because he didn't want anyone else talking to his good friend from Transylvania, who was just as scared of the light as Gideon. But that's another story, and not one for today, I'm afraid." Dylan laughed again.

"I'll look forward to hearing it." Electra yawned, u-nable to stop herself anymore.

"Come on, I'll walk you home," Vagan yawned as well, putting his arm around her shoulder. "Thank-you, Dylan, for saving me, for saving us."

"Well, that was my pleasure. Sleep well, beautiful ones, and I'll see you soon." Dylan told them. "If not at school, then at the wedding."

Neither of them responded, as they watched Dylan climb into his car, and drive away into the night. Both of them were tired, but looked at each other, trying to decipher his words. But it was late, and the rain was back, getting heavier, so they started on their way back to Steiner Street. When they reached the door, Vagan kissed her good night, no longer afraid of the people beyond the door. Their lips lingered a while, and when he left, she could feel them there still.

Vagan made his way back to college, where he would spend the rest of his time there with no days lost, becoming technically better than he ever thought he could. He lost no more time, spent no more hours in the darkness, waking in the shack with no way of knowing what he had done.

In that night, the intertwined lives shifted. Electra went back to her old life, knowing that it would someday lead to her new life. Geena Du Pré got over all her problems, finally sleeping unhindered by her dreams, which drifted away like feathers on a breeze. Dylan decided it was time to take a trip home, sometime soon. And Vagan's aura turned momentarily pure white, before settling on a rather passionately loving red.

Epilogue

The ice was perfect under the low lights in the arena. Electra stepped out first, pulling Vagan behind her as she moved out into the centre of the rink. The music started slowly, becoming faster as they moved closely, dancing across the smooth surface together.

They became lost in the music. They hadn't taken the time to practice, knowing that their abilities were so in tune with each other that they had no need to. They had been together for long enough to know each other's moves before they were made. As he threw her into the air, millions of people across the world held their breaths. As he caught her, the world sighed at the beauty.

"Ladies and gentlemen, this is our gold medallist, Electra Philips, and partner." The announcer told the audience, "We actually don't know who the young man is, but we appreciate his style."

The voice was lost in the air that whipped around their heads, and the music that filled their bodies. It had taken them a long time to reach this stage in their lives, but it had all been worth it. Now, they barely recalled the months where darkness had filled their lives, remembering only the first stages of their love.

Somewhere above them, the small booth where the Olympic announcer had spent the past weeks commentating on all the action was being invaded. "I know who he is."

"Well, ladies and gentlemen, we have a young man here who says he knows who our mystery skater is. Please, enlighten us." The commentator requested. Cain Philips stepped forward to the microphone, feeling braver than he had for some time.

"His name is Vagan Elison, from here in Utah. I'm Electra's brother, Cain, and she and Vagan have been dating for a little over four years, now. They're getting married in June." Cain told everyone.

"Well, there you have it, everyone. That's one really lucky young man."

"Yeah, he is, and so am I. Sorry, I'm sure you don't mind. I have to say this, before I have time to think. Mom, dad, I'm gay." Cain announced, before walking back out of the booth. The man behind him laughed into the mike.

Back on the ice, the music was coming to an end, and as it trailed away, Electra and Vagan came to a slow stop, holding each other on the ice, their hearts beating in perfect time with each other, breathing rapidly. The spotlight glinted off the ring on her finger, shining through the globe shaped crystal she wore at her throat, creating rainbows on the ice.

"I love you." Vagan whispered, kissing her gently as hundreds of flowers and soft toys hit the ice around them.

"I love you, too." She whispered back, returning his kisses with her own.

Although the events that had originally brought them together still remained in their memories, they rarely thought of the dark spells that had filled the early days of their affair. Time had given them perspective, and Electra had not mourned the loss of her cousin for long.

There had been questions, of course, but they had been dealt with by the enigmatic young man from far away, who knew far too much about the world he had lived in for over two centuries. Maggie's death was not thought of by many, and the police stopped bothering the innocent parties. Life went back to degrees of normality for all involved. Because time passes.

Eventually, June came. The wedding was small, and simple, just as was foreseen. It was the perfect start to their married life together. All the most important people were there. Devon wore a skirt. Dylan was there, finally back from his travels, but those are another story, and not one for today.

Soon to come from the same author

Cats Eyes

High on a cliff over looking the pacific, stands Tarot house. Catalina Tarot has lived there very happily for her entire life, but this summer, things are going to change for her forever. The arrival of summer guests brings Guy Marin, the mysterious young man who keeps his thoughts to himself, even if he doesn't realise it. As the long hot days of their summer together dwindle, Cat and Guy find their way to each other, but their happiness is not meant to last.

The Scream Within

If only someone could hear her scream, night after night, perhaps she could get through it. But who is there to listen? A father who works all hours of the day to forget his past failings? A brother so disturbed by life that he has gone hundreds of miles to escape it? A mother who has been gone for so long that few even remember her name? Perhaps Gabriel Estevez? Until she can stop, she can never move on, so she'll continue to struggle through.

Ma Vie D'enfer
(My Year in Paris)

A year in the City of Lights was all the Jasmine White ever wanted. She had no idea it would turn out to be torture. Looking after the vile little Vallette, and her brother Stephané, Jasmine learns that the city can be both beautiful and terrible, as they put her through as many hideous experiences as possible. So, with dealing with them, and her growing infatuations with just about every male she meets in the city, it seems she will never get the peaceful year she longs for.

Once upon a time, Lyndsay Tobiyah Coomber knew exactly what she wanted out of life. Only recently did she get it. Now, of course, she is happier than she has ever been before. If you are lucky enough to know her, then you will understand. If not, too bad. So yes, this book was once dedicated to someone else, because it took a long time for her to realise that there was really only one person it was ever meant to be for. Hopefully, he will understand, and she will be happy for a long time to come. If not, too bad. She should find out soon enough.

www.ingramcontent.com/pod-product-compliance
Lightning Source LLC
Chambersburg PA
CBHW071806020726
47502CB00004B/1023